Sunrise at Sunset

By
BJ Barnes

D1522795

Sunrise at Sunset
By: BJ Barnes

Sunrise at Sunset is a work of fiction. Any reference to real people, events, establishments, organizations, or locations is intended for adding authenticity alone. In addition, each character portrayed is fictional, not intended to portray any real person or persons.

ISBN: 9798580523439

Dedication

To the men and women of Law Enforcement who put their lives in harm's way, every day.

Acknowledgements

Dena, my bride, my rock and best friend.
Carol, longtime friend and mentor.
Stephanie and Chris my beautiful daughters
My mom who kept me centered.

Chapter One

The rising June sun was proceeded by a warm glow of reddish light that would take your breath away. The glow foretold the beautiful day ahead. Rising slowly over the Atlantic Ocean off the coast of North Carolina, the sunlight bounced off the waves causing a shimmering effect that only God could produce. The rays pierced the morning, adding light to darkness as it swept across Bird Island and then across the Intracoastal Waterway. All this was the free light show TJ Slone watched every chance he got. Sitting on the deck watching this spectacular event Sheriff TJ Slone reminded himself why he bought this place so late in life and why he was in debt. He couldn't imagine a more perfect view or one that showed the wonder of God's creation. Sunset Beach was the location, a small coastal town between Calabash, the self- proclaimed seafood capitol of the world and Ocean Isle. Ocean Isle was just as nice as Sunset, but more commercial. Buying this place was part of his future retirement plan.

TJ was the longtime sheriff of the third largest county in the state. He was in fact at the end of a very successful career. He could retire at any time, he didn't because he loved the job, the people he worked for and with. He was respected in the law enforcement community as well as the halls of the US Congress and North Carolina legislatures. TJ was the longest serving sheriff in his county's history which meant the citizens obviously appreciated the work he was doing as Sheriff. His tenure was especially impressive since he was a Republican in a Democrat county, yet consistently won by 20 points or more. All that seemed so unimportant as he sipped a cup of decaffeinated coffee, sweetened with honey and French vanilla creamer, watching this glorious sunrise.

As he watched the sunrise, a Carolina Skiff pulled into the day dock on the Intracoastal Waterway behind the condo. TJ watched as the skiff, which he estimated to be about sixteen feet in length, pulled up and tied to the dock. The occupant of the skiff was probably a fisherman, returning from a night of flounder gigging, a popular way to fish in the shallow waters close to Tubbs Inlet at low tide. TJ had fished this way before, but it was not his favorite way to fish. Standing knee to waist deep in water lit by a floating light looking for the impression of a flounder hiding in the sand. Wading in water holding a 6' flounder gig, while all around you was darkness. Hiding in the shadows were things looking for the chance for a meal, things like sharks and barracuda. Sharks would look at TJ's 6'8", 290 pounds as a buffet. TJ was afraid of no man but had a healthy respect for anything as fast and as aggressive as a bull shark at feeding time. He loved to fish, but not that way, more power to the fisherman who did.

He heard, then turned to see door to the condo open.

Tina Slone joined her husband TJ on the deck as she sipped her own cup of coffee. Tina was just as accomplished as TJ, having retired as a very respected nurse. She started a second career as an elected official. She served at different times as council person, mayor and mayor pro tem on the council of their small town in Guilford County. If you can call little pay and a bunch of headaches a second career.

Tina was the glue that held the family together, everybody liked Tina, with few exceptions. She was active in the Republican party serving as an officer on the National Federation of Republican Women and had served numerous times with the group at the local and state level. She was the mother of two beautiful girls, Monique and Louise. Both TJ and Tina had been married before and each brought a daughter into the mix; it was Tina that made the mix work.

This condo was to be their forever home. They owned property in Summerfield but decided to take on another mortgage by buying their place at Sunset Beach, a place where, when TJ retired, they would end up. Tina was ready now, but TJ still loved his job, the people he worked with and for, so they came to the beach as often as they could, but it got harder and harder to return to Summerfield after each visit.

This time of the morning was special to both. A time where they would watch the world wake up. A time and place where no matter the problems, they seemed to be small compared to the view and salt air they shared in their special place. TJ and Tina had been married for 36 years. They both left their first marriages with little in the way of material goods but found a rich life together with both good times and bad, and always an appreciation of what they had. Their life and marriage were special, as were these moments.

TJ was not the easiest person to live with. He was opinionated, independent and held himself and others accountable. His expectations of people and family were set very high. He gave his best, he expected nothing less. TJ's Marine Corps background, being raised by a single parent, his mother, was a big part of his thinking and his life. Tina on the other hand was the opposite, she was a Libra. She was easy going and did not push people like TJ, and sometimes would balk at TJ's opinion. This made for some interesting conversations between her and her husband. She was tough in spirit, gentle in nature and together they made a formidable team.

Most mornings like this one were spent in silence, enjoying the view and the sweet taste of the coffee. After so many years together, the couple could and often would finish the other's sentences. This morning was different, this morning had a particular urgency to it.

"What time are Matt and Belle going to be here?" Tina asked as she sipped her coffee.

"I don't know." TJ responded. "They'll call with the time later."

This answer did not please Tina, she had groceries to get, meals to be planned. Men thought or believed things just happened by magic, not realizing the planning that needed to be done. Matt and Belle were their good friends, she wanted everything perfect and despite the men involved, it would be.

Matt Hart was the Governor of North Carolina, Belle his lovely wife. Matt was not only the Governor, a state leader, but a leader on the national scene as well. So much so that Matt was on the short list to be appointed Vice President of the United States. This was only speculation by many, but TJ knew Matt was actually on a short list.

Former Vice President Mark Elliot was now president, after the recent assassination of President John Turnage. President Turnage had only been President six months before he was shot by an Islamic radical. His short tenure had been eventful and aggressive in attacking issues such as fair trade, terrorist activity, taxes, immigration and health care. He was making headway and making a huge impact, but not without making enemies. His biggest enemy being the media who daily fed the hate and discontent of the people who did not care for the changes President Turnage had in mind. Even in his short six months he had made a difference in the stock market and the US standing among the other nations in the world. President Elliot would continue President Turnage's short legacy. He began by being just as aggressive in working on his agenda. John and Mark made a great team, had made a great team and now that President Elliot needed a new partner, Matt Hart was on the short list.

Governor Matt Hart was a second term Governor and had made a huge impact in his first term. His innovative, progressive ideas had brought the state into a solid financial position. He had moved the state's ranking from the bottom half to the top ten. He was not afraid of controversy but was also not afraid of compromise. He had solid credentials having served as the mayor of one of North Carolina's largest cities. He was well deserving of being on the short list, though TJ knew Matt was not anxious to take the job. Belle definitely was not. Belle was a great partner for Matt, but she was a hesitant participant in the political arena.

Belle Hart was the poster child for what a southern belle would be. She was a tall, slender, attractive woman who had an easy smile that hide the mischievous part of her personality. That demure look and gentle demeanor would often lure people into thinking there was little substance to her, a bad mistake. Belle Hart had a very sharp mind and was truly a great supporter of her husband and his ideas. She didn't seek the limelight, in fact shunned it. She worked in the shadows in the political arena but in the forefront when it came to her passion, animals and animal rights. Belle was a little skeptical about an appointment as Vice President. She understood the toll public life placed on relationships and was not sure the price was worth it.

The governor's arrival at Sunset Beach was going to be a lowkey event. Though lowkey, it still required a bit of planning. There would be a security detail made up of two officers. TJ felt more would be appropriate and if Matt accepted the position, there would definitely be more, but Matt insisted it be lowkey. Matt wanted one more event that would be as close to normal as normal could get for a governor.

TJ had talked with Thomas, the condo caretaker. Thomas was a friend and asked few questions of TJ. Thomas know whatever TJ asked for was needed and appropriate. Thomas issued the parking passes needed on any vehicle left overnight in the parking lot. Though Thomas didn't ask, nor was he told, when TJ asked for two parking passes for two SUV's, he figured the Governor was coming again. The request for the guest suite available to residents, that sealed the deal in Thomas's mind. It would be for the Governor's security detail. Thomas had been through this before, he had even had the chance to meet the Governor and his wife in the past. Thomas liked the Governor and his wife, hell, he even voted for him, though they were from different political parties. He suspected their dog would be along too. The dog was the only thing that was a little disruptive. People in the other units were not used to seeing it, nor the strange men who walked the dog. Strange because they seldom spoke and always wore lightweight jackets no matter what the temperature.

They often inquired of Thomas, asking things such as "Do we have new tenants?" Thomas's answer was always the same, "No, just friends of TJ's." It amused Thomas they went away still not having the answers they were looking for.

In fact, most of the residents knew these guys were security for the Governor. The permanent residents had asked, and he told them who his guests were. He trusted them, they were good people, and he knew they would respect the Governor's privacy, though he was sure they would have loved to meet and spend time with him. Every one of the condo owners were successful in their own right.

Chapter Two

As the boat glided toward the dock, Number *One* looked toward the condos that faced the Intracoastal waterway. The boat, a 16 ft. Carolina Skiff, had been docked at the canal home he and his friends had acquired the night before. It was acquired by Number *Two* killing the two occupants when they opened the door for what they thought was a pizza delivery. They had not ordered a pizza. They probably figured the delivery person was at the wrong house. Underneath the pizza box was a model 422 Smith & Wesson with a silencer. The owner of the house answered the door with a friendly voice and smile, saying he had not ordered a pizza. For his trouble he got two 22 caliber bullets to the chest at point blank range, straight to the heart. Number *Two* had actually pressed the gun to the homeowner's chest in the area of the heart and pulled the trigger. Pressing the gun to his chest caused the sound to be even more muffled. His wife came running to the door after hearing the muffled shots. As her husband fell, she got a single shot to the head before she could cry out. Both dead in a matter of seconds.

The canal home was chosen a mere 4 hours before the occupants died. The house was chosen after a recon mission by Number *Three*. Number *Three* whose actual name was Maria Garcia was a true believer who had converted to the radical Muslim faith. She was undocumented and had been in the shadows her entire time in America. She was chosen because she was attractive, efficient and when needed, brutal. She followed orders, doing what Number *One* asked her to do. Things that sometimes included providing sex when he desired it, plus she could cook. She was no stranger to hiding from the law and she was very smart in a common-sense way, if not from an academic standpoint. Just hours before their death, Number *Three*, Maria, had knocked on the door of the canal home holding a large box of laundry detergent and a clip board. She explained to the house occupants the purpose of her visit was to offer the detergent to the homeowner if they would answer a few questions and send in a review of the product after they used it. The detergent had been purchased that morning from a local store. The information gathered by Maria told Number *One* the man and wife lived in the home alone. Seemingly innocent banter sealed their fate.

The homeowner was a semi-retired real estate broker who managed his own properties. Their nearest family was in New York, and through friendly banter, Number *Three* found their family had just left from a visit. Their family usually came twice a year, once in June and again at Christmas. It amazed *One* the information these Americans would give out when it was a pretty face asking and they thought they were being helpful or getting something for nothing. The homeowner being helpful caused her to be graveyard dead, just hours after the survey.

The house was in a perfect location. The houses on each side were empty and for sale or lease. The canal at the back of the house held a dock and a 16 ft. Carolina Skiff. Not the right size boat, but the house and location were perfect. Few chances to be interrupted and easy entry from the water since it was located at the end of the canal nearest the Intracoastal Waterway. It was located just a few miles by water from the condo that was the true target. The canal home would work as their base, so the retired couple had to die.

Number *One*'s actual name was Azil Mohamed Adula. He had put his five-person team together with purpose. He alone knew their true names. Of the five team members, the only person who knew his true identity was Number *Two*. The rest of Azil's crew did not know *Two* was Azil's brother. *One* assigned each their number, and they would refer to each other by that number, his orders. The purpose was to protect the team in case anyone was captured or if someone decided to betray the operation, they would not know who their other team members were. *One* cautioned them not to discuss any conversations between him or them and not to discuss their true identity. Azil told them he knew who they were, what they could do and that was all that they needed to know. It was a safety precaution and Azil was a very cautious person. A cautious person with a secret.

Number *Two* was Kareem Adula, brother to Azil, a true believer in the Islamic faith and Jihad. Kareem and his brother had trained in the deserts of Iran and Iraq. Azil and his brother had quickly distinguished themselves as being ruthless, brutal operators. Azil was a team leader responsible for many successful Jihads against western targets. Azil included his brother in every one of his operations.

Kareem knew he could trust his brother and he knew how his brother operated. He was also not one to question his brother; he had every confidence in the fact he would be taken care of.

Two was a believer, Radical Islam was his life. Both brothers were experts in small arms and explosives. They were part of a group dedicated to the overthrow of the American government. Kareem Azil believed, should he be killed, he would receive his promised 72 virgins and place with Allah. Killing Americans was part of the deal, killing the couple just added two more to those he had killed before in the name of Allah. Allah Akbar.

Two trusted his brother with his life and had many times in the past. *Two* would follow his brother thru the gates of hell and be happy to be there.

The rest of the team consisted of numbers *Four* and *Five*.

Number *Four,* Jerry Blair, was a true believer who had been converted on the internet. This was his first operation with Adula, whose reputation had not escaped the young American. In terrorist circles Adula was a legend. *Four* was honored to be asked to be a part of the team. He was from New York, looking for chance to prove himself as an Islamic warrior. In NY he worked in a dead- end job and had few friends. His training was not as intensive as *One* and *Two*, in fact it consisted of a little time with small arms at a local range before moving to New York, but he was good enough to be of use. Little did *Four* know, to Number *One* he was cannon fodder, meant to be sacrificed if needed.

Number *Five,* Juan Santigo, was a mercenary. He had no beliefs that drove him into any cause, except money. He was recruited because of his knowledge of explosives, mountain climbing and repelling. He also knew how to drive a boat, a boat like the 16 ft. skiff. As far as *One* was concerned, *Five* was also cannon fodder, he would be sacrificed in a minute.

Five had served in the Special Forces in the army of El Salvador. He was a gang member as many in the El Salvador Army were. He was illegally in America and had settled in the Los Angeles area because it was a sanctuary for many illegals such as himself. It was also full of rich victims just waiting to be taken advantage of.

Five had crossed the Mexican border into America illegally and entered into gang life in America, committing violent crimes for pay, acting as an enforcer for the drug cartel, or as a Coyote bringing humans illegally across the border.

He had no loyalty to anyone but himself. He was a brutal man and Number *One* needed his expertise, which included driving a boat, but *One* knew *Five* had no loyalty in him. Like the others, with the exception of his brother, *One* felt they were all cannon folder.

This team, not known to each other. would pull off one of the biggest terrorist victories since 9/11 and *One* would be paid well.

Number *One*, Azil Mohamed Adula was no longer a true believer and he too was a mercenary. He kept this from his brother. He had lost his faith. The others, except his brother, would be sacrificed as needed. If they died, he did not have to pay them, meaning his bottom line increased.

As a warrior *One* had seen the millions of dollars being amassed thru the drug trade, the kidnapping business and the contributions from the faithful who supported the cause. He also saw much of the money collected was going into the leader's private offshore accounts. *One* decided it was time he got his share and this operation was going to make that happen.

The boat softly bumped into the dock. *Five* knew what he was doing *One* thought. *One* looked up at the condo which was about a hundred yards from the docked boat.

At the target condo, he could see a male sitting on the deck of the top floor. *One* knew that male would be TJ Slone. His research told him

Slone was not going to be easy. His intelligence research stated TJ was the longest serving Sheriff in the history of Guilford County, a career law enforcement officer. That didn't happen unless he knew what he was doing. No, TJ Slone was not going easy, but going he was.

One had decided TJ Slone was going to die. Slone was a former Marine, that in itself was enough to give any terrorist pause and reason enough to decide Slone would die. Marines had a history of being fierce in battle and tenacious in protecting their country, their fellow Marines and America. Their motto Semper Fidelis, meaning Always Faithful, was ingrained in their DNA. In *One's* mind they were idiots. Idiots that needed to be respected, dangerous idiots. Since Slone was a former Marine, *One* knew, unless they took him out first there would be problems. He knew that once a Marine, always a Marine.

One looked down, trying not to show interest as he helped *Two, Three* and *Four* out of the boat. As they walked up the dock gangway toward the condo, each carried black duffel bags, trying to be inconspicuous, *One* took a final look at his target.

Five pulled away from the dock to go back to the canal home they had acquired earlier. He would join the team later after securing the boat, taking one of the two cars belonging to the dead couple. The car they had been using was a rental which *One* had turned in since they now had the dead couple's cars. The rental was an unneeded expense and attracted curiosity.

The boat could not stay docked at the condo. The dock was a day dock for the use of the condo owners during daylight hours only. Leaving the boat there after dark would draw attention. *Five* would return to get the boat when needed. He would join the team at a condo located on the top floor, the same floor as TJ Slone's condo. Another condo was secured the night before using the same ruse used for the canal home: the phony survey and the phony pizza delivery with the gun hidden under the empty pizza box. The same ruse using the laundry detergent survey.

Establishing the condo on the same floor as Slone's lessened the chance of being discovered. Add two more lives to *Two's* long list of

Americans killed. The body count for this operation was now four innocents.

Five had plans before returning, he intended on searching the house for any valuables he could find and take. He had tried to do this the night before, but *One* had stopped him, not approving of robbing the dead. *Five* had no such reservations. He would take anything he could find of value. He would even violate their dead bodies if it pleased or amused him. He would not be back right away. He was going treasure hunting.

Chapter Three

Tina got up from the deck giving TJ the kiss that seemed just as fresh all these years later as the first one had been. They had truly found their soul mate in each other. Yes, they argued on occasion, but it never lasted long. Both had been married before and were determined not to make the same mistakes this time.

They argued and were both strong personalities, but they were committed to one another's happiness. When he asked her to marry him and said he had nothing to offer but the promise she would never be hot, and never cold or hungry and he would make her laugh. He had kept his promises.

"I'm making a grocery list, anything special you have in mind?" Tina asked.

"No, just remember we are feeding four extra mouths, five if you count Mo," was TJ's answer.

The five extra mouths were Matt and Belle Hart, their dog Mo, a black lab getting on in age, and two State Highway patrolman acting as security for the Governor.

One of the security team would be on duty 24/7. They alternated resting in a suite located on the property which could be rented by the condo owners for overflow guests. Normal guests TJ and Tina would take out to dinner, but as Governor, especially a Governor who may be the next Vice President of the United States, it seemed more prudent to eat at home. Security was the reason, a necessary inconvenience and would only get worse if he was appointed Vice President.

* * * * *

Tina left, list in hand, to shop at the Lowes grocery in Little River just across the state line in South Carolina. Tina liked to shop there because it was easy in and out, great parking, there was a gas station on site as well as several different shops and restaurants and it was just a short ride away.

TJ remained on the deck, on his cell phone, reviewing calls the Sheriff's Office had been answering or was answering now.

He loved technology when it worked. On his phone or laptop, he could monitor what every one of his on-duty officers were doing. He could send them notes or inquiries about a certain case and could access any data he needed. He could do all this without interfering with their workflow. He could interject himself if needed from the keyboard on his phone. He was seldom needed. The officers at the Sheriff's office were professionals. Training was a big part of TJ's administration. He knew they knew their job. TJ let them do it, they knew he was there to support them if needed and they knew he would, he had many times before.

TJ called his Chief Deputy Thomas "Tom" Powe. Tom and TJ had been deputies together. They had worked together in Raleigh for a former governor. Tom's wife and Tina had worked together as nurses at the hospital. He and his family were more like family then boss and employee, but neither TJ nor Tom let their friendship interfere with their job. The members of the sheriff's office, including their leaders, were professionals.

TJ called Tom on his Sheriff's office phone, knowing how he would answer.

"Colonel Powe, how can I help you?" the chief deputy answered.

"Tom, how is it shaking, anything happening?" TJ asked, as he always did.

Colonel Powe knew the sheriff already knew if anything was happening, knowing he had already reviewed the calls. The sheriff also knew if anything happened, Powe would have called him. Powe knew the sheriff was reviewing calls and the activities of each of the cars, he always did. The sheriff insisted on knowing when anything newsworthy or out of the ordinary happened. There was hell to pay if anything happened and he did not know. It didn't matter if it was the middle of the night, he wanted to know.

The Colonel replied "Yeah, the Martians have landed, I was just getting ready to call you."

TJ laughed and replied, "Send their little green asses home unless they have legitimate business here. They're not causing my crime rate to go up, we work too hard to keep it down."

The Colonel laughed and gave the sheriff a rundown of the nights reports which TJ had already reviewed, nothing outstanding, the usual calls.

The sheriff asked the Colonel to keep it in the middle of the road just as he did at the end of each call when he was out of town and just as he knew his chief deputy would. The Colonel transferred TJ to his administrative assistant Debbie Lynch.

Debbie had been with the sheriff the entire time he had been sheriff. It was a joke between Debbie and Tina that Debbie was the office wife. She was efficient and knowledgeable and was a big part of the successes at the Sheriff's office and TJ's other right hand. Debbie repeated the phone messages sent by email for TJ to respond. It was just the normal stuff for what would turn out to be a very unusual day.

The Sheriff's Office operated like a well-oiled machine. Each section had a captain that was responsible for their area. If anything happened in their section, they knew there was no cover, they were responsible. TJ Slone was a fair man. He gave you every opportunity to succeed, but he also held you accountable for your area. He did not like excuses, nor did he accept failure. If you couldn't do the job, you did not keep the job. Everybody knew that, everybody respected it.

Chapter Four

Tina returned from her shopping trip, gathered up her grocery bags and walked into the lobby which held the elevator and mailboxes for their building. Waiting outside the elevator was a tall, muscular Hispanic looking man in his late twenties. Tina smiled and said hello. The young man did not reply, which Tina thought a little odd. Although the lack of response was a little strange, the fact she had never seen him before did not alarm her. She and TJ were not permanent residents, so seeing a stranger was not unusual. She thought it strange, but she guessed he either did not hear her, did not speak English or was just not talkative. He punched the top floor, the same floor she lived on.

Five was nervous. He tried hard not to show it. He had not counted on anyone being at the elevator, especially not the wife of Sheriff TJ Slone. *Five*, like the others, knew who she was from the intelligence file containing photos shown to them by *One*.

Five was returning from the canal home with the dead couple's car. Their bodies were double wrapped in large outdoor trash bags and rested in their closet. They had not objected to him doing whatever he wanted, dead people never did. While there, alone with the dead couple, *Five* searched their closets and took whatever valuables he could find. He even took the college class ring from the big man's dead hand, his watch off his wrist. The ring and the more expensive pieces he carried in his pocket, the rest he hid to retrieve later. He could hear the metal as it rubbed together, he hoped Slone's wife could not.

Five had parked the boat to be used again later as part of their exit plan and had driven the Lexus SUV belonging to the couple back to the condo. All had gone smoothly, the drive back, parking in front of the condo, all as planned. Now he shared an elevator with Tina Slone a woman who would see her life change in a few hours. Five did not respond to her greeting because he did not know what to do. He had not planned on her being there.

When the elevator stopped and the door opened, *Five* quickly exited to the left, knowing his fellow passenger Tina, would go to the right after gathering her packages. He knew this because *One* had gone over the floor plans the night before. When Tina turned to go into her condo, she glanced in the direction her fellow passenger had gone, but the man was not there.

TJ was talking on the phone when Tina entered the condo and placed the groceries on the kitchen counter.

"We'll be looking for you, everything is ready, see you in about twenty minutes."

Tina gave TJ one of her famous looks, the kind that could kill or seriously wound. She forgot about the elevator and the young Hispanic man she rode up the elevator with.

"Twenty minutes, that's great." She really didn't think it was great. "I need a little help here." She added.

TJ got up to help, this was no time to try to joke your way through, and asked what she needed him to do. Tina got down to business, the man on the elevator was forgotten, the Governor would be there in twenty minutes.

Twenty minutes later the doorbell rang. Trooper James Drey stood in the door as it was opened. Behind him was Governor Matt Hart and wife Belle holding the leash of their black Lab Mo, bringing up the rear was a young trooper named Billy Scott.

"Come in folks!" was followed by hugs for everyone except the troopers. The relationship between TJ and the Governor went back to their high school days. TJ had actually graduated with the Governor's sister, the governor was several years younger, but the friendship was decades old.

Tina and Belle immediately retreated to the deck with Mo.

They started talking like they had just seen each other the day before even though it had been weeks. That's what friends did. TJ and the trooper Scott retrieved the bags from the car.

TJ then took Trooper Scott to the suite he and Trooper Drey would be sharing which was located by the common area of the clubhouse, where residents held gatherings. Trooper Drey had been there before, Scott had not.

TJ was given a portable radio just like each trooper had, so they could communicate if needed. One trooper would be in the parking lot in front of the condo all during the visit. The only time they would leave the vehicle was to escort whoever walked the dog. Before any dog walking occurred, a radio call was made. The plan was that the Governor would stay on site the entire two days of the visit, the rest of Friday and Saturday night, leaving on Sunday.

TJ excused himself leaving the troopers to their post. Billy Scott went to the vehicle, Drey settled in the guest quarters until he and Billy were called for dinner. He and Billy would join them for dinner at the insistence of TJ and Tina, as well as the Governor, although it wasn't what he liked doing or expected. Knowing TJ from past visits he did not argue, it would not have done any good, he always provided their meals though the state provided them a meal allowance. On any visit anywhere else they would be responsible for feeding themselves, but TJ Slone was not that kind of guy. Drey actually knew TJ was all cop at heart and he looked at other cops as a brother or sister in arms. He suspected that was acquired from his Marine Corps training, but it did not matter, he liked it.

TJ came back to the condo to find Tina, Belle and Mo still on the balcony, Matt Hart was on the cell phone in deep conversation about legislation, probably with the chief of staff or the leader of the house or senate.

The rest of the day was spent by TJ, Tina, Belle and Matt catching up and sharing memories and making new ones all in the confines of the condo. As the evening approached Tina and TJ fixed dinner. Tonight, would be shrimp and baked flounder. The seafood was fresh, having just been caught that morning and purchased from Amanda, a close friend who owned and operated the Island Seafood Company, Tina had picked it up on the way back from grocery shopping. It was going to be good and the summer corn on the cob, coleslaw and baked potato would round out the meal. For dessert, a key lime pie freshly made by Amanda's mother-in-law with real key limes brought up special from Florida. The pie was a little pricey, but today was a special day, they just didn't know how special.

After dinner, Drey went back to the guest quarters, Billy back to the car. Belle and Tina took Mo for a pee stroll, with Trooper Scott a respectful distance behind, watching, but not intrusive.

After clearing the dinner table and loading the dishwasher, TJ fixed drinks which they took out to the 5th floor veranda overlooking the beautiful view of the Intracoastal and Atlantic Ocean. Belle and Tina joined them after returning from Mo's stroll. They had barely sat down when Matt dropped the bomb.

"TJ, Tina, let me get straight to it. I have been offered the job of Vice-President. I just have to accept. I, we, wanted to talk it over with you guys, well, because you are valued friends and Belle and I value your opinion and thoughts." said a pensive looking governor.

"Of the United States?" said a joking TJ Slone.

"Yes, asshole, the United States" the governor laughingly replied.

The job of Vice President was his he explained, he just had to say he would take it. It was Friday and he had until Monday morning at 9 o'clock to give the President an answer. When he answered, if the answer was yes, he would be picked up by a secret service detail immediately. In fact, the detail was already in Raleigh in case the answer was yes. He would be flown to Washington, DC on Air Force One on Monday afternoon for a joint news conference and introduction to the country. This was all hush hush. Air Force One routinely made touch and go landings in Greensboro and Raleigh, so it being there would not draw attention and the Secret Service would get him on board quietly.

As Matt explained what was happening, TJ watched Belle. Belle watched he and Tina to see their reaction. Matt went on to explain if he said yes, this would be the last opportunity to act like real people or as close as a Governor could act like real people being who he was.

TJ's next question went straight to the point as so often his questions did. "Are we celebrating or are we still in the thinking phase?"

Belle responded for both "We're in the thinking phase. He wants to do it, I'm not sure. We wanted to talk to you guys, we value your friendship and your opinion." She repeated.

The conversation lasted into the evening, with both sides being reviewed. Governor Hart felt he had the obligation to serve and felt he was a good match for the job, the prestige having nothing to do with the consideration. He just wasn't that kind of guy. Belle looked at it from the side of a loving wife who had spent the biggest part of her life sharing her husband with an adoring citizenry. She admitted her response was selfish, but she just didn't know if she wanted to deal with the additional pressure and scrutiny. After a couple of hours conversation and what if's, along with several Gentleman Jack mixed drinks and Dirty Martini's for the girls, it was decided the conversation would resume in the morning. It was 12:30 am, it had been a long day.

Chapter Five

Five entered the condo and quickly closed the door. As he leaned against the door his demeanor and apparent frustration caught *One's* eye.

"What's wrong?" One asked.

"I just rode up in the elevator with Slone's wife." *Five* said. *Five* knew who Tina Slone was because of *One's* intel packet with photos of TJ, Tina and the Governor and his wife. He knew it was her. *One* had more than just photos and bio's in his intel package, he had the inside track from a source close to the President.

He knew Matt Hart was on a list of one for the job as Vice President. In fact, he knew he had been offered the job. He knew it was his to take or not. He also knew from this same source the Governor's plan to visit his friend TJ Slone. This intel was from a person so close to the president it could not possibly be wrong.

One felt sure it was right, but this development concerned him. "She say anything, is she suspicious?" *One* quizzed his fellow terrorist.

"No, she had a load of groceries, I don't think she thought anything about it," *Five* replied.

Azil thought, a load of groceries. Company is coming, just as his source had said it would. Now the plan was truly on track. Everything to this point was based on intel, now it was no longer a plan, it was an operation.

One ordered *Four* to sit in the car *Five* had just arrived in.

He was to avoid suspicion and let him know when two SUV's arrived. He ordered *Four* to take the stairs, no more surprises were needed. He knew it would be two cars because that was standard procedure. In one of the SUV's the Governor and his wife would be riding. The second SUV would only hold a single trooper. His job was to take the Governor, who was referred to as the "package", if the Governor's car was incapacitated for any reason.

After entering the parking lot, the Governor's vehicle parked while the spare vehicle cruised the parking lot, checking out each vehicle and also taking a video of each license number with an automatic license reader. The license numbers were checked automatically against a data bank to see if any vehicles were stolen or part of an alert. All this would be done in seconds. The canal couple's Lexus would not draw any attention. In fact, it fit in with the other vehicles in the lot.

If any suspicious vehicle was identified the Governor would not get out until the suspicious vehicle was cleared. If nothing was found, the "package" was allowed to leave the vehicle.

Four had barely entered the parked vehicle when he saw two black Chevrolet SUV's entering the parking lot. The lead vehicle found a parking place just in front of the door to the condo. The other vehicle slowly drove through the lot. *Four* called *One* and reported in.

One hung up the phone. It had begun, the clock was ticking. He instructed *Four* to come up to the condo ten minutes after the Governor entered the Slone condo and the trooper parked and sat in his car. He ordered *Four* to use the stairs and be careful not to draw attention to himself. He gathered the rest of the team around the dining room table. His team and the two dead homeowners, having been placed in the master bedroom closet, stuffed in black plastic heavy duty leaf bags were now in a waiting game.

Each condo had the same floor plan as the one TJ Slone had. The same floor plan *One* and his team were in. The condo they occupied was a mirror of Slone's. *One* started a walk thru with his team on what would occur.

One looked at the front door and decided as a last resort they would kick it down. The first plan was to go across the roof, drop down to the condo deck and see if by chance the patio door was left unlocked. Often people who lived on the top floor left their door unlocked thinking, being so high they were safe. In fact, the couple whose condo they occupied had a veranda door that was not locked. *One* knew the chances were slim, Slone being a law enforcement officer. His vocation caused him to think security, but it was worth a try. The master bedroom was at the rear of the condo that faced the coast. If they had to kick the front door, the distance from front to back would give Slone a chance to arm himself. *One* had decided to use *Five's* expertise as a climbing expert to try the patio entrance. He would send his brother with him. His brother could pick the lock if by chance it was locked.

One, Three and *Four* would wait at the front door, hopefully to have the other two unlock it and if not, to kick it. Upon entry, they would secure the Governor and his wife. Duct tape would be used across the mouth and used to secure their hands. Slone was to be shot by his brother and *Five,* first thing. TJ Slone was to be the only one shot. Mrs. Slone was to be taken as a hostage, getting the same duct tape treatment as the Governor and his wife. They practiced the scenario multiple times in the condo as they waited for early morning.

After securing the three hostages, they would bring the hostages down the stairs at the end of each condo floor. They would take the hostages to the boat dock to the boat *Five* would have brought back. They would then take everyone to the canal house. If it went as planned, they were hours from a successful operation and a very rich and happy ending, especially for *One.*

The plan was pretty simple, it just had to be carried out, and needed to be done quickly. The entire kidnapping should take less than three minutes from time of entry to heading for the boat, as well as everything else that was getting ready to happen. Before the actual plan would be started, there were three things that had to be taken care of. The two security guards and a little matter of a diversion. The two security guards were first.

Billy Scott had not been a trooper long and this assignment on the Governor's Protection detail was heady stuff for a young trooper. This was a plum assignment as far as he was concerned. It meant a lot to his career, but it was also a high profile and glamourous assignment He did not know why he had the job, other than the fact he was a hard charger and looked good in his uniform or business suit. He was inexperienced, having never done investigative work except accident investigations. His lack of experience would be fatal for him tonight.

Billy listened to the radio as he sat in his car. It was after midnight, in fact, almost one in the morning. The lights in TJ Slone's condo were out, he figured they were in bed, so the rest of the night would be easy. He would be relieved by Drey at 5 o'clock. Four more hours. The beach music station, 94.9 The Surf, was the station of choice. Beach music was not his normal choice, but he liked it. It fit the assignment. The SUV window was down since the warm night salt air just added to his euphoric feeling. He thought he had it made, it was a perfect evening, he had the perfect job.

Billy did not hear or see the El Salvador Special Forces trained soldier slipping up beside his car. *Five* was very good at his job. Billy never knew what would take his life. For a fraction of a second, he may have thought something was wrong, as the ice pick pierced the side of his head into his brain with all the force *Five* could muster, but probably not. Billy Scott sat in his car, straight up as if on guard duty, the beach music played, but Billy was graveyard dead.

Just before killing Trooper Scott, number *Three* had gently knocked on the door of the guest quarters located beside the condo's clubhouse community room. The soft knock woke a lightly sleeping Trooper James Drey. Looking at the clock he could see it was after midnight. He knew it wasn't Billy because he had a key and protocol required him to call before coming in. Failure to do so could get him shot. Besides there was no need for him to come in, the clubhouse had a restroom if he needed one.

Trooper Drey put on his pants, took his gun out and went to the door.

Peeping out the door peephole he saw a young Hispanic female, attractive and obviously in distress. Trooper Drey could see her mascara was streaked from tears coming down her face. She was holding what appeared to be a child tightly against her chest. With his limited vision thru the peephole, he saw nothing else in the hall. Drey placed the Highway Patrol issued 357 Sig Sauer in the waistband in the small of his back and opened the door. Before he could say how can I help you, the supposed child fell from in front of the woman to expose a silenced Model 422, 22 cal. silenced automatic. Not the most powerful handgun, but one favored by assassins for close range killing. Trooper Drey and Number *Three* were very close and in a fraction of a second, she had placed three muffled shots straight into his face and head.

Death was instantaneous.

Five stepped out of the shadows and helped drag Drey's body from the open door further into the room. He collected the trooper's gun and car keys, as well as his portable radio and his wallet. The wallet had no tactical value except for the credit cards and cash, and for *Five* it was all about the cash. With both of the security team out of the picture it would only be a short time before the rest of the plan would be put into motion. The walkie taken from the dead trooper would let them monitor any request from Slone's condo. If there was a request the plan would be aborted, they would take the condo by force, hoping surprise would be on their side.

Three went back to the condo with the rest of *One's* team.

Five took the canal couple's vehicle and went to get the boat. Before he left, he took the car keys he had removed from the trooper's room and placed a small block of C4 explosive with a remote detonator inside the dead trooper's car parked in front of the condo. He then drove the Lexus SUV to the canal home to retrieve the boat.

Three entered the condo joining the rest of the team. *One* looked at her and said, "How did it go?"

She simply replied, "It's done." Maria did not like to kill, though she was no stranger to it. She had killed many before this Trooper. It did not escape her that she had taken advantage of a person who had been willing to help, after what he saw, what he believed, was a person in distress. His kindness and training as a law enforcement officer was the cause of his death. She took some solace thinking his last few seconds, thinking he was helping someone may help him with his God. She thought about that and then thought, no matter, it's done.

Five arrived back at the dock with the 16 ft. Carolina Skiff.

He had been gone about thirty minutes. He backed into the boat slip so when they loaded, he could drive straight out. He left the key in the ignition as instructed. He walked up the gangway to the security gate which he propped open, so they would not have to use the security fob to enter on the return trip with the hostages. He then walked up the stairs to the top floor and into the condo holding the rest of the team. It was a little after 1:30 am on Saturday morning, in less than an hour the operation would begin.

* * * * *

Five reported all the lights were out in the target condo. He jingled when he walked, the noise coming from all the jewelry he had stolen from the canal home, as well as the condo they were using as a base. The others looked at him with distain. He didn't care what they thought.

Chapter Six

One looked at the clock on the wall, it read 2:10 am. He felt they would be asleep by now. Looking down from the top floor condo veranda, just a few condos from the Slone home he could see the pathway lit by solar lights leading from the pool to the condos and from the pool to the boat dock. There were a few lights on in some of the other condos that he could see. He felt the lights that were on were probably either lights that were on by mistake or were left on to act as night lights.

The parking lot was full, but that was not surprising, it was the middle of June and school was out. Sunset Beach was a popular family vacation spot. Not as large as Ocean Isle, but close to Calabash, the self-proclaimed seafood capital of the world and just across the state line from Myrtle Beach.

After tonight, it would be remembered for a far different reason. After tonight it would be known as the place Governor Matt Hart, his wife and Sheriff TJ Slone's wife Tina were kidnapped and several people, including Sheriff Slone, were killed.

One looked around the condo at his team. They busied themselves attending to their gear. They didn't know each other by his design, but they did know their job. *Five* was going over the rappelling harness with Azil's brother *Two*. *Two* was familiar with the rappelling process but not as much as *Five* who was military trained. *One* often wondered why the El Salvador army trained for repelling work, did they really have the need for such training.

How many all buildings or mountains did they have? No matter, he was glad they did. It really wasn't as much a repel as a drop. The pair would climb onto the roof from a roof entry point located by the elevator. The ladder to the roof door was locked but that was easily defeated with bolt cutters. After reaching the roof they would quietly walk to the roof just over the patio Slone was sitting on just hours before. They would secure a rope and drop about 12 feet onto the deck. Once on the deck they would try the door, hopefully finding it unlocked. If not, Kareem could pick the lock, training he had received in the deserts of Iraq. After the door was opened, each with night vision goggles provided by *One,* his brother *Two* and the mercenary *Five* would enter the condo. *Five* would go into the master bedroom and *Two* to the front door to let the rest of the team inside. It was a good plan, if it worked.

Once everyone was inside, Slone was to be shot through the head. The Governor and his wife as well as Slone's wife would be taken from the condo to the boat. They would be transported to the canal location. Each prisoner would have their mouths duct taped as well as their hands. The duct tape would be wrapped around the head and mouth, hair and all.

The alternate plan was not as quiet and was far more chaotic. They would kick the doors and rush in from the front and back. *One's* team would take the Governor's room which was the left front bedroom and the second team made up of *Two* and *Five* would take the master bedroom where Slone and his wife slept, killing Sloane and taking his wife. No matter which plan they used the time allocated for the whole operation once inside the house was 180 seconds. In and out in 180 seconds, three minutes, an eternity when gunfire was involved.

One said, "It's time, everybody ready?" They didn't answer with words but by action. They got up and grabbed their gear. They left the "borrowed" condo in a mess. They had made themselves comfortable, eating the dead couple's food, watching their TV. *Five* had been through every drawer, taking jewelry and cash. *One* didn't stop him, what would be the point, the man was a pig, he had no honor, but he was good at his skill and *One* needed that skill. They left the two dead bodies in large black leaf bags in the master bedroom closet. So far, this operation had cost six lives, Slone would be the seventh.

As they walked the few steps to the elevator's location, *Five* raced ahead, pushed the elevator button to call the elevator to the fifth floor. While they were not going to use the elevator, they didn't want anyone else to use it either. When it arrived, he pulled the stop button, locking the elevator on the fifth floor. He then cut the lock on the ladder leading to the roof. He and *Two* climbed the ladder and disappeared on the roof, closing the roof door behind them. The rest of the team walked to the stairwell beside Slone's condo. They quietly waited. *Three* and *Four* waited with a roll of duct tape in their hand. When they rushed into the bedroom occupied by the Governor and his wife, they would be covered by *One*. They waited in silence.

Two and *Five* walked across the metal roof as quietly as they could. The combat style boots had rubber soles much like a running shoe, making little noise except when they stepped on a loose piece of metal. *Five* jingled when he walked because of the jewelry he had taken from the condo and the canal home. The noise was not very loud, but loud enough to aggravate *Two*. He did not like this man and wondered why his brother chose him.

What little he knew about him showed the man knew his craft, he killed efficiently and quickly. He was good, but after this operation if he never saw *Five* again it would be OK with him.

TJ was not sleeping well, he seldom did when he had strangers in the house. The Governor and Belle were not strangers, they were valued friends, but for the purpose of a good night's sleep, they were strangers. TJ was also thinking about the fact his longtime friend was getting ready to be the second most powerful man in the world, if he accepted. He had little doubt Matt would take the job. His sense of duty would rule the decision and Belle would come around, she was a good supportive wife, but one that just for fun would make her husband sweat a little first.

It was also unusual to have a dog in the house. Tina and TJ had not had a dog since they had to put down their fourteen-year old Doberman. Diamond was her name and she was a great dog, just as the first Doberman Duchess had been. They missed them both. The reason they had not gotten another was because of the toll their loss had taken on each of them. They both agreed, the time needed to have a dog was not in the cards. That, plus the fact the condo rules did not allow Dobermans, a fact TJ found narrow and short-sighted. The few times he had ever been bitten, it was by a small dog, not by big, gentle, loyal dogs like Diamond or Duchess.

Mo, the Governor's dog seemed restless. TJ could hear the soft pacing of his paws on the hardwood floors. TJ thought Mo may have trouble sleeping in a new place, with new sounds and smells. As he listened Mo seemed more and more agitated. TJ got up and went to the living room. Mo looked at him with little interest. He continued pacing looking at the ceiling, then the front door. He let out a quiet whimper. TJ knew dogs well enough to know the dog was concerned about something. He returned to the bedroom, went to his secret hiding place and pulled out a Glock 43. It held seven rounds counting the one in the chamber, had night sights and was a gun TJ shot at the expert level. TJ was acting on instinct, that and the fact that a dog has far better hearing and smell than a human. He didn't know Mo that well, but he knew caution was in order.

Five tied the rope to the vent stack pipe coming from the roof. He tied a second rope to another vent pipe. He was not taking a chance on one pipe holding two men. When he finished tying the ropes, he handed one rope to *Two* and kept the other.

They attached the ropes to the harness each wore and sat on the edge of the roof, their legs dangling over, plainly visible from the condo if anyone was awake.

Mo became a little more agitated, his whimper a little louder. It was as if he was saying to TJ, "look at this dummy, I'm trying to tell you something." TJ looked out the patio doors and saw two pairs of legs hanging off the roof. What the hell, TJ thought? Before he could answer his own question, one pair of legs dropped from the roof and slowly eased down to the patio railing.

The silhouette of a man showed against the starry night sky. TJ could see out the door thru the sun blocking shades. TJ doubted the intruder could see into the dark living room. The lights from the pool below the condo illuminated *Two* as he swung from the roof. The figure climbed onto the deck, unhooked his harness and headed for the veranda door.

Two eased onto the patio railing, quietly slipping his foot over the top railing, sliding onto the floor. This was easier than he thought. He was doing this. Next it was his job to open the door.

The night vision goggles gave everything a green tint. He really didn't need them outside because of the pool lights, but he would inside. *Two* placed his hand on the door about the same time the second pair of legs with man attached dropped from the roof.

No sooner had *Two* grabbed the door then Mo let out a growl and bark.

Two backed from the door and grabbed from a sling around his shoulder what TJ recognized was a MP5 type assault rifle. TJ did not give him a chance to use it. He pulled the trigger on the Glock 43, putting two shots into number *Two's* chest, just as TJ had trained to do all his adult life. The safety glass in the door shattered into a million pieces as the rounds hit, exposing a clear sight of the second intruder hanging in mid-air. The second intruder was attempting to get the handgun he carried in a chest holster similar to what TJ's special ops team wore. TJ did not give him the chance. The second intruder's hand had just grabbed his pistol when TJ's third and fourth rounds caught the hanging intruder in the chest and top of his head. The head shot was a result of *Five* dropping his head after the first round penetrated his heart. It was not meant to be a head shot, but it worked, it finished what the first shot started.

TJ did not have time to survey the damage or the results of his actions, the front door slammed open with a crash having been kicked by even more intruders. As he turned, he could see Mo was heading for the black clad intruders. For an old dog he moved pretty fast. Mo was just not fast enough. The man standing in the door shot him with a double tap from his handgun. TJ could see two more people behind the first. As he started to turn his gun to engage these new targets, he saw the muzzle flash from the first and second person firing at him and then everything went black.

Chapter Seven

Where the hell did that dog come from, nobody said anything about a dog. *Four* didn't mention anything about a dog. If he had known there was a dog, he would have approached this whole thing differently. As he kicked the door, he saw the big black dog running toward him. Well placed shots stopped him in his tracks, but the lack of knowledge about the dog had taken a toll. As he looked beyond the dog, he could see TJ Slone, gun in hand. He fired as did *Four* who was right behind him. They both fired at the same time and TJ Slone, gun in hand fell motionless to the floor.

One headed to the master bedroom, stepping over the bodies of Mo and TJ. Each were being engulfed in pools of their own blood. *Three* and *Four* turned into the bedroom occupied by the Governor and Belle. As *One* headed for the master bedroom, looking through the veranda door, he saw what he knew was his brother, lying in a pool of his own blood. Hanging from a rope dangling 50+ feet in the air he could see the lifeless form of *Five*. The late TJ Slone was good, he had taken two of his team out in a matter of seconds, and one of those was his brother.

As *One* ran into the bedroom he ran into Tina Slone, phone in hand. *One* knocked her to the floor using both his hands and body weight. The phone was knocked under the bed. *One* did not know if she had called 911 or not, it didn't matter, the clock was ticking. He quickly wrapped duct tape around her head and mouth, tightly to stop any noise such as a scream coming from her. There had already been too much noise, he did not need a screaming woman. Tina Slone was in a daze, so putting the duct tape around her hands was easy. He jerked her to her feet and started dragging her toward the front door. As he guided her around her husband in the floor with an ever-widening pool of blood, he could see her eyes widen. *One* could feel her pull back, but he just jerked her harder. He pulled her past Mo, lifeless in the floor, and was met at the front door by *Three* and *Four* holding both the Governor and Belle, both, duct taped, both compliant, having witnessed the carnage in the living room of the condo.

One led the group to the right, taking the stairs, just as he had planned all along. They dragged their captives from the top floor to the bottom. The speed was faster than the barefooted captives felt comfortable with, but *One* didn't care about their comfort. Less than a minute before he had a living brother, now, to the best of his knowledge, he didn't.

As *One* reached the bottom of the stairs he turned, dragging his captives to the right, heading for the boat dock. He reached into his pocket, pulled out a remote detonator and pushed the button. The explosives planted in the trooper's car by *Five* exploded, destroying the car and both cars beside it, as well as damaging the front of the condos three floors up from the explosion. It was the diversion needed. It would give them the time they needed to get away without being noticed.

One looked up at the condo they had just left and could see *Five* limply swinging. You could not see any blood because of the darkness but he could not see any movement. He knew his brother was lying in the pool of blood he could see when he went in to retrieve Mrs. Slone. The death of her husband, Sheriff TJ Slone, was some consolation, but not much. This operation had cost him more than he wanted to pay, because of Slone and that damn dog.

They easily passed through the security gates leading to the boat, docked pointing out to the Intracoastal Waterway. *Five* had propped the security dock doors open. Now if that pig Juan Santigo, *Five,* had done as instructed and left the keys in the ignition they would be good to go. *Five* had done as instructed.

One started the boat and gunned it into the waterway.

Four barely had time to untie the boat before *One* gunned it turning left toward the Sunset Beach bridge. As *One* looked around he could see the light from the fires caused by the explosions at the front of the condo. He could see every condo had lights, but he saw nobody looking his way, the distraction had worked.

When they arrived at the canal home there was little resistance. A pistol across the face of the Governor had gotten the attention of everyone in the boat. The Governor made a feeble attempt at resistance which *Four* quickly met with a backhand pistol slap across his face drawing blood. *Three* explained to the three captives that if they resisted or did not follow instructions the consequences would be bad, very bad. At the canal home the boat was docked after several failed attempts. *One* had not planned to be the boat driver but because of the death of *Five*, it was now his job. Besides, you didn't get much practice driving boats in the desert where he came from. His fear was all the racket trying to park the boat would draw unwanted attention. The fact the houses on each side were empty gave him the cover needed.

Number *One* and his crew took the captives into the house. The Governor and wife were placed in one of the bedrooms and duct tape secured their feet as they were placed on the queen size bed. Their hands were duct taped behind their backs. If they tried to move, they would fall from the bed alerting the team.

They were placed facing away from each other and duct tape was placed around the eyes and head to match that around their mouth. Duct tape held their hands behind their back and their feet were bound. Now they could not move their arms and legs and they could not speak or see. One more indignity was placed on Belle Hart. She was given a shot of a sedative by Maria, Number *Three,* which knocked her out. She could feel no pain, hear nothing and see nothing.

Number *One* took Tina Slone into a separate room down the hall. The bed had been taken apart and placed against the wall leaving a big empty space in the center of the room. The mattress, placed in front of the window, would help deaden the sound, if any escaped the duct tape. In the space where the bed had been, a simple office style wooden chair set. Tina Slone was roughly pushed into the chair. Her hands were freed from the duct tape only to be taped to the arms of the wooden chair. She was taped in such a way her fingers could move, but nothing else. Her legs could not move because they were taped to the chair legs. Her mouth which was already taped had matching duct tape around her eyes, the duct tape circling her head involving her hair. It was going to hurt when it came off, if it came off. She was not able to make a sound, nor could she see or move. Ear plugs were placed into her ears, the foam type given away at loud venues such as concerts, car races and shooting ranges.

It was like she was in a world all her own, a world of pain.

Tina thought about the last thirty minutes of her life, that's all it had been, thirty minutes, give or take one or two. Was TJ dead? The love of her life, her best friend and partner lay in a pool of blood when she last saw him. Please God, don't let him be dead Tina thought. Who were these people, they seemed pretty well organized and trained, but who were they? Tina was sure it had something to do with Matt and his probable appointment, but what were they expecting? Ransom was out of the question, the United States government didn't pay ransom, and with the resources this country had, their chances of being caught were great. If this was just a suicide mission to show they could take out our leaders, why not just kill us, the point would be made? Tina could not figure out the angle. TJ can't be dead, Tina thought, not like that. She saw the person at the door and the one hanging from the roof.

How many more were part of this operation? Was it just the three in the boat with them? She suspected the troopers were dead.

What was the explosion she heard as they went to the boat? Why had they separated her from Matt and Belle, were they alright? So many questions. Little did she realize answers were coming soon.

Chapter Eight

"TJ, TJ, can you hear me?" Sheriff John Pass said with desperation in his voice.

TJ opened his eyes looking straight into the face of his longtime friend and fellow sheriff. The pain was excruciating as the EMT medic wiped blood away from the head wound over his left ear. It was just a crease, he was informed. It looked bad, bled like hell, knocked him out and caused a terrible headache, but it didn't kill him.

"Where's Tina?" TJ asked immediately.

With a look of sorrow John replied, "She's gone."

TJ attempted to sit up, but the medic and John held him down as he said, "Gone, what do you mean gone?" thinking his friend meant dead.

"They took her, they took the Governor and his wife also. Their dog is dead, they blew up a couple of cars and it looks like you got two of them, but they've got Tina, the Governor and Belle."

John knew about the Governor because as a professional courtesy TJ had told him he was visiting.

"John, what about the Governor's security detail?" TJ asked, his head pounding with each question.

"Both dead, the young man in the car appears to have gotten an ice pick to the head, looks like something out of a third world killing. The trooper in the guest suite looks like he took three small caliber rounds to the face, very professional." Sheriff Pass said with just a hint of professional appreciation for what he knew to be a heinous act.

"Who are these people John?"

"I don't know, but we will find them. We will find Tina," the last part said to comfort TJ, but it didn't work.

The medic said," Sheriff we need to get him to the hospital, he's lost a lot of blood."

"TJ, I'm going to follow you in, we'll talk more at the hospital."

TJ insisted on having his phone, knowing the Sheriff's office would have the condo locked down to complete their crime scene investigation. Sheriff John Pass got him his phone. He knew it was of no value to anyone but TJ. It was not needed for the investigation.

As they carried him from the condo to the ambulance, he could see the carnage caused by the explosion, an explosion he did not hear, He could also see Billy Scott sitting in his SUV, head slumped down like he was sleeping; he was, an eternal sleep.

On the ride to the hospital, over the objection of the medic, TJ called his Chief Deputy Thomas Powe. It was just after three in the morning, so a groggy sounding Chief Deputy did not surprise him.

"Tom, wake up, I need your full attention." If the ringing phone did not get his attention, the story about what had just happened did.

"Tom, I need a quick reaction team on the way here in less than an hour. Go to the fleet manager office and get the spare set of keys to my vehicle, put one of the team in it and have them bring it to me, along with their vehicles. In the package you send, I want hard chargers equipped with our best toys, including a K-9 and the drones. In the morning, first thing, I want our forensic team in the office waiting for anything we need checked, and yes, I know it's Saturday. Before you ask Tom, no, you can't come, I need you there to coordinate. Brief our attorney first thing when you get off the phone with the reaction team. I will have a mutual aid agreement to cover our guys within the hour. Let the county manager know what's happening after seven o'clock. Tell him to keep it to himself. Nobody is to know other than those I spoke of. The bad guys probably think I'm dead, I want to keep it that way for now. Tell our team to bring their equipment, but civilian clothes, I don't know where we will be based out of yet, but I will let them know before they get into town. Tom, tell them to hurry."

As he hung up the phone, he looked at the medic who looked at him with amazement.

"I guess we can rule out a concussion." He said.

TJ's look and response were meant to send a chill down the medic's spine.

"Son, you need to forget everything you just heard. They have my friends and more importantly, they have my wife. If anybody gets in my way getting them back, they will have a bad day, which could well be their last, do you understand?"

His response was short, "I pity those guys, whoever they are."

So do I." said TJ.

TJ was taken straight from the ambulance to an examining room. When the emergency room doctor walked into the examination room, he immediately requested TJ to lie down. TJ said no.

"Doctor, I know what's getting ready to happen in your mind. You're going to remove these bandages and look at the bullet crease on the side of my head. You're going to tell me how lucky I am it was not worse. Then you're going to say you want me to stay for 24 hours for observation, just to be safe, am I right Doc?"

Sheriff John Pass walked in just as TJ started his statement to the doctor.

The doctor looked at John, smiled, it was obvious they knew each other, and responded, "Yeah, something like that."

"Well Doc, it's not going to happen, I will be walking out of here in less than an hour, I hope with both of your cooperation, but walk out I will. During your examination if you find something we'll talk, but if it's just observation, I'm walking.

John, I'm not going to ask either of you to lie, but I need you to report there was one survivor in what appears to be a kidnapping at the condo belonging to Guilford County Sheriff TJ Slone. I don't want you to give the media any indication on who that survivor is. That knowledge could be the edge we need to save the lives of the Governor, his wife and Tina."

The doctor agreed, Sheriff Pass just said, "We need to talk."

After the doctor finished his examination, he agreed to TJ's demands but not without some stipulations. Sheriff Pass was a little harder sell. He understood the circumstances and what was at risk, but to say this was unorthodox was a gross understatement.

In less than an hour TJ and John walked to John's SUV. The hospital had a room in intensive care locked down with a Brunswick County Sheriff's Deputy standing guard outside. The room was empty. TJ had a mutual aid agreement giving his officers authority in Brunswick County faxed and emailed to his office and attorney. Three Guilford County vehicles were moving at emergency speed down Highway 220 heading for Brunswick County. Inside the vehicles were five Guilford County Quick Response team members and a K-9 deputy.

The doctor had cleared TJ. He had him sign a release for his safety and the hospital's. He said the ache would be there a while, as would the bloody bandage, which needed to be changed often, the doctor explaining head wounds bleed, a lot. The doctor wanted him taking plenty of fluids and Tylenol for the pain. He cautioned TJ that if he felt any dizziness or nausea to come back immediately and he was not to drive for at least 24 hours.

Right now, he didn't need to drive, he needed his phone. He remembered and believed, as President George H.W. Bush once said, you need a good rolodex, meaning you need to be able to reach out to your contacts to make things happen.

TJ reached out to longtime friends, Dave and Katy Cates who had a beautiful six-bedroom home located on the west end of Ocean Isle. He and Tina had stayed there often before buying their place at neighboring Sunset Beach. The early morning call explaining what had just happened and asking to use their home as a base was met with the affirmative answer TJ hoped for. In fact, when they arrived at the home within minutes of the call, Dave was loading the car and Katy had put on a pot of coffee and had a tray of pastry out beside the coffee pot. Katy was always prepared, just as every southern woman was.

TJ explained they may hear he was dead or at least the inference he could be. He asked them to keep to themselves they knew different, they said they would. Amazing friends who understood the gravity of the situation and wanted to help.

John was on the phone when TJ got back from seeing the Cates off.

"I know he's the Governor Mark, but it's still my jurisdiction, my case, my four dead bodies, and three kidnapped victims, a wounded person, not counting a dead dog. I've got blown up cars and buildings and I'm not giving up my responsibility. We'll talk about it when you get here, but I'm telling you I don't want anything released until we do, not by you, not by anyone. Call me when you get in county and I'll tell you where to come." As he hung up the phone, he looked at TJ.

"We have an hour tops, before Mark Sturgis, Director of the State Bureau of Investigations gets here and he's already making noises like he wants to take the case."

John's news was not unexpected. The Bureau had the jurisdiction or at least concurrent jurisdiction because Matt was the governor, but they didn't have the momentum, or the local knowledge John and his office had. The easiest and most politically expedient thing for John to do was pass it off.

TJ knew he would never give up the case and he knew John was not going to either. Sheriffs have a special connection to the citizens they work for. Sheriffs were truly the people's law enforcement. They didn't work for anyone, except the people who elected them, the good ones knew that and took it seriously. John was a good one.

Captain Sonny Young looked at the screen of his phone and saw it was the sheriff.

"Yes sir" he said after pushing the answer button. As the sheriff spoke, Captain Young entered the address the sheriff was giving him into the vehicle GPS. "The GPS says we will be there in 40 minutes barring traffic, and we have the road to yourself except for the black SUV we picked up after Highway 95. Don't know who is, but he's hanging tight, appears to be law enforcement, been following several miles and hasn't called in any other units yet."

Sheriff TJ Slone sighed saying "That's probably SBI director Mark Sturgis, we'll call and tell him to follow you in, so let him hang with you. I'll let you know if it's not him."

"Yes sir, see you soon." the captain replied and hit the off button.

Captain Sonny Young was a matter of fact, no nonsense team commander. He was one of the Sheriff's office federal Joint Terrorism Task Force members and had been since the 9/11 attack on the World Trade Center. He and other members of the sheriff's office were committed to a safer America. Captain Young was very good at what he did, as was his team. He had hand-picked each member with each member as dedicated as the captain. His second in command, Lt. Ron Jarrett, was a hard charging former Marine. He still looked like a Marine and acted like one, just in a Sheriff's office uniform. Jarrett was both respected and feared as was the captain. Not feared in a bad way, but in a good way. The team members feared nothing except letting the team down, no team member wanted to let the team down, to be the weak link.

The rest of the team consisted of Sgt. Jenkins, Cpl. Howell, Cpl. Jackson and Cpl. Jackson's K-9 Drake. Together this team was one of the best law enforcement had to offer. Their jurisdiction was Guilford County, but now as they sped down Highway 74 into the early morning, each silently thinking about the task ahead they knew they were part of a bigger picture. It was what they trained for.

After hanging up the phone with Captain Young, TJ turned to Sheriff John Pass and said, "You might need to call Mark, I think he's fallen in behind my guys on Highway 74, if he's in a black SUV."

John said "Damn" as he started pushing buttons on his phone. The call was picked up after the first ring.

"Director Sturgis" was the curt answer.

"Mark, John, are you on 74 behind some SUV's?" "Yeah, who are they, their tags are not in file?"

"They are TJ's quick reaction team, just follow them in, they have the address, TJ and I are waiting."

A frustrated SBI director said in a voice a little above normal, "TJ's people, a little out of their jurisdiction, aren't they? And what do you mean you and TJ are waiting, from what I understand he was shot and should be in the hospital. John, his wife and friends were kidnapped I hope you and he don't think he is going to be part of this investigation, that is not going to happen. He's a victim and victims are not part of investigations except as witnesses."

Sturgis's rant was not unexpected, in fact Sheriff Pass would have been disappointed if the SBI Director had not said what he did, God knows he had said the same thing to TJ a short time before, but TJ made some valid points, the same points he was getting ready to make to Director Sturgis.

"First off Mark, they have a mutual aid agreement I have provided, so they have the same authority I give my guys, as does TJ. Second, the Governor and his wife, are just as much friends of ours as TJ's and we are not removing ourselves from the case. As for Tina, yes, she is TJ's wife, but again she's your friend as well as my friend. You and I, as well as TJ, will be working this together, and together we will decide what needs to be done. If you have a problem with that, you tell TJ he's out, I won't."

Mark Sturgis listened and thought about what Sheriff John Pass just said. Sheriff TJ Slone was a true professional, so was Sheriff John Pass. In fact, TJ was offered the job as SBI director before he was, if he had accepted, Mark would be working for him. TJ turned down the Governor, even though the director of the SBI made more money, especially with the retirement TJ would draw from his years as sheriff. For TJ, it wasn't about the money, it was the people. The people he worked for, and the people he worked with. He was loyal to both. Mark also knew TJ's team, his entire staff were some of the best in law enforcement, hell, TJ had even hired some of his people. They had the best equipment. His guys took a lot of money from drug dealers through the asset forfeiture program and TJ was not shy about spending it for the good of law enforcement. In fact, since his office was the first in the state to get Rapid DNA testing equipment, he could test quicker than the state lab. All this and the fact that TJ was respected by state leadership as well as the federal level. A call from him usually got answered.

No, he was not going to tell TJ he was out, but the media optics would be a killer if not handled right. Sheriff Pass was right, all parties involved were friends. If we took all the people out of the mix who had a personal link, then the investigation would be hindered greatly. TJ was in, but he was going to have to be tempered and that, with TJ Slone, was like trying to put out a forest fire with a squirt gun.

Chapter Nine

One looked out the front window to the street below. It was still very early in the morning, the houses he could see were still dark. The canal house was silent and dark except for the soft glow of the TV with the sound off. It was a huge TV on which he thought a soccer game would be fun to watch. He suspected the Americans enjoyed watching baseball games since that was the sport in season. He had ordered the house to go dark until morning so as not to draw the attention of some patrolling police officer.

Now was the time for caution. His captives were duct taped in different bedrooms. They could not see, move, or speak.

Three and *Four* watched the silenced TV, reading the closed caption, to see if the news carried anything about the morning's kidnappings, but nothing was showing. This was a small media market and would not have 24-hour news. He imagined the first news would be at 6 am, a good hour away. He suspected it would be the news for the next several days. He would be long gone by then, his mission complete.

Now, it was time to get started with phase two.

Governor Matt Hart could hear movement around him in the adjoining rooms. He could not see anything because of the duct tape around his head and eyes. He couldn't speak because of the tape around his head and mouth. He couldn't move his arms and legs because of the tape around them. Belle was lying beside him, but she was not moving. He had tried to get her to move but she wouldn't or couldn't. It was like she was drugged, she was breathing, just not moving.

One opened the door to the Governor's room. In the dark, he could see the Governor had heard the door open because he looked in the direction of the door when it opened, even though the tape stopped him from seeing. *Four* walked past *One* and jerked the Governor up from the prone position and into a sitting position, in not a gentle way. He cut the tape around his feet and jerked the tape loose from his legs and the pajamas he was wearing. He cut the tape around his eyes and jerked the tape from his head and eyes. The tape pulled hair from his head and his eyebrows. The pain was tremendous, but the tape around his mouth stifled the scream he was trying to make. *Four* jerked him to a standing position. Matt Hart looked back at his wife Belle. She had not moved. *Four* pulled him to the door, past what the Governor imagined to be the man in charge. *Four* took him into a room, two doors down from the room he and Belle were in. The man who he thought was in charge got very close to his face. His breath was not pleasant, but neither was his message.

"Before we finish you will either be cooperative, or you will be dead. This will happen in the next few hours. As you can see, you cannot be protected from us. We can get to you, your family, anyone we want, anytime we want. We have leverage as you will see in a moment. I will be showing you how serious we are. You will be the master of your own fate as well as that of your wife and the widow Slone. This first lesson is to get your attention."

Widow Slone, so TJ was dead. Matt was not sure, but this confirmed it.

Four opened the door. Inside, Matt could see Tina sitting in a wooden chair, her hands and legs taped to the chair. Her eyes and mouth were taped as his were. The only thing you could see on her beautiful face was her small delicate nose.

The man who was in charge walked over to her chair, stood in front of her and lifted her chin where she was looking up at him though the tape stopped her from seeing anything. He then viciously backhanded her across her face, causing that delicate nose to spray blood across her face and body. The force of the blow caught her by surprise, the scream she tried to utter was muffled by the duct tape. He grabbed her chin though she tried to pull away and struck her again, just as hard, just as squarely across the face. The nose was damaged but did not appear to be broken. The swiftness caught the Governor by surprise and though the strikes were not on his face, he felt the pain as he watched his friend being abused.

Four pulled him out of the room as the man in charge followed. When they got back into the room he and Belle shared, *Four* pushed him into a sitting position on the bed. The man in charge bent down and again said in a low voice.

"We will talk again, soon." He then placed tape across Matt's eyes, this time not around his head. He taped his feet together and pushed him back into a lying position. He lay with his hands taped behind his back, his feet taped together unable to speak or see. He was completely helpless, and he knew it.

Three called, the news was on. As *One* predicted the local six o'clock morning news showed live shots of the condo they left hours before. The photos showed little since the crime scene tape kept the reporters and cameras far away from the actual scene.

The reporter said there was an explosion and they had four dead bodies and one seriously injured person. They were giving no names or other information at this point, citing a continuing investigation.

Someone lived, was it his brother, did Slone survive, surely not, he was bleeding profusely. Was *Five* still alive? Could the living person have any information that would compromise the operation? If Slone lived, he knew nothing. His brother and *Five* did. His brother would not say anything, *Five,* was a mercenary dog who had no loyalty. This operation was on a tight timetable and *One* needed to know who was in the local hospital and he knew who he would be sending.

One told *Four* to stay alert and asked *Three* to follow him. He led her into what was the master bedroom of the canal home. In the closet were two black plastic trash/leaf bags containing the bodies of the owners of the canal home. *One* shut the door and sat on the edge of the bed.

"I need you to go to the hospital, I need to know who is still alive. Is it part of our team or is it Slone? I need to know their condition. I need you to be careful and not cause any suspicion.

Do nothing. But find out who is still alive."

Three responded, "I cannot go like this. I have no other clothes." Her dress was combat gear. Black pants and tee shirt and combat boots with a web belt. She was right, she looked like a soldier. *One* pointed to the closet.

"*Three,* you have a whole closet full."

Three walked into the closet and searched thru the clothes hanging neatly on the rack. She had to step around the trash body bags. She paid them no mind. She pulled out a hanger containing a jogging suit, gold in color. She reached to the floor picking up a pair of white running shoes and came out of the closet placing the clothes on the bed.

Three swiftly pulled her black tee shirt above her head, exposing her sports bra which compressed her ample chest. The sports bra could not hide the nipples which protruded at an odd angle because of the compression. Odd angle aside they were very sensuous and did not escape *One's* attention. Her next move caused even more attention. After removing her boots, she dropped her pants and there was nothing underneath the black pants. *One* could see her clean-shaven pelvic area, clean shaven except for a thin straight line of hair pointing down to the treasure chest below. This was no mistake, she did it on purpose to say without saying, I care about myself and how I look, I am sexy.

This was evident to anyone who knew Maria Garcia. Her light brown body was well formed. Nothing was out of place, nothing too little, nothing too big, it was a perfect body, and she knew it. Although she was a believer, her body was something she was not ashamed of and she did not mind it being noticed. This was one of her vices, one not approved by her religion.

One noticed and motioned for her to step over. His hands made short work in removing the sports bra and cupping her firm round breast. *One* pushed her to the bed, spread her legs and roughly entered her motionless body.

Sex with *One* was not something which made the world stop for Maria. They had sex before, in fact often. After all, he was in charge, he was a man, she could not, would not dare refuse. Another tenet of her religion. The sex was not memorable. She never felt warm, loved or worshipped. She felt used. She knew she could not resist. She must comply. Her faith told her she should be subservient and give in to the desires of the man. She did those things, but they left her feeling empty. She wondered if the feelings other women from other cultures had told her about would ever be her feelings. She longed for just such an experience, but it did not happen, not today, not this time, not ever before.

One watched as *Three* got dressed. They had sex before, he was satisfied and felt she had been too, this time was no different. If she wasn't satisfied it did not matter to him, it was pleasurable to him and in his mind that was what mattered. He had no feelings for Maria, this was just for lust, to satisfy his desires. She was expendable and if she survived this it would be a miracle. He was not tied to her or anyone.

The jogging suit she put on was too big. The woman who owned the clothes was obviously about two sizes larger as were her feet, but it would do for the recon mission she was going on.

Three picked up the keys to the couple's car from the counter and walked downstairs to the car. She raised the garage door by pushing the remote on the visor. and backed out from under the canal home as the sun was just starting to rise. It was going to be a beautiful sunny June day.

Chapter Ten

The four black SUV's pulled up in front of the beach house on the west end of Ocean Isle. Along with Sheriff Pass's black SUV it made the parking area look like a black SUV convention. It would have been funny if the situation was not what it was. TJ, bandaged head and all, waited on the stairs. SBI Director Mark Sturgis was first up the steps, greeting TJ with a heartfelt hug, saying he was sorry this was happening. TJ thanked him, knowing he meant it, also knowing it changed nothing. He motioned Mark inside while he waited on his team to make the top of the stairs.

Each carried their gear in large black duffel bags, each greeted the sheriff with a hug, but few words. Nothing really needed to be said. As they walked into the room Sheriff Pass got off the cell phone he had held against his cheek. His face was ashen in color.

"Gentleman, we have two more bodies." Sheriff Pass explained officers had canvassed the whole condo complex, waking those who were not awake, which were probably none. Residents of each condo were interviewed. They found the maintenance man and had him unlock all the units that did not answer the door, using the emergency doctrine of the laws of search and seizure, fearing for the safety of those residents who lived there. Those responding to the knock on their door were deemed to be all right. Those not responding had their condo searched to make sure they were not in danger. In a unit down from TJ they found the bodies of Sharon and Frank Shapiro. Both had been shot thru the head with a small caliber handgun. They were placed in black plastic bags and placed in the master bedroom closet. It appears they were robbed since the jewelry box was empty. Sheriff Pass also said one of the suspects TJ had shot, the one hanging from the rope had a pocket full of jewelry.

Director Sturgis immediately jumped in and said, "So this is a bunch of jewel thieves."

TJ shot him a look that cut straight to the bone.

"Wake up Mark, jewel thieves don't kidnap and kill people or hang around for a second job if they did. They damn sure don't blow up cars."

Mark Sturgis wished he were dead. He knew immediately he had stepped in it. Captain Sonny Young smiled to himself, this was about to get interesting.

TJ Slone asked Sheriff Pass if he could see the jewelry. He also asked Sheriff Pass to allow his K-9 to get a whiff of Tina's clothes and see if he could run a track.

Sheriff Pass looked a little perplexed but said he would make it happen. He had dogs. They could run a track.

Cpl. Pat Jackson and K-9 Drake left with a Brunswick County deputy heading for the crime scene. After they left, TJ asked John Pass and Mark Sturgis to follow him to the widow's walk on top of the house. As they walked out on the widow's walk the new morning sun was just beginning to show what a beautiful day this was going to be. It was close to six o'clock. TJ looked across the inlet and Intracoastal toward his condo. He could see remnants of smoke, or at least in his mind's eye he could. It may have been his imagination filling in what he knew to be there from the exploded vehicles.

TJ began by saying, "Guys you need to know. Matt wasn't here for just a visit. He came to talk about an appointment as Vice President."

Sturgis spoke up, "Everybody knows he's on the short list, but the decision has not been made yet."

TJ smiled. He didn't want to burn him again, but here goes. "Mark, the decision has been made, he came to tell me the job was his if he wanted it. He had until Monday morning to turn it down. If he did not, he was to be in DC for an afternoon news conference." The silence was broken only by the sounds of the waves crashing on the beach.

Finally, Sheriff John Pass broke the silence, "Damn, damn, damn, you know what this means. We're going to be knee deep with FBI wanting this case, this is going to be a cluster in a hurry."

TJ knew his comments had gotten the reaction he wanted. "They can't take the case unless you guys are willing to give it up, it's your jurisdiction, not theirs. Matt has not accepted the position," TJ said.

"I don't know about you guys, but my people are just as good as theirs and I don't want to give up anything. We can offer them a liaison spot if you like, but we don't need them in our way."

Both Sheriff Pas and Director Sturgis agreed. Both knew the disaster that accompanied the FBI taking over any case where they had to work with local law enforcement. They took out all the air in any investigation and gave little back. It was like the locals were not as good.

As predicted a call from DC offering to assist in the investigation came straight from FBI headquarters. Sheriff Pass's offer to have someone act as a liaison was not met with much enthusiasm, and the FBI's request to hold off on the crime scene until they arrived, which was declined, was met with even less.

They said they would be sending a deputy director on a bureau aircraft within the hour. Sheriff Pass thanked them and said give him a call when they got here.

Sheriff Pass and Director Sturgis left TJ Slone on the widow's walk. TJ dialed his cell phone. You could not tell by looking at the phone, but its internal make up had special features allowing it to be scrambled and encrypted so it could not be hacked. When it was answered, TJ entered a four-digit number followed by a verbal password followed by another four-digit number and waited.

A voice on the other end of the call responded. "TJ, I'm glad you are ok. Didn't know what was going on."

TJ thanked the voice and explained what was going on. He also told him who was involved including the deputy director of the FBI on his way down from DC. "We may need some special help. Can you convene and see if the others agree? I don't know what we have, but I do know it has something to do with the Governor and his probable appointment. I also know I'm too close and should not be involved in the decision, I will abide by whatever you guys decide."

The voice at the other end agreed. "I'll send someone your way if everyone else agrees. They will call your number and give the usual identifier. You won't hear from me, but from him if it's approved. Good luck TJ." The line went dead.

The jewelry arrived and was spread out across the dining room table. There were several rings, earrings and necklaces, a Rolex watch and various jewel incrusted pins. TJ did not know what he was looking for but felt he needed to be doing something.

Sgt. Jenkins looked down at the table and said, "Sheriff, you notice those rings are different sizes?" Sgt. Jenkins was right. TJ quickly sorted out the men's rings, of which there were several into two separate piles, by size.

TJ looked at John and asked. Is Mr. Shapiro a small or large man?" John's call to his detective established Mr. Shapiro was a small man, 5'6", weighing about a 135 lbs. There were two rings that were at least a size 13, one a class ring from East Carolina from 1969. Inside the ring were the initials HWS.

Sheriff Pass picked up his phone and called his Chief Deputy telling him to immediately contact Pitt County Sheriff's Office to have them pick up a 1969 East Carolina annual, pronto. TJ was on the phone with his Chief Deputy Tom Powe, telling him to research any property owned by any male with the initials HWS living in a fifty-mile radius of TJ's condo. TJ knew it would take time, but he knew his chief deputy could do it.

When he hung up the phone, he looked at John Pass and said, "My friend, we may have more bodies."

TJ had a little down time, so he brought his team together, all, except Jackson and K9 Drake, who had gone to run a track at the crime scene. They gathered in the bedroom at the top of the stairs.

"Guys, first off, thanks for coming. I don't know what we have or where it's going to go. I know you signed on as a Guilford County Deputy, yet here you are in Brunswick County. I'm not going to ask you to stay unless you want to, and any man who doesn't will have no hard feelings from me. I know you're the best, that's why I called for you, but this is not your fight, not your jurisdiction, not your responsibility. You may be placed in harm's way, but because of all I just said, you need to decide. If you decide to leave, do it with my blessings and appreciation."

Nobody said a word. TJ knew, as did his team, he meant what he said. There would be no hard feelings, no repercussions if they did not stay. They had watched their sheriff agonize each time they were sent into harm's way, hell, sometimes he even went with them, putting himself out there.

Lt. Jarrett looked around the group, he spoke for everyone. "We're family, we'll stay."

Chapter Eleven

Cpl. Jackson arrived at the crime scene and went immediately to the sheriff's condo. He asked one of the deputies to go to the master bedroom closet and bring a piece of woman's clothing, preferably from the dirty clothes. In short order the Brunswick deputy returned with a blouse he found wadded up in a white basket he assumed to be the dirty clothes. Jackson took the blouse and placed it under the Plott hound's nose.

The Plott hound was the NC state dog. It was bred as a bear hunting dog, was fierce and had a keen nose. Jackson whispered "Hunt" in his ear. Drake immediately perked up. This was what he lived for. It was time to play. He put his nose to the floor and went immediately toward the condo. Jackson pulled him back. Drake realized he needed to be looking in another direction. He dropped his nose to the floor and went toward the steps leading down from the top floor. He had a strong scent. Jackson knew because of the intensity he was pulling. He wanted to find the person this clothing belonged to and he wanted his reward. The trail started down the stairs, all five floors. Went through the yard, past the hanging terrorist, straight to a security gate going to a walkway leading to the dock. Jackson called another deputy who found a security fob to open the gate. Drake went straight to the end of the dock, turned left and stopped at the last boat slip. Drake looked disappointed. The trail was gone. Jackson knew his partner had done his job. Jackson called Sheriff Slone.

"Sheriff, they left the condo and went down to the boat dock, They left by boat."

"Are you sure?" TJ asked, "yes" was the answer. TJ was sick to his stomach. John Pass looked at him and saw something was wrong.

"TJ, what is it?"

"I saw the sons of bitches, I watched them get out of their boat yesterday morning at sunrise. I thought they were flounder fisherman coming back from night fishing. They were dressed in black and now I don't remember seeing any fishing gear. I just wrote it off as I enjoyed the sunrise and my coffee. I saw the bastards and wrote it off."

Nobody said anything, it was one of those things that happen, something that would haunt TJ.

John asked, "Do you remember anything that might help?"

TJ responded, "Yes, there were five of them and one was smaller like a child, probably a woman. The boat was a 16-foot Carolina Skiff, because I thought that boat is too small for that many people."

Sheriff John Pass picked up the phone telling his Chief Deputy to research boat registration and get him the name of every 16-foot Carolina Skiff owner in this and every surrounding county. He knew there would be hundreds, if not thousands, but it was a clue. He instructed his chief deputy to check both the Wildlife records and county tax departments. Since this was Saturday people had to be gotten out of bed and brought into work. It didn't matter, the clock was ticking. Every law enforcement officer knew that after 72 hours without a suspect, your chances of solving a murder case were slim. In a kidnapping, the chances of finding the people kidnapped alive was also slim. Almost six hours had passed; time was not their friend.

When the information started coming in, it came in droves. Guilford County Chief Deputy Powe called back to say there were 63 pieces of property in the general area with owners with the initials of HWS, the initials found on the ring in the dead suspect's pocket. He was sending the list by email.

Pitt County called back after waking up the college president who in turn woke up the school registration manager.

They found they had three people who graduated in 1969 with the initials HWS, two females and one great big hunk of a football player. John took a leap of faith and asked for the name of the football player. With a size thirteen ring it was a safe bet. The football players name was Howard Wayne Swanson. The email came in from Chief Deputy Powe, listing the 63 pieces of property. Nine of them belonged to Howard Wayne Swanson, all of them were on the water. It seems Mr. Swanson was a real estate investor and this time of year his properties were probably occupied by vacationers from all over the country. When the boat registration came, one 16-foot Carolina Skiff was listed to Howard Wayne Swanson. There wasn't a single lead, there were ten, counting the boat and they all needed checking.

The team was divided up. Each team got an address to check out. They were to observe only. They were not to approach any of the properties. Nobody was to go around any of these locations in a black SUV. There was a rush to find plain vehicles.

Brunswick County Chief Deputy Roy Ingram walked into the hospital to check on his uniform officer guarding the empty hospital room. The officer guarding the room wasn't normally a uniform officer. He was a seasoned detective assigned to uniform this day to watch for any person who might have a little too much interest in the person who was supposedly in the empty room.

Detective Tim Nelson sat in a chair squarely in front of the room designated as the room of the imaginary patient. His job was to appear to be guarding the room. He was an imposing figure.

Professional in demeanor, a big man, very intimidating, even when sitting in a chair. He watched everything that went on around him. He wasn't sure what this was all about, but he was sure there was a good reason. The sheriff's office didn't waste resources such as manpower and they certainly would not waste a seasoned detective such as himself unless it was important. Chief Deputy Ingram approached his detective who rose from his seat immediately upon seeing him.

"Tim, how's it going, anything unusual going on?"

"No Chief, just staff scouring around, it's still a little early yet for anyone but staff, but it will pick up." Said Detective Nelson.

"Tim if you see anything, no matter how strange or minor it may be, I want you to call me. Let us, together, decide if it needs checking out. I will be in my car in the parking lot, so call my cell. If you need to use the bathroom, call, I'll relieve you. Again Tim, anything strange or unusual, call." The Chief Deputy said these things with a voice that said he thought something would happen. Suddenly Detective Nelson felt, maybe, this wasn't a waste of time, maybe he was going to be in the mix, contributing, making a difference.

Sheriff John Pass called his dispatcher and asked for all vehicles listed to Howard Swanson. A computer search found Swanson had two, both registered to his office address which was located on Ocean Isle. The office itself needed to be checked as well as the nine houses. It was probable the vehicles would be located at one of the nine houses he owned and was used as his home, but everything needed to be checked.

SBI Director Mark Sturgis called and ordered the agency surveillance plane to be stationed at the Ocean Isle airport. It was a small airport, so it would only handle a small plane. The plane could carry two people, a pilot and an observer. It also carried some of the most powerful surveillance equipment in use today.

It had cameras and could provide a live feed to a command post or the house acting as a command post. It had the capability to see in complete darkness and could determine heat signatures inside most buildings. It didn't tell you who they were, but it could tell you where they were in the building and if they were moving. It did this all in real time. It did this high enough to not be noticed unless you were looking for it. Director Sturgis felt vindicated by providing the plane, at last he was helping in some way. The plane would not be used unless needed. This area had heavy jet traffic because of the Marine Corps Air Station at Cherry Point. Sturgis knew a phone call could get the plane in the air and all other planes out of the air. He had felt like a third person on a date with both sheriffs making things happen. It was obvious watching them in action they were hands on in their management style. He admired that and realized how much he missed being in the hunt, being involved. He made himself a promise, he was going to be more like them.

Chapter Twelve

One looked at his watch. It was time for another lesson for the Governor, a lesson he was sure would seal the deal. He thought the Governor was a weak person, driven by his compassion for other people. He found most Americans to be weak for the very same reason. They did not have the stomach to do whatever was needed to reach their goal. He did. If it meant death and destruction, so be it.

Four opened the door to the bedroom with the Governor and his wife. The wife was still motionless except for shallow breathing.

The Governor again looked at the door. The sound of it opening causing him to react. He could not see thru the strip of duct tape across his eyes but looked toward the sound.

Four jerked the Governor to his feet, then ripped the duct strip from his eyes. It didn't hurt as much this time, but the removal of the tape caused his eyes to have to adjust to the light. The Governor could see a window in the room with light coming in around and through the closed blinds. He looked at his wife, still lying in the same position they had put her in hours before, still breathing but not moving. *Four* cut the tape from his legs, jerking the tape causing him to stumble. *Four* then jerked him toward the door. As he walked thru the living/dining area he could see a TV which showed the condos he had been taken from earlier. There was no sound, but he knew the story was about his kidnapping.

One pushed open the door to the room Matt Hart knew was the one Tina Slone was sitting in. When he looked into the room, he saw the same set up. Tina sitting in a chair in the center of the room. This time there was an identical chair sitting directly in front of her. Governor Hart was pushed into that chair. His arms and legs were taped just as Tina's arms and legs were taped. They were within two feet or so of each other's face, knee to knee.

Four ripped the tape from Tina's eyes and head. Matt knew it hurt. It had hurt him. It hurt him again watching this happen to her. The pain, the light, it all hurt Tina. Her muffled scream was gurgling in her throat and chest, but little or no sound was heard. As her eyes adjusted, the first face she saw through her teary eyes was that of her friend Governor Matt Hart. She looked and saw two other faces, those of the people who hours before had entered her home killing her husband and the Governor's dog. She could see one of the kidnappers was definitely American or European, and the other seemed to be middle eastern. Tina didn't know what this was about, but she suspected it was about the Governor and his pending appointment to be Vice President. What she did know was she was both mad and scared to death.

Matt Hart looked into the face of his friend. He could see and sense the fear she felt. He felt those same fears. He also saw a flicker of defiance and that look gave him pause. Her nose had stopped bleeding, but the tape across her mouth was streaked with trails of dried blood. The flicker of defiance was what really had his attention, not the bloody tape, she was mad, really mad.

Matt Hart thought as he looked into the face of his friend, this woman is phenomenal. How can she have any reaction other than horror and fear, seeing what she witnessed. The thought was interrupted by his sense of smell. Matt could smell heat. It smelled like something was burning. He looked around the room and found the source of the smell. An electric heating iron burned red hot in the corner of the room, plugged into the outlet on the outer wall.

The iron was the type used to burn wood from a wood burning kit similar to one he had as a kid. The iron could get red hot. This one was red hot. He looked at Tina and saw she was looking at the same thing, both with a sense of dread.

One calmly walked beside Tina's chair. In his hand, you could see a hand garden shear like the ones used to cut small limbs from bushes and small trees. It was efficient on trees and bushes a half of an inch or less. He grabbed Tina's left hand. She saw what was coming. Her muffled screams and look of terror were testimony to the horror that was about to occur. She tried to pull her hand away, but the tape was just too strong. Her arm could not move, could not be pulled away.

One picked the little finger apart from the others. With a swift cut *One* sheared the little finger off just below the nail and above the first joint. Matt could see the pain rush across the face of his friend, he could feel in his own throat the scream the tape would not let out. The blood spurted from the cut and bone could be seen. *Four* handed *One* the red-hot iron which he pressed to the cut finger, letting out a hiss as the hot iron met the wet blood, sealing the finger where her fingernail tip had been just seconds before. Again, Matt heard the muffled scream of his friend and then she passed out. This horror show was meant to terrify him, and it was working. What was next? Were they going to do the same to him?

Four placed a strip across the eyes of Tina. No longer around her head, just across the eyes.

One cut the Governor's arms and legs loose from the chair he was sitting in. He took him by the arm and led him to the dining room table and sat him down in a chair with arms. *Four* who had followed behind him, taped him to the chair by his arms only. For a brief second, he thought about diving out the window before they secured him, but he was not going to leave his wife or Tina and he doubted such a move would work. It was a desperation move, but in truth, he felt desperate.

One pulled his chair up close to Governor Hart's chair.

Four stood behind him holding a cell phone size instrument with two probes sticking out of the top. He pushed a button on the side and an electric arc joined the two probes.

One said in a low voice "Governor, I am going to take the tape off, so we can talk. If you attempt to scream or call out, he will shock you with that electric taser. It will not allow you to scream and will incapacitate you. We're going to talk, there is a way out of this for both you and your wife. If I don't get the answers I want, the way out will be death. If I get the answers I want, the answers that will be beneficial to me, you, your wife and Mrs. Slone, then everyone wins. Now again, do not cry out or scream, do you understand?"

Matt Hart nodded yes. *One* took the duct tape from his mouth with one swift jerk.

Matt ignored the pain and immediately asked "Who are you, why are you doing this and what have you done to my wife?"

Silly American. The answers were simple. I'm the guy holding you captive. I'm doing this for money, and I've drugged your wife. That's what he wanted to say, but instead he answered. "I'm the guy who has your life and that of your wife and friend in my hands. I want your cooperation. Your wife has been given a sedative which will make her oblivious to pain unless you don't cooperate. I believe you have seen what I'm capable of. The same pain your friend has endured can be inflicted on your wife or you, it's your choice."

Governor Matt Hart knew he didn't want Belle or himself subjected to the same pain and abuse inflicted on Tina. He hated the thought, he hurt for his friend. He hated the fear and hated the helplessness he felt.

"What do you want?" Matt asked.

"I want you to be a hero, I want you to be Vice President, I want us to have a long and fruitful relationship."

"You killed my friend, you killed my dog for God's sake, you just cut off part of my friend's finger and you want to be friends, are you crazy?" Matt blurted out before he thought, the adrenaline causing him to speak quickly and without choosing his words carefully. The whole thing just seemed so absurd.

One smiled, he had made the impact he wanted. "OK, we can't be friends, but we can be business partners and we will, or I will kill you all. In fact, I would be happy to bring Mrs. Slone back around and remove another part of her finger to show you how serious I am if you would like?"

Matt had no doubt he would, he didn't answer, he just shook his head no. When he finally spoke, he simply asked what he wanted?

"As I said, I want you to be Vice President, I want to provide you with information of mutual interest when you become Vice President. I want you to be President some day and we continue to be partners. I want you to succeed, but I want you to be my and my employer's secret friend. We want to have mutual goals and accomplishments."

"You really are crazy, why would I do that? What makes you think

I'm going to be Vice-President or President? Even if I were, even if I agreed, what makes you think I would keep such an agreement once I'm free. This is nuts," was Matt's answer.

"If we can't reach an agreement, you don't live. If we reach an agreement and you don't live up to the agreement, we will target your family, your wife's family. The most distant cousin to your closest relative or any family member will not be safe. I will be keeping Mrs. Slone and remove a piece of her body until you comply. I will do this until there are no more living pieces. Then I will leave her dead body in the street somewhere and you will know you did this. Then, I will take someone else you know and start all over again. You should already know I will take a life. Just so we could have this conversation, eight have died, not including your dog. If we cannot reach an agreement, then you and your wife as well as Mrs. Slone will die. To be honest Governor, I would just as soon kill Mrs. Slone now and you as well, but my employer does not wish it. Your friend the sheriff, probably killed my brother, before I killed him. Killing his wife now would not even the score, but it would give me great pleasure. The only reason I will keep her alive is to keep you focused on our deal, or if you would prefer, I can keep your wife." The look on the Governors face said no well before his words did.

"You said probably, what did you mean?" Matt asked. "Your news media said someone survived, it could be my

brother. If it is, I can assure you he will not talk. If it is my brother, he knows nothing that will compromise this operation. None of my associate's know anything except what their assignment is. They do not know by design. If it is your friend the sheriff who lives, the media says the person is in serious condition. If it is him, he will be dead before you are sworn in, either by his wounds or by my intervention. Neither your friend the sheriff nor your government can help you. I have run many operations in and out of your country and your government has never come close to catching me. Your FBI is too bogged down by your silly laws. I don't play by anybody's rules but my own."

One's answer did not lack confidence and Matt did not doubt he would attempt to carry out his threats. Matt was looking for a way out and his captor was giving him nothing.

One said, "You have an hour to think about my offer. I will be giving you another piece of Mrs. Slone to think about and we'll talk again."

Matt's arms were cut from the chair and he was jerked up from his chair by *Four* before he could reply. He was taken into the bedroom and duct taped next to his drugged wife again.

Chapter Thirteen

Number *Three* parked the car in the hospital parking lot. She adjusted the ill-fitting gold jogging suit and headed for the front door. The parking lot was empty except for employee cars, as was expected, it was very early in the morning. In the parking lot was what *Three* thought was a police vehicle. The car was parked with a clear view of the main entrance and there was a white male sitting in driver's seat of the vehicle. Tactically it was a typical cop move. *Three* noticed but tried not to be conspicuous, as she walked to the entrance. *Three's* intention was to walk each of the four floors until she found a room guarded by a police officer. It was early, too early for visitors, so the reception desk was not occupied. *Three* walked straight by the empty reception desk. She didn't know who to ask about anyway, so it worked out better this way. She figured they would have the patient under a false name anyway, another precaution she knew the police would take. If stopped, *Three* was going to use the excuse she was looking for her friend's room and there was no one at the reception desk to ask. She got on the elevator and pushed the button for the floor marked Intensive Care. If the survivor was in critical shape, they would be on that floor.

Detective Gene Nelson sat in front of the empty room, leaning back in the metal hospital chair provided by staff, drinking a cup of sorry tasting hospital coffee. He had seen nothing out of the ordinary and really had not expected to. It was very early.

Only hospital employees made up of doctors, nurses and cleaning personnel. There were a few family members who were sitting with other family members who were patients, but none appeared the terrorist type, and all could be traced back to an actual patient. This was a long shot anyway, but his bosses, Sheriff Pass and Chief Deputy Roy Ingram did not leave anything to chance. If there was a hole, they wanted it plugged. He understood the Sheriff of Guilford County had been shot, TJ Slone was part of the investigation, even though he was also a victim. Gene had heard of him, who hadn't. He was loved by his deputies and feared by his enemy's and that was as it should be. His sheriff and Sheriff Slone were close friends, both being active in the North Carolina Sheriff's Association, both active with Sheriff's Training and Standards. Gene had often thought if he ever left the beach and Brunswick County, Guilford County would be a great place to work.

The elevator door opened causing Detective Nelson to turn and look. Out of the door stepped a young, Hispanic women. She appeared to be in her late 20's, early 30's. She was very attractive and wearing a gold colored jogging suit. She was the type of woman any man would be proud to be seen with, but, something about her hit him as not being right. Was it his normal detective suspicion or was it the male hormones causing him pause? He couldn't put his finger on it. She had his attention, but he didn't know why. He wasn't sure if the attention was because of her looks, his boredom or what.

Her looks he thought. It was her looks. The jogging suit was too big, that was what caused him to be suspicious. Why would a woman as attractive as her wear something that obviously did not fit? He started to rise from the chair as the woman turned to go down to the hall opposite the room he was sitting in front of.

Before he could get out of the chair, the nurse manning the nurse's station stopped her. Detective Nelson heard the nurse ask the woman if she could help her. He stood and listened. The young woman said she was looking for a friend's room. The nurse asked if the friend was in Intensive Care to which the woman replied, she did not know. She said there was nobody at the reception desk she could ask. The nurse asked the friends name and the woman responded, Jill Long.

"I'll check the computer for you." The nurse said. "We'll see where she is located."

The woman had already turned back toward the elevator, "That's OK, I'll go back to the reception desk and wait, it's probably too early to visit anyway." She quickly walked away.

She looked straight at Nelson and smiled as she hit the elevator button. The door opened, since little time had passed since her exit from the same elevator. She quickly entered, the door closed, and she was gone.

Detective Gene Nelson did not feel right about this. He asked the nurse to check the name the woman had provided. Her check, which took only a minute on the computer found no patient named Jill Long in the hospital. Detective Nelson knew this was the only hospital in the county. Ill-fitting clothes and looking for a patient that did not exist, fit the bill for contacting the Chief Deputy who was in the parking lot.

His call was answered on the second ring. "Chief, I might have something, or I might not, but a woman in a gold jogging suit was just on the floor asking for a non-existent patient. She first caught my attention because she was wearing a jogging suit that did not fit. Like I said, it could be something or it could be nothing."

"Gene, that woman just come running from the hospital and got into a white Lexus crossover. I thought it was a little strange because she was running from the hospital she just entered. I wrote it off to her being young and in a hurry. She pulled out of the parking lot a minute ago."

The chief deputy started his car heading for the exit. The time it took to check on the imaginary patient gave *Three* the chance she needed to get to her car and leave. When the Chief Deputy reached the exit, he found it empty. He could go right, or he could go left, he chose right, Number *Three* had gone left.

It did not take the Chief Deputy Ingram but a few miles to realize he had chosen the wrong direction. At pursuit speed, had the suspicious woman gone to the right he would have overtaken her. It was an educated gamble on his part. FBI research has shown the normal criminal will make right turns when trying to get away since it is usually the path of least resistance, you don't have to cross over any traffic lanes. This time of morning there was no traffic to have to wait on. It was an educated guess, it was wrong. He had a fifty-fifty chance and he lost. Chief Deputy Roy Ingram headed back to the hospital, where there was hospital video to look at. During the drive back, he called Sheriff Pass to report what had happened, it was a call he didn't want to make, he felt like he had failed, the clock was ticking, and this suspect if captured could have been a game changer.

The explanation of the events reported to Sheriff Pass were not good news, but he understood.

"Roy, shit happens, don't worry about it, you could have been right just as easily. Get me a photo, run it thru your counterpart in Guilford, they have facial recognition capability, let's put a name to this woman, we're getting closer." Sheriff Pass hung up the phone. He knew his Chief was beating himself up bigtime, he also knew he would work his ass off to get a photo and the suspicious female identified.

At the hospital, Detective Nelson had already begun pulling the surveillance video. The hospital had state of the art equipment and the hospital security team had already isolated the parking lot and identified her vehicle as a Lexus crossover and the white vehicle the Chief had been trying to locate. They also tracked her movement from the parking lot, into the hospital and into the elevator and out onto the Intensive Care Unit. It showed her confrontation with the ICU nurse. She tried to hide her face, but too many cameras allowed security to provide a clear photo of not only her car, but her face.

Chief Ingram called Chief Deputy Thomas Powe, his counterpart in Guilford County. They had known each other for years, often venting to each other over similar issues each faced in their respective jurisdiction, not the least of which was their similar bosses. Both worked for hands-on sheriffs who insisted on everything being done quickly and done right, two traits that were sometimes not the easiest to accomplish. After venting about losing the suspect and Chief Powe lamenting the fact he was not there, they got down to business.

"I'm sending you a photo of the suspect. I understand you guys have access to photo recognition and can get me a name.

According to Sheriff Slone there are five players involved and she is one," reported Chief Ingram.

"It may take a little time, but I will get back to you as soon as I can hook up and get you an ID. If she's been arrested or gotten any form of government photo taken, we'll find it" was Chief Powe's response. He would put every effort into identifying this woman. He just regretted he was not there. Two hundred miles away did not give him the satisfaction of being a part of it, like being there would. He forwarded the photo he received to the Special Operations Division to begin their magic, he just hoped they could do the trick.

Three pulled down the canal street, pulling into the next to last house on the canal. It was still early and there were very few lights on in any of the residences. The lights burning were probably nightlights, so they were nothing to be concerned about. She pushed the button on the remote hanging from the visor of the Lexus and watched the garage door open. She stopped the car inside the garage and pushed the door remote again and watched the door close. She knew she had not been followed because she had taken evasive measures. She had failed in her mission, but it had not been compromised. She hoped *One* would not be too upset. They still did not know who had survived just hours before.

Was it *Two* or was it *Five* or was it the Sheriff? This operation was perfect, had it not been for that damn dog. The sheriff should have been asleep, they should have had the element of surprise.

Instead they left two of their team behind. She did not know either of them well, she suspected that was by plan. *One* was a hard man to read, but he was no dummy. She had been on missions with him before and had heard of his exploits and of course he had taken her sexually several times. She knew she was just a distraction for him, there was no love. It was not like she could refuse. Her religion and position in the group dictated she comply. She longed for experiences such as other women had described the feeling of warmth from a relationship that had mutual respect and caring, but from past knowledge of *One,* it was not going to happen with him.

As she reached the top of the stairs from the garage *One* opened the door, and his question was as expected. "Who is alive?"

"I don't know." replied *Three.* "The room in ICU is guarded by a deputy sheriff outside the door. At this time of day, the hospital is empty. I was stopped as soon as I left the elevator and questioned by a nurse about who I was looking for. I gave her a name and she offered to look it up, I thanked her and said I would go check at the reception desk. I left the floor and the building. There was a cop in the parking lot, but I left him there. I suspect unless we got lucky the name I gave is not in the hospital" "Were you followed?" An anxious *One* asked.

"No, I am sure I was not."

One regretted sending her on what turned out to be a fool's errand, but it was done. Hopefully, nothing would come from his foolish mistake.

Chapter Fourteen

Sheriff John Pass picked up the ringing phone, TJ watched as his friend's face took on a strained look. He just shook his head as he hung up.

"It's the FBI, we got an Assistant Director from DC coming. He's in the air now, couldn't get everyone on a plane small enough for our airport, so they are coming by helicopter, which will take a little longer. They're bringing a whole team from DC."

Like John, TJ was not happy. Anytime the FBI gets involved things seemed to turn to molasses as it related to movement. They do not play well with others and acted like their opinion was the only one to be considered. All they needed was a group of bureaucrats who had been riding a desk in DC to be interjected into the investigation. He was sure they had also alerted their Wilmington and Charlotte offices and had folks coming from those locations as well. The investigation was about to be asshole deep in FBI agents. Both sheriffs had great working arrangements with their local agents, but heavyweights from DC seemed to not be as interested in solving crimes as they were in advancing their careers. Both sheriffs realized things were about to become more complicated, and it didn't have to be.

"John, they're going to try and take over your investigation.

They have jurisdiction because of who is involved, and it is a kidnapping, but John, it is still your investigation, you have dead bodies. They can't cut you out," Sheriff TJ Slone stated, even though he knew Sheriff Pass was well aware of his position.

"Any suggestions on how we handle this?" was the response from Sheriff Pass.

TJ's response was quick. "Yeah. Let Mark Sturgis with the SBI deal with him. The two can handle the media and keep them off us. This should feed the FBI's ultimate goal which is to advance careers. The media thinks if it is coming from the FBI it's gold, let them handle that, it only slows you down when you have to do it. You can still appear with them, but let the FBI do the talking. It will feed their egos. We'll brief them and use their resources but if they have any sense, they will realize they have a great opportunity here and will stay out of our way. We've got movement, we've got leads and I don't want to get bogged down in the quicksand that is the federal bureaucracy. Who are they sending?"

Sheriff Pass smiled, the kind of smile that had a smirk built in, the kind that said you are not going to believe this.

"Deputy Director Steve Dunham."

TJ took a deep breath. "What an asshole!" Dunham was the most disliked bureaucrat in the FBI administration. If it had not been for the turmoil involved with the assassination of President Turnage he would have been replaced long ago.

Dunham knew he was a dead man walking in this administration and jumped at any case he could use to gain points to try to save his job. TJ knew, as did Sheriff Pass, Dunham was going to try and do the same with this case, to him it was about career, not justice.

TJ and John's plan for Director Sturgis to keep Dunham busy was met with the resistance they expected. Mark was a good guy, but he hated intrigue and he knew by reputation Deputy Director Steve Dunham was an intrigue kind of guy. He hated the idea, but he would do it, he still had a cop's heart and knew sometimes you took one for the team. He left for the airport to meet the helicopter, his facial expression looking like someone had knocked his ice cream in the dirt.

FBI Deputy Director Steve Dunham looked down from the helicopter window at the Ocean Isle Airport. It was a small private airport that serviced the local homeowners. It was not big enough to handle the size plane he thought a man in his position should be arriving in. Instead he was arriving in a loud, cumbersome, slow- ass helicopter. This was not his usual job, field work, in fact as far as he was concerned, this was beneath him. He was here because a possible Vice-President, his wife and the wife of a county sheriff had been kidnapped. He would not be here except for the fact the possible future Vice-President, Governor Matt Hart could make his career and reputation if he solved this case and by chance rescued the governor. Even if he didn't rescue Governor Hart, the media exposure would give him the chance to get in front of the new President and if he could do that, he could parlay that into a good career opportunity. If he was the man who rescued the Vice President, he could be the next appointed FBI Director, it could happen. Now he just had to make it happen.

Deputy Director Dunham exited the helicopter to be greeted by the Director of the North Carolina State Bureau of Investigation, Mark Sturgis. They had met before at different conferences and law enforcement events. Dunham was not impressed. He felt even though a Director, Sturgis was beneath him.

Mark Sturgis watched as Dunham filled the door of the helicopter. He surveyed the area like he was looking over his domain. To Mark he looked like a pompous asshole. His look of impatience showed he felt being met by one person without fanfare was not appreciated. Mark thought to himself, his friends the sheriffs knew this. This guy is not going to fare well. Southern hospitality was not going to be to his liking.

Captain Young stood on the widow's walk looking toward the only vehicle access to the house. The street was guarded by a gate controlled by a code access. It was a quarter mile to the house located at the end. There were speed bumps along the quarter mile. Even if someone were to try to gather enough speed to crash the house they would easily be stopped by the fully automatic rifle at his feet, resting on the floor out of sight. The widow's walk would always be manned. Facing the water on two sides and the neighboring house on the other, a camera watched the road and all sides through a monitor located on the widow's walk. Nobody was going to get close without being seen and stopped if needed. As he looked down the street, he could see the black SUV which he knew belonged the SBI Director Mark Sturgis. He also knew the FBI Deputy Director Steve Dunham would be inside the vehicle. He called Lt. Jarrett to relieve him, he knew the next few minutes when Dunham arrived would be interesting, and he was not going to miss it.

When Sturgis pulled up to the house, he saw nobody was there to meet the Deputy Director of the FBI. He, knowing Sheriffs Slone and Pass, knew it was intentional. Their conversation was going to start with the Deputy Director being pissed, they didn't care and to be honest neither did Sturgis. From a psychological point of view, him being pissed would play right into their hands.

Steve Dunham looked from the SUV and saw there was no greeting party, just as there had been nobody but the State SBI Director at the airport. These locals were about to be schooled on who they were dealing with. He knew Sheriff Pass was popular in his county but was not a player on the national scene like he was. He knew Slone was more of a player, being friends with the kidnapped Governor, so therefore friends with the next potential Vice President. He had heard he was also friends with the prior president, the now sitting President and Attorney General, but he did not know to what extent. It didn't matter, they would soon learn as the old saying went, there's a new sheriff in town, pun intended, the thought of that made him smile.

Dunham and Sturgis walked into the house and saw Sheriff's Slone, Sheriff Pass and a man he did not know standing around a large table containing a computer and papers. Outside were three other men, dressed in civilian clothes but obviously cops, though they were trying not to look like cops. It wasn't the look, but the attitude that gave them away. You could tell they were not missing anything going on around them.

"Deputy Director, welcome to the fray," said TJ Slone as he looked up from the Surface tablet computer in front of him.

Slone had a bandage around his head that showed a faint hint of blood staining the bandage, he was taller than Dunham remembered. "I believe you know Sheriff Pass. This is the Captain of my Sheriffs Emergency Response Team, Sonny Young," Said Slone as he motioned toward his Captain.

"Your team, why your team, a little out of your jurisdiction aren't you?" said Dunham.

Before TJ could answer, Sheriff Pass responded. "No, they have authority here just like everyone else in the mix. We have a mutual aid agreement."

The look on Dunham's face screamed he was not happy.

The mutual aid gave him two sheriffs to deal with, not one.

Dunham turned to the table, saying "What have we got?" Dunham was briefed on what had occurred about six hours before. The kidnapping and the deaths of the two Highway Patrolman, the two suspects and the two condo residents. He was told how they figured there were at least five suspects, now minus the two TJ had killed. They explained how they had not announced who was killed or who had survived and had placed a guard on the empty hospital room to see if there was any interest from the suspects.

They told Dunham they felt the female suspect had been at the hospital but left with nothing as to who had survived. She could see there was a guard posted outside a room on Intensive Care, but nothing else. They felt she was part of the terrorist team. She was driving a vehicle they believed belonged to what may be one more victim, that being Howard Wayne Swanson or Swanson could be part of the plot. More than likely he was not since they had his ring, taken from the dead suspect's pocket. Swanson owned a car similar to what was seen driven by the female and a boat similar to what was used by the suspects. All this told them the suspects may still be in the area. The owner of the vehicle and boat also owned nine properties in the area and a business. The sheriffs stated they did not know which, if any of those properties Swanson may be living in. The boat and cars came back to the business address which they had staked out. The electric and water bills for the homes all came to the business address. The business was set to open at nine this morning. If he showed, he would be watched until they decided what to do, if he did not show they would reassess.

Each of the properties were getting a drive by to see if they could gather any information that might be helpful. The two dead suspects were being processed for identification, their fingerprints and photos as was the photo of the female were being checked thru the facial recognition and fingerprint data base. Dunham was told how they identified Swanson. They explained how to them, it was obvious by the killing methods and how the explosion was used as a distraction, they were dealing with professionals.

Deputy Director Dunham had to admit he was impressed. They had gotten a lot done in six hours. Impressed, but he was not going to let them know that.

Sheriff Pass's phone rang, it was his Sergeant who had put together the surveillance teams for the nine properties owned by Swanson. Since it was the beginning of summer vacation, as best they could tell, each property was occupied. They could see the vehicles at five of the properties and had ran the tags to establish they were not local but were from all across the eastern part of America. Not unusual for June. There were no vehicles spotted listed to Swanson, but there were four properties listed to Swanson that had enclosed bottom portions of the home. This was not unusual since all houses on the beach or canals were raised to protect against high water during bad storms. Many homeowners enclosed the lower portion to act as a garage or storage area, this was the case in four of Swanson's properties. Each of these properties were located on the canals on Ocean Isle. Sheriff Pass ordered those four be checked by boat to see if they could spot the boat used by the suspects during the kidnapping. He reminded the Sergeant to use a private boat with civilian dressed officers.

Chapter Fifteen

One was not happy. *Three* had not found out anything on her trip to the hospital. He did not like the fact she spotted a cop in the parking lot and in the hospital, though he really expected nothing less. Her appearance at the hospital was possibly raising suspicion at this moment. He was sure they had photos of her and the vehicle she drove.

He had to tie up some loose ends. He ordered *Three* to stay with his captives and ordered Number *Four* to take the vehicle *Three* had just driven and meet him at a marina located just across the state line, in South Carolina off 13th Ave. It would be a short boat ride for him. He would leave the boat there and be long gone before they discovered the boat or tied it to this operation and location. He just wanted the boat away from his location.

One also needed to meet with the sea plane owner for final arrangements for transportation tonight. The sea plane operated out of Little River, SC, which was halfway between the marina and the canal home. The marina was also near a local sports bar and restaurant, Boardwalk Billy's, where he had the first meeting with the sea plane owner. *One* had visited there since that first meeting. He liked the place as many folks did. It was always crowded, always had great food and if you had to wait, it was worth waiting for. He had taken his team there the night before this operation began. Its location was one close to the marina and *One* knew Number *Four* could find.

Four was waiting at the marina as *One* pulled the boat to the dock. His boat ride had taken him by the condos he had left hours earlier. The smoke and smell from the explosion could still be seen and smelled. *Five* still hung from the roof, verifying he was dead. He knew because otherwise, they would have cut him down. He wondered if his brother still lay on the veranda deck or if he was the person in the hospital room guarded by the deputy.

One parked the boat in a spot reserved for temporary parking to allow the boat owner to get bait, ice, drinks and snacks. He hoped it would not draw any attention until later in the day and he would be long gone. He had checked the boat registration and saw it was registered to Swanson's business address, as was his car. He hoped they would not tie the boat to the house they were at, at least not until he was gone.

Four moved from the driver's seat, letting *One* take the wheel of the white crossover Lexus. Jerry Blair, Number *Four* was a good soldier, a true believer, thought *One*. It was a shame he was so expendable. He was not going to survive this experience, he was cannon fodder and at the end of the day if he did as he was told, he would be dead. *Four* had replaced the tags on the vehicle they were in with tags he had stolen the night before from a car located at a local garage being repaired. He had put the Lexus tags on that vehicle, all this had been done after they returned to the canal home before daylight. Even if *Three* had drawn attention and they got her tag number, they would get nothing of value from it until they checked the garage. With luck the tag switch would not be noticed as having been switched. The boat was a different story. It came back to the man in the leaf bag at the canal home. *Four* definitely had talents and followed instructions well, except he did not mention that damn dog, if he had, his brother *Two* and *Five* may still be alive.

No matter, his brother may still be alive, he didn't know who was in the hospital. It had to be his brother or Slone, *Five*

was swinging in midair when they left the condos. He still hung there now. He was sure *Five* was dead, not so sure about his brother and Slone. Had *Five* not been dead the cops would have taken him down, tried to save him. Slone was bleeding from a head wound. His brother was lying outside the door on the balcony. He should have put another round in Slone's head, but he didn't. That was a mistake. Time did not allow him to check on Slone or his brother's condition. There were three hostages and three of them and time constraints did not allow the checking of the dead or wounded.

Five pulled into the Sunny Side Café in Calabash, NC. It was located within a couple of miles of the condo they had left just hours ago. It was also halfway between the Marina and canal home they occupied now. Going back to the canal home he would take the back way, knowing the route in front of the sheriff's condo would be blocked. *One* instructed *Four* to stay in the car.

When *One* walked into the café, he immediately spotted Mac Samms, the sea plane captain sitting in a corner booth. The café was full of vacationing tourists, and Samms looked out of place sitting in a four-seated booth alone, especially since there were people waiting. *One* slid into the bench across from him.

"Good morning, Mr. Samms, how are you today?" asked *One*.

Mac Samms did not answer the question but asked one of his own. "Who's your friend, and why did he not come in with you?"

One smiled and thought to himself, Mr. Samms is a cautious man, a man no stranger to covert activities, which was why he was chosen.

One replied, "An associate, Mr. Samms, who has no business knowing our business."

Mac Samms was no stranger to intrigue, he had been smuggling, using his sea plane to bring into the country or out of it whatever his employer wanted. Whether it was legal or not was not his concern, he was in it for the money. Besides if it were legal, they would not need him.

Samms said, "You asked me to be available tonight, I'm available. Where do you want me and at what time? How far are we going? How much does the cargo weigh, including passenger weight?

One smiled and answered. Samms was straight to the point, he liked that.

"At the boat landing in Ocean Isle at midnight. There will be three passengers and the total weight will be less than 500 lbs. We will be going approximately thirty miles out to sea, where we will land on the water to meet a freighter going south. Flight time less than thirty minutes at max speed. I will give you coordinates tonight. A lifeboat will pick us up and your job will be done. I will pay you $10,000 now as you require and another $40,000 when we get to the boat. Should you not show up, I will hunt you down and you will not like the results. Should you not get me and my passengers to my location, you will not like the results. Any other questions?"

Samms was not impressed, all these smugglers liked to make threats. "I'll be there, make sure you are. From your description, I would guess this whole transaction should be over in an hour or less. Is there anything else I need to know?"

"No, just be ready to pick us up at midnight, exactly, and I expect to be airborne less than five minutes after that. Not 12:01 or 12:02, but 12:00 midnight." Said *One* as he passed an envelope containing ten thousand dollars across the table.

One placed an order for five steak, egg and cheese sandwiches to go, along with five coffees. Five sandwiches though he knew Belle Hart would not need one and doubted Tina Slone would. The small talk continued between the two until he was told his order was ready. He left the table, picking up Mr. Samms check to pay along with his own.

"See you tonight," were his parting words. That and a look meant to intimidate.

Samms watched as *One* entered the white Lexus. He wondered who the other passengers might be. He wondered if the man would be one of the passengers. He wondered if this man had anything to do with the excitement going on just a couple miles away. He wondered, but he didn't care. He knew he was going to make $50,000 for about an hour's work. That was all he really needed to know.

One pulled into the garage under the canal home. As he drove in, he noticed a boat similar to the one he had just left in South Carolina in the canal behind the house. It was pulling into the main channel, probably a couple fisherman getting a late start.

The Brunswick County Sergeant pulled his fishing boat from the canal into the main channel. This was the last of the four properties Swanson owned that were in question. None had a boat docked behind the houses on the canal. He only saw life at one of the properties and it appeared to be vacation families sharing the house. There were toys on the back deck and young kid's clothes and towels hanging on the rail. It wasn't his call, but if it were, he would take that one off the possible list. He would report his findings back to Sheriff Pass.

One brought the sandwiches and coffee up the stairs followed by *Four*. *Three* reported everything was quiet. The news had no new information, just repeating the same story over and over, just with different people telling it. *Three* had turned the channel from local, which was now sporadic to Fox News which was full of talking heads giving their opinions on what happened and why. *One* knew if these talking heads went on long enough, it would be bad for his cause. He wanted the Governor to be seen as a heroic victim, if this went on too long the governor would turn into a sympathetic, abused victim. It was time to see if the governor was a player or a casualty.

One finished his sandwich and coffee and instructed *Four* to bring Tina Slone back around from passing out after round one. It was time for round two. *Four* had scoffed his sandwich down. He took another drink of coffee and went to the room Tina Slone occupied.

One went into the room occupied by Governor Hart and his wife Belle. Belle was still lying motionless, but there was a wet spot where she had pissed herself in her stupor. *One* set the Governor up and took the tape from his eyes. When the Governor's eyes acclimated to the light, he could see *One* held a sandwich and cup of coffee in his hands. *One* explained that he was going to loosen his hands and take the tape from his mouth. If he shouted out, if he tried to resist, tried to get away, the penalty would be harsh, and he would kill his wife out of spite. He was to nod if he understood. Governor Matt Hart nodded.

The sandwich was cold, but tolerable. The coffee was warm and black. Neither was to his liking, but it was something, and nothing in the past few hours had been to his liking. When he finished *One* taped his hands so he could not move and cut the tape on his feet so he could walk from the room. He once again taped his mouth. Again, he was led to the room occupied by Tina Slone. As he entered the room, Matt Hart could see the same set-up. He was placed directly in front of Tina again. He could see the same heating iron and could smell it was glowing hot, but this time the room had the smell of burning flesh. As he sat in front of Tina, the other male in the room ripped her tape from her eyes. This beautiful woman looked like hell and that was exactly what she was going through. The little finger *One* snipped before was oozing. A small pool of blood was on the floor below where her hand was taped to the chair. Tina looked around the room, she looked at Matt, she looked at *One,* she knew something bad was getting ready to happen, again.

One stepped forward, grabbed the same little finger and cut it off just above the middle knuckle. Matt heard the scream that did not make a sound because of the tape. He heard it though it could not escape the tape. Before Tina passed out, he saw and felt the immense pain she felt. She looked directly in his eyes showing terror and pain. *One* picked up the heating iron and closed the wound with the same sickening hiss he had heard before. The smell of burning flesh intensified, but Tina felt nothing. Pain had caused her to pass out again, taking her out of this final misery.

Four took Matt back to his and Belle's room and secured his feet so he could not run, but he did not put the tape across his eyes. *One* came into the room and sat a chair in front of him. He told *Four* to leave the room and close the door behind him.

Governor Matt Hart realized he had just pissed himself. Fear had caused the involuntary reaction.

One, in a soft voice, almost a whisper said, "Let me explain to you your options. By options I mean what is going to happen.

Before this is over you will either cooperate with me or you, your wife and Mrs. Slone will die. Now, I know you are thinking I will say or do whatever I need to, to get out of this mess. You could do that, but at the end of the day, only you and your wife will be leaving after we make a deal. I will be keeping Mrs. Slone and every time you don't comply with what I want, another piece of Mrs. Slone will be taken. If you assist us and follow instruction then she will stay just as she is now, just missing part of her little finger. Now if you tell anyone about our little arrangement, then Mrs. Slone will be killed immediately and someone in your family, could be an aunt or uncle, brother or sister, mother or father will meet an untimely death. I think I have already proven you can't be protected. Revenge is a big part of our religion. Now our goal is for you to be president. Our requests of you will be few and far between. When you become President, we will look to you for help in securing our rightful place in the community of nations.

Now I can't stress enough how the safety of your family and Mrs. Slone depends on you. Should you decide at any time you are not going to participate, then you and your family are going to be in our sights, my sights. Mrs. Slone will be sacrificed, she's already lost a husband and part of a finger, what else she loses is dependent on you. Now, your wife has been drugged, she knows nothing about what has happened or about our deal. You should not tell her a thing. You will be rescued, by your law enforcement, if you agree to our arrangement. You will be a hero. Of course, you will say you do not know what happened to Mrs. Slone. It will be the truth. You will not know for sure. You will promise to leave no stone unturned until she is rescued. You will accept the position of Vice President. A position we know you have been offered. We have people in place who will let us know if you do not stick to our deal. We have spies everywhere who are friendly to our cause, even in your White House. Now I'm going to take the tape off your mouth. Be very careful to not cause yourself and your wife any more pain then is necessary."

One removed the tape with a single swift jerk.

"Are you crazy? This will never work. I can't make policy as Vice President. A Vice President carries out the President's policy, not make his own. How can I know Tina is safe? I'm supposed to believe you will not kill her? You could kill her as soon as you leave, how would I know?" Matt blurted out.

"She will be kept safe Governor, I can assure you the parts I take if needed, will be fresh, as will the pain she will endure. I will send a photo by text on the phone every three months, which you will immediately erase. In the photo will be a Washington DC paper from the day before the photo is taken. Not the day of because the paper will be brought into the country she is held and that will take a day. When you are rescued, Mrs. Slone will be safely on a boat with me, heading to a safe location where her comfort will be dependent on your actions." answered *One*.

"Within hours after we leave, she will have excellent medical care.

As I told you, we will wait until you become president, which may be even sooner than you might expect. Presidents have died before in office. It happened recently, which is why you have been given this opportunity. Remember, I told you, we have a long reach."

Governor Hart knew he was trapped, his options were to live or die. If it had only been his life the decision would be easy, but he had the life of his wife and the life of his dead friend's wife. If it was only him, he would lie and agree to anything, but this man had leverage. The life of his friend and family were at stake.

"How am I going to be a hero? How am I going to be rescued?" asked the Governor.

One simply said, "This will be explained to you when the time is right. Do you agree with the plan, or are you wasting my time? Should I wake Mrs. Slone and demonstrate again how serious I am, or maybe your wife should see what she's been missing?"

"No, no, don't do that. I will go along, don't hurt anyone else," pleaded Matt Hart.

One replaced the tape on the Governors eyes and mouth and laid him back down beside his wife who slept oblivious to the world full of pain.

Governor Matt Hart was getting ready to betray everything he stood for to save his wife, his friend's wife, and his family.

What options did he have, his captor held all the cards? He was right, they had gotten past all his security. They could do it again. They knew entirely too much about what was happening in Washington, about the offer made to him. Matt knew keeping secrets in Washington was like plugging holes in a boat with a sponge. Eventually it leaked. Even if he and Belle got out of this, his captor was very clear, they would kill Tina and members of his family. All the people he loved and cared about could not be protected, not all of them, not all the time. He did not want to betray his family, his country, but it seemed he was going to betray somebody, or he was going to die, along with his wife and his friend's wife.

One left the room knowing this operation was going to be a success. Even if the Governor changed his mind and did not follow instructions, he would have been paid. *One* would be hired to exact revenge if Governor Hart, soon to be Vice President, did not comply. If the Governor, Vice President to be did comply, he would be hired to pass on instructions and again he would be paid. The Governor was his retirement plan. Now to put the rest of his plan in motion. This operation would be over at midnight, tonight.

Chapter Sixteen

Chief Deputy Ingram walked into the Cates house which was ground zero for the investigation. Sitting around the table were Deputy Director Steve Dunham, Sheriff Pass, Sheriff Slone and Captain Sonny Young. Corporal Howell sat in the living room working on what Ingram knew was a drone, but a drone unlike any he had ever seen. It had four blades and was bigger than the average four bladed drone. It needed to be, to carry all the equipment it had brackets for. This drone had an infrared thermal camera which seemed much more intricate then any infrared he had seen before. This thing looked like military grade equipment he had heard about, but never seen. The blades were coated with a special coating that increased efficiency and reduced noise.

Ingram had heard of this type of drone. Drones were not supposed to be able to see into homes, this one could, or so he had been told. It was not to be used to gather evidence, unless you had a search warrant, but in emergency situations could be used to save lives.

Ingram hoped this one would save lives. It was an expensive piece of equipment. It was painted sky blue camouflage, there was a twin to it sitting on the floor painted in the same hue. He suspected either would blend with the sky no matter whether night or day. Nobody was going to see or hear this thing unless they wanted it seen.

Ingram looked at his sheriff.

"Sheriff, I have news. The recon mission showed no boats at any of the four houses Swanson owns with enclosed bottom garages. They also said one of the houses was probably a no go because of the toys and children's clothes on the deck, that leaves three possible targets."

TJ pulled out the map and said, "Chief, show us where the three are located."

Chief Deputy Ingram looked at the map and pointed out the three locations, circling each. Each house was located within a quarter mile of each other. If joined by a straight line, they formed a triangle.

Corporal Howell looked at the map and noticed almost dead center of the three houses was the town water tower.

Howell said, "Sheriff, I can fly from that water tower and watch each one of those houses. I have a 45-minute flight time before I need to change batteries and I have enough batteries for four and a half hours, longer if I can re-charge as they are replaced. I can fly continuously."

TJ was glad he spent the drug forfeiture money on those drones, drones like no other agency had. Drones he had access to because of connections out of DC. He looked at the corporal and said his normal response to his team. "Make it happen."

The phone rang in TJ's pocket. He picked it up and heard Chief Deputy Powe say "Sheriff, your ears only."

TJ knew what that meant, he had information that needed just his ears, until TJ could decide who should hear the information. "OK, go ahead" was his short response.

"Sheriff, we have identified the shooters you killed. We did it thru facial recognition, fingerprints and DNA. One shooter is Juan Santigo. He is a El Salvador Special Forces mercenary. He is known to work for anyone with the money to pay. He is here illegally, has a lengthy criminal record and has been connected to some Islamic terrorist organizations in the country. The second shooter is Kareem Adula. He too is associated with some Islamic extremist who have carried out operations against the United States Government around the world. Both are bad people. Both are on the radar of the Joint Terrorism Task Force."

The chief deputy knew this because, like the Sheriff, he had secret clearance. He could access the information that was known only to the task force members. TJ also knew that was exactly why the chief had said for his ears only. Nobody got that information unless they were cleared.

TJ ended the conversation saying, "Thanks, I'll get back to you."

The chief deputy responded, "Sheriff, if the feds have this information, you know the deputy director had this information." TJ knew. His response was short. "I'll take care of it" and hung up the phone. TJ looked straight at Deputy Director Steve Dunham. The look of distain did not escape those sitting at the table.

TJ's voice was low and menacing as he said, "You knew who we were dealing with, you got off that damn helicopter knowing or having a strong suspicion who and what we were dealing with. You took our information and you said nothing.

You left us in the dark and yet you still said nothing. Deputy Director you are about two seconds from me kicking your ass."

Deputy Director Dunham knew exactly what he was talking about. It was his FBI that identified the suspects TJ had shot. It was his FBI that Chief Deputy Powe had run the photos, fingerprints and DNA data through. Of course, they could not have done it without the locals, but the FBI had the data base, so they controlled who got access. TJ was a member of the task force as was his chief deputy and Captain Young, but the information requested was given to him before anyone else, on his orders, and yes, he did know before he got off the helicopter. He chose his next words carefully.

"Sheriff Slone, you can have access to the information because you are task force certified and have top secret clearance these others do not."

The look on Sheriff Pass's face was pure disgust and his response to Dunham left no doubt about his thoughts on the matter.

"You pompous asshole, we've got six dead bodies, maybe more, three kidnapped victims, exploded vehicles and a community that doesn't have a clue why their peaceful world has been splashed all over the national news, and you are holding out information."

Deputy Director Dunham without blinking said, "You are not certified, this is above your clearance."

TJ got up from his seat, leaned across the table and in a voice that could have stopped a man's heart.

"You are a deputy director of the FBI. You can make the call to share information. You can make this happen. If you don't have the guts to make that call, I can assure you I can get somebody on the phone that will. I may not have the president take my call, but I can assure you the guy standing next to him will and he will pass the president the phone. When I get through telling them how you are not helping with this investigation you will be lucky if you get an assignment in Boise, Idaho. I will also walk out the front door of this house and hold a news conference and tell the media how the FBI Deputy Director is stonewalling information that could help solve this case. I'm going to make that phone call in about two minutes. That's how long I'm giving you to make that executive decision to do the right thing."

Deputy Director Dunham did not know if Sheriff Slone had that kind of clout, he suspected he did. He did know he had the reputation of doing what he said. Deputy Director Dunham took a deep breath and begin to speak. He didn't need the two minutes.

"Kareem Adula is on our watch list, as was Juan Santigo. They are the two people killed by Sheriff Slone. They have been involved in numerous terrorist activities around the world. Kareem is a true believer, Santigo is a mercenary, military trained and in it for the money. His vices, women, and gambling keep him working. Neither is a leader. Kareem is known to only work with his brother Azil Adula. Azil is a leader, in fact he heads up a cell of ISIS terrorist known to have been responsible for a mass vehicular attack in London and a subway attack in New York. He has been mentioned as being involved with the assassination of the president. You can be assured if he is involved, he is the leader of this kidnapping. He is known to be extremely brutal in dealing with his victims and has no hesitation in killing. We figure he has personally been responsible for killing hundreds if not more. We don't know who the other two may be, but be assured if Azil recruited them, he did it because of their skills. The Bureau has a secret list of the most wanted list of terrorists. Bin Laden was on the list, Azil is number three working toward number one on the list."

The table was silent, what was to be said. The stakes had risen with this news.

For TJ, the need for speed in finding Adula just became even more intense.

TJ said to nobody in particular, but to everyone listening. "You know we are going to have to kill him."

Chapter Seventeen

One looked out the front window. Ocean Isle was coming alive. He could see vacationers pulling beach wagons loaded with chairs and coolers heading for the beach, which was a short walk away. It was 9 am. In twelve and a half short hours, he, *Three* and Tina Slone would be leaving for the meeting with the sea plane and pilot Mac Samms. *One* intended on getting there early to make sure nothing suspicious was going on. He knew American cops were overworked, but if they had an operation, such as a raid, they would stage first. They were predictable. *One* intended on leaving *Four* to guard the Governor and his wife. He would leave instructions that the Governor was to be protected at all costs. His instructions to *Four:* no harm should come to the Governor or his wife until his return. One knew he was not returning. He also knew the police would be coming to the house. In the process of taking the house, *Four* would probably be killed trying to protect the Governor. Even if he was not killed, *Four* knew nothing of his plan. He also knew *Four* would have no idea where he, *Three* and Tina Slone were going.

One knew the police would be coming. He knew because he was going to call them and report the house as being the location of an active domestic violence situation. When they knocked on the door, *Four* would panic, he would probably fire the first shoot. The police would retreat and start negotiations to end the situation. It would become a barricaded suspect call which would end up wasting time, taking up resources, causing confusion using up even more time and law enforcement personnel. This was meant to be a diversion, so he could leave without incident. He would make the call at 9:30 pm after leaving the house. It would take the police an hour or more to prepare to enter the house by force, after the first shot was fired. They would regroup and all available officers would be utilized to secure the area before they went to the house. American police always worried about collateral damage, warriors such as himself did not. It was the cost of war, if some innocent person died, so be it. It was the cause, the mission that was important, not someone's pathetic life. *Four* would be collateral damage. As a true believer, he would give his life for the rewards coming, rewards *One* no longer believed existed.

Three was in the master bedroom when *One* walked in.

She was nude from the waist up, exposing her breasts as she changed from the ill-fitting jogging suit. He said nothing, walking toward her and cupping her breasts in each hand, He caressed her breast as he whispered in her ear. "We are on schedule, say nothing to *Four*, but you, Tina Slone and I will be leaving at 9:30 tonight."

Three did not ask any questions, did not say anything. She knew if he wanted her to know anything, he would have told her. She just breathed a sigh of relief, that there was not going to be another round of meaningless, unfulfilling sex. She resented being used, but she knew in her position, she had no choice. She was a professional and knew she was as good as any man, but in her religion that belief was best kept to herself. *One* watched as she finished dressing in her black gear, the same gear she had worn during the raid and kidnapping earlier that morning.

One instructed her to give Belle Hart another shot. It was important she stay sedated. *One* also told her to clean Mrs. Slone up as best she could. She was beginning to smell because of the burnt flesh, dried blood and human waste, all which had accumulated in the few short hours she had been taped to the wooden chair. This was woman's work. He was glad *Three* was there to make these things happen.

When *Three* left the room, to clean Tina Slone as instructed, *One* went to the room occupied by the Governor. *One* propped Governor Hart up and removed the tape from his eyes and feet. He walked the Governor to the door of the room occupied by Tina Slone.

Matt Hart prayed this was not going to be another object lesson, another painful moment for Tina. As he looked into the room, he saw the Hispanic looking woman he had seen before gently washing the mutilated hand of his friend. He could see *Three* had already cleaned Tina's face of the dried blood from the vicious slaps across her face.

This was a relief because of what he was afraid he was going back to the room to witness. *One* took him back to the room where his wife lay in the same position, she had been in the entire time they had been there.

One ordered *Four* to go down to the car and listen to the car radio, searching for any news stations and see if they had any news not being shown on the TV. *Four* did as he was told. *One* did not need *Four* to hear him telling the Governor what was going to happen to he and his wife and what was going to be the end for *Four*. *One* told the Governor to listen and listen carefully. His voice almost a whisper.

"Governor at about midnight tonight, you will be a free man and you will be a hero. The local police will be heroes and your future, your families and your friends will be in your hands. You double cross me and I can assure you the deaths of your family and friends will be very gruesome. In the near future, a man will approach you and say you have mutual friends from Ocean Isle. He will be at an event, such as a fundraiser where you will be working the crowd. You will make some excuse to speak with him as privately as possible. His sole purpose is to deliver a cell phone to you. He knows nothing other than he is to give you the phone which will be used when a message is sent. The cell phone will only be used to send you a text message which will have a phone number. You will call this number privately, from a secure phone, within three hours of receiving the phone number.

You need to make sure the call is private. You try to have it traced, you let any of your law enforcement know about the call, I will know. Somebody will die because of you. Mrs. Slone will lose a body part. The call is to a phone router which will send the call to several different phone locations before you actually talk to me. This will be done in seconds. Our conversation will be short. The number and routers will be changed every time we talk. It will be impossible to trace. The contact number will change each time. You will need to keep the phone given you charged and ready to respond, again within three hours. If you call three hours and one minute, I will take a body part from your friend. If you do not call then I will kill a family member, it may be a cousin, an uncle or a niece or nephew and I will kill your friend Tina, in a long and painful way."

The governor had no doubt he would do as he said, he had no choice. He swallowed hard and asked, "How do I know you will treat her humanely, how do I know you will not torture her and make her life more miserable then you already have? What happens if the phone you give me fails or is out of area to receive the transmission?"

One was growing impatient, this American like most Americans thought they had options, that they were in charge. "Your friend will be treated well, as long as you cooperate. She will be in a warm, pleasant location and a doctor will be treating her wounds within twenty-four hours, just a short boat ride. I assure you she will not be harmed. I will text you a photo every three months with proof of life. As for the phone, we know your location always and know if you are in a service area. We will not call unless you are. If it fails, we will receive a notice the phone is out of service. Another contact with another phone will be made just as before. If we find the problem was on your end, a family member dies. Say nothing to the man I leave you with. He will protect you with his life. When you are rescued you will tell them what happened here, everything except what you and I have discussed. You will answer their questions about the kidnapping and what we look like and what we did. You will tell them what I did to Mrs. Slone. You will tell them I had a strong dislike for Sheriff Slone, which is why he was killed, and his wife tortured. The police will figure I killed Slone's wife and will be looking for a body. You will never discuss with anyone what we discussed.

Do you understand?"

The governor only nodded. He looked at his wife once more before his eyes were covered by the tape and his legs and feet were bound once again.

Four listened to the radio in the car, constantly changing channels, looking for news channels. He grew weary of pushing the button going from station to station. *Four* recognized he was very low on the pecking order. He didn't know what *Three* knew, but he did know he knew nothing. He did not know what their exit plan was. Why had they not taken the hostages further from the condos? Why were they torturing only the one, why not the Governor, and why was his wife kept sedated? Was this some kind of test for him and if it was, how was he doing? *One* had told him nothing. *Three* barely talked to him and it seemed like there was some kind of sexual tension between *One* and *Three*. Not that he wouldn't like for the same to be happening between he and *Three*. *Four* pushed the radio buttons, he had heard nothing that was any different from what he heard on the TV news.

Four knew better than to ask what the plan was, he would be told when *One* wanted him to know. *Four* came up from the garage and car, after an hour and reported he had nothing new to report. *One* thanked him and told him to have a seat.

"*Four*, I want you to get some rest, tonight I will have an important mission for you. You need to prepare your weapons after getting some rest, I will wake you in a few hours.

Four got up from the chair, went to bedroom *Three* and *One* had shared earlier. Though the bed was messed up, he did not mind. As he lay his head on the pillow, he could smell the essence of *Three*. Thoughts of her would help him sleep.

Chapter Eighteen

It was the middle of the day and TJ realized they had not eaten anything since the breakfast pastry and coffee Katy had made before she and Dave turned over their home to the team. TJ said out loud, where it could be heard by the entire room, "Corporal Howell, it would be a shame for you guys to come all the way to the beach and not get some seafood. I need you to make a chow run."

Corporal Howell, got up, knowing he was getting ready to go somewhere for food, and his stomach did not mind.

"Go across the bridge and turn left at the first light, just across from the airport. Go down a couple of miles on your right to a place called Island Seafood Company. Go in and ask for Amanda. Ask her for five pounds of fresh shrimp, tell her that a friend of hers, TJ Slone told you about her and her place.

Corporal, the seafood will be so fresh it will still be gasping for air when you get it. Bring it back and I'll fix up a shrimp boil. Listen to what Amanda tells you, she will know what the town is talking about and what she says may be of value. She will have heard what happened to me, she will know if I sent you that we are friends. Don't let her know you work for me or that I'm alive.

Just listen. Knowing Amanda, she will have something to say and you can count on it being gospel. After picking up the shrimp and any intel, stop at the Crab Shack at the bridge and pick up slaw and French fries for everyone, and don't forget the hushpuppies."

Corporal Howell did as was requested, returning in less than an hour. The water was already boiling, waiting for the seasoning and shrimp. The shrimp would be ready in minutes. Howell reported that Amanda was very concerned about what had occurred at the condo and was upset that she did not know the condition of TJ. She told him she had just sold Tina some seafood for a special guest, and she understood now, that guest was the Governor and his wife. She had heard that you had killed at least one of the kidnappers and she was glad. Her exact words were, "she hoped the son of a bitch rotted in hell."

Amanda was a friend, her concern was appreciated, TJ hated to keep her in the dark, to keep everyone in the dark, but hopefully it would be over soon.

After lunch, Corporal Howell and Corporal Jackson left for the water tower located in the center of Ocean Isle. It stood 200 feet in the air, was round with a platform built on the top. The platform held antennas for cell operations as well as repeaters for the police and fire radio systems. Just as important, it had a solar powered plug to be used for the drone batteries. The climb was a struggle for Corporal Jackson because he did not like heights.

Once they got their gear to the top of the tower, they placed themselves square in the center of the platform. This position placed them out of the sight line of anyone on the ground. They laid rubber mats on the platform and covered them with a small pop-up tent to block the June sun. It was going to be hot and a metal water tower soaked in the heat. Howell and Jackson began putting the drone together. Once launched it would provide a live feed back to the water tower as well as to an I-pad located with the others at the command house. Howell would program the drone to go to a height of 1000 feet, which should allow him to get a view of all three of the target homes. The three homes were located on Monroe and Concord streets. It was still unknown which house, if any, Swanson lived in. They hoped the drones would narrow the three to one. The camera could zoom in and would provide live action. The drone would fly for 45 minutes and then return to the tower where a battery would be switched out. The second drone would take its post. Watching again. The entire battery switch would take less than two minutes, but the drones would cool down between flights. There was a drone always ready as a spare. The Lieutenant was stationed at the bridge going off the island, the only way off, nobody was leaving these houses or this island without the drones or the Lieutenant knowing. Especially not a white Lexus SUV. If they were even on the island. All their eggs were in this basket. They had nothing else.

TJ's phone rang again, it was Chief Deputy Tom Powe. TJ answered the phone on speaker, now that there had been a come to Jesus moment with Deputy Director Dunham, there was no reason not to.

"Sheriff, Tom, we've identified the female at the hospital." "Anyone we know Tom?" TJ asked, knowing Tom would have everything he could find ready to share. He knew TJ did not like partial answers, he wanted as many facts as he could get as fast as he could get them. Early in their relationship, TJ had burned him more than once asking him questions he should have known the answer to. Chief Deputy Powe made a promise to himself, never again.

"Ears only Sheriff."

"It's OK Tom, we've gotten beyond that."

Powe answered, wishing he had been part of that conversation.

"Maria Garcia, she is here illegally of course, and according to the Task Force has been suspected in multiple terrorist activities around the world. Her specialty is close quarter assassinations using a small caliber handgun."

The entire group immediately thought of Trooper Drey, killed by a small caliber handgun, shot directly into his face.

The couple at the condo also.

"OK, Tom, any ideas on who she may be working with now?" though TJ expected he knew the answer.

"As a matter of fact, yes. Intelligence said they had word she was recruited for a special operation along with a kid by the name of Jerry Blair. An American kid from New York, who was self-radicalized. They were recruited by none other than Azil Adula, so sheriff, I guess that makes up the five on their team counting the two you took care of. I'll send you the latest photos of each, should be there as soon as they download."

"Thanks Tom, you've earned the big bucks I pay you" said TJ with a hint of laughter.

Deputy Director Dunham was already on the phone, calling DC with a report to the Director of the FBI. He knew the information had come from the bureau task force. He also knew he had instructed them to tell the members requesting the information first, so he did not incur Slone's wrath. They would not report up the chain, leaving that to him. That was just the way he wanted it. In his call to the FBI director, he did not mention anyone by name, referring to the information gathered as a "we" product translating out to it being a "me" accomplishment, which in his mind and later reports would be all his accomplishments. TJ didn't care, Dunham could take all the credit he wanted, just stay out of his way.

Sheriff Pass was also on the phone, talking to his chief deputy. After hanging up, he turned to the group with a look of concern. "We have a problem. The media is getting restless, they are pushing about who's alive and who's dead at the condo.

They've even gone to the trouble of filing Freedom of Information requests, something, they've never had to do with any on-going event in my county."

TJ suspected he may have the same problem. A phone call, to his Administrative Assistant Debbie Lynch confirmed it.

Debbie didn't work on Saturdays, but this Saturday was different. He put her on speaker phone and asked her to have Chief Deputy Powe to join in, for their ears only. They both huddled around her phone.

"What you got Debbie?"

"We are getting requests for information from all over the world it seems, to see what we know. It is time consuming and stressful. I'm not used to lying, that's not what we do. Sheriff my hardest job is lying to your daughters. They want to know. They know their mother has been kidnapped but they want to know if their father is dead. Monique especially, she's pushing hard.

Sheriff, I've known those girls most of their lives, I don't like lying to them, especially about this."

Tom Powe added. "Sheriff, I've gotten calls from every elected official in this area and beyond, all wanting answers that I can't give them. The Democrat commissioners want to know who's in charge, they say they are sorry if you're dead or injured, they just want to know who's in charge of the third largest sheriff's office in the state."

TJ smiled; the vultures are circling.

"Debbie, I know it's hard to lie to family and friends, but we need a little longer. Information such as who's dead or alive could give us an advantage. I know it's stressful on you and I know Monique can be a handful. It is hard on both she and Louise as well as the grandkids. Hang in there a little longer. We'll take the heat off you by diverting it down here." That last statement drew a grimace from Sheriff Pass.

TJ knew his daughters were devastated. He also knew that the knowledge he was alive would get out if they knew. They didn't involve themselves in politics and didn't have a clue about investigations of any kind. They were both professionals, in the medical and management fields. Their pain and confusion associated with the kidnapping of their mother and possible death of their father was not the way he wanted their Saturday morning to begin. He hoped they would forgive his decision to keep them out of the loop. Getting their mother back was foremost in his mind right now. His hope was they would understand why he did what was best. Debbie was right. Of the two girls, Louise was the most pragmatic, Monique the most emotional. He knew if they did not show the proper level of concern, indignation, hurt, the media would pick up on it. He needed that advantage a little longer, just a little longer.

After hanging up the phone, Sheriff Pass jumped right in. "So, you're going to divert it down here are you. I'm a little over-worked and a little understaffed. Just how is that going to help the situation?"

"We're going to let the state and feds handle it." He looked around the table and saw he had Sturgis and Dunham's attention. "You are going to just be there to introduce them and thank them for being here to assist in this case which has national implications. You are going to let them take the spotlight. Schedule a news conference and let them tell the media what we want them to know. You just stand there for window dressing. You've done it before, hell, we all have. You're not a media hound, like some of our peers."

Director Sturgis knew TJ was not talking about him, Director

Dunham did not have a clue. TJ continued, "Dunham and Sturgis will tell them there will be an update provided every three hours if new information is available. It's logical. It gives the media the optics they need and keeps them off our ass for at least three-hour blocks of time."

Mark Sturgis was not happy with this plan, he was still a cop at heart. Steve Dunham loved the idea. it would get him back in front of the camera which was going to do his career wonders. He was starting to like TJ Slone a little better. Sheriff Pass like TJ and Director Sturgis had a different agenda than Dunham.

Dunham was looking for glory. Pass, Sturgis and Slone were looking for justice.

The group set down and mapped out the information that would be provided. It was bare bones. Sheriff Pass would start off and turn it over to Dunham who would fill in some information then pass it to Sturgis who would open it up for questions, always a slippery slope. The news conference would be held in one hour, at 3 pm. This would give everyone a chance to hurriedly get ready, which gave them an hour of talking heads trying to forecast what would be said. The news conference would be followed by another three hours of talking heads discussing what was said.

Then the process would begin again. They would not identify who was dead or who was wounded at TJ's condo until the second news conference. Just the troopers and Juan Santigo would be identified then.

Santigo because his photo was already flashing on the media as being dead, but unidentified. Several of the residents had taken phone video and photos and made them available to the media. Each channel showed the video or photos after cautioning the viewer, they would be graphic. TJ doubted if there was anyone in America with a TV who had not seen Santigo swinging in the wind. TJ doubted if anyone knew who he was, except himself, the members of the team, the FBI and Azil's team. The media knew this was good for ratings and they were eating it up. It wasn't that they were insensitive, he had many friends in the media and he knew they were caring people. But this was news/show business and the old saying, if it bleeds, it leads, was certainly true in this case.

Chapter Nineteen

Three called out to *One*, "they are showing it again." *One* came into the room to see *Five* hanging by his harness, off the roof of the condo. It was just as obvious now as it was that morning, he was dead. If not, they would not have left him hanging there. *One* felt no remorse, the man was a dog, he had no honor, he stole from the dead and was only interested in money. *One* missed the irony, that money was the motivation now driving him. *Five* would have been helpful in getting Tina Slone into the car after she was drugged, but now that job would fall to him and *Three*. His original plan had been to leave *Four* and *Five* at the house, to fend off the raid he knew would be coming, but *Five's* death changed those plans. *One* was left to wonder who was in the hospital, was it his brother or was it the sheriff. He could not be concerned. His brother knew the risk. If he survived and was tried as an enemy combatant, he would end up with many of their warrior brothers in Cuba at Guantanamo Bay. *One* took some solace in knowing he and his brother would be on the same island, separated by a fence.

The news conference was set up at the condos, which were still cordoned off by police tape. A podium had been set up by the Brunswick County Sheriff's Office. In front of the podium was a semi-circle of news cameras all hooked into their individual sound trucks. The satellite dishes on their roofs would send a live shot to their stations. TJ was not there, but he could see the set up from a Skype video being sent him by Capt. Young. He instructed Sheriff Pass, Director Sturgis and Deputy Director Dunham, he was going to watch on the big screen at the house, just a call away. TJ was a little apprehensive about this news conference. The wildcard in the whole thing was Deputy Director Steve Dunham. TJ didn't like him, didn't trust him and he damn sure didn't respect him. He hoped Dunham would take his early warning to heart, a smart man would.

"Ladies, gentleman. My name is Sheriff John Pass, Brunswick County Sheriff. Thank you for being here and thank you for your patience during this trying time. I will begin by giving you an update on what we believe occurred this morning, followed by a synopsis of where we are during this investigation. That will be followed by a few words from Deputy Director Steve Dunham of the Federal Bureau of Investigation and Director Mark Sturgis of the North Carolina State Bureau of Investigation. That will be followed by a question and answer session.

"Let's begin. This morning at approximately 2 am we received a call reporting an explosion, the results which you can see behind me. Upon arrival, we found several cars engulfed in flames, again the results you can see behind me. The explosion was caused by persons unknown. It was part of what we believe to be a terrorist plot and kidnapping. So far, we have confirmed six dead and three kidnapped. We also have a survivor who has been wounded and is in the hospital in a protected room. We will not be releasing the names of the dead or the wounded pending the notification of next of kin and family. Again, we will not be releasing any names pending notification of next of kin and family. The kidnapped victims are Governor Matt Hart and his wife Belle, and Tina Slone, wife of Guilford County Sheriff TJ Slone. I believe this would be the best time to say, this is a very tragic and unusual event for Brunswick County. We have a peaceful community, and I want to assure everyone, it will be again. I'm afraid this is a sign of the times we live in, as tragic as that is, a reality we in law enforcement deal with on a daily basis. We have received no notification about any demands from the kidnappers, nor had there been any intelligence before this event about any plot against the Governor. I can say this was a well-planned assault on the residence and subsequent kidnapping. As you will hear from Deputy Director Dunham and Director Sturgis, we have the full cooperation of each of our law enforcement partners. Having said that, let me turn the podium over to FBI Deputy Director Dunham."

And with that Sheriff Pass stepped away from the microphone.

Deputy Director Dunham walked to the microphone and adjusted it to his height, since Sheriff Pass was taller. He asked, "Can everyone hear me?"

TJ thought as he watched the big screen TV, what an ass, he just heard John talking on the same microphone, he knew he had a problem with this guy and all guys like him. TJ Slone did not suffer fools well.

Dunham continued. "I wanted to reiterate what Sheriff Pass said. The FBI and our local partners are working non-stop to solve this crime and return the kidnapped victims to their families. We have all the resources of the bureau at our disposal and are prepared to use whatever means necessary to bring this investigation to a successful conclusion."

Inside TJ was screaming, what an idiot, he had said nothing that wasn't obvious to anyone who had a brain. He really didn't need to speak, but his need for recognition and to be in front of the TV camera required him to say something. He capped off the inane speech by saying, "For you who don't know me, I'm Deputy Director Steve Dunham, spelled D U N H A M."

Mark Sturgis walked up to the microphone Dunham had vacated without introducing him.

"I'm SBI Director Mark Sturgis, I really don't have anything to add to what Sheriff Pass said, except to say we will be taking questions now and if there are additional developments, we will be having another briefing in three hours."

TJ had not missed the slight Sturgis had just sent Deputy Director Dunham's way by not acknowledging him, but he was sure Dunham did. The man was a narcistic idiot. TJ thought, now it was getting ready to get interesting, these questions would be fast, furious and to the point. TJ was sorry he was not there to participate. He loved the give and take, and had made many friends with the media, along with an enemy or two.

"Buck Roberts, Fox 8 from Guilford County. This question is for Deputy Director Dunham."

TJ watched as Dunham stepped to the microphone with a self-assured, pompous look on his face. TJ knew that look was very premature. Buck was a very competent investigative reporter. He was used to dealing with bureaucrats and had a reputation of being fair, but persistent. Dunham was going to have his hands full right off the bat.

"Deputy Director, why is it taking so long to notify the next of kin? This event started about thirteen hours ago and I'm sure you have notified the next of kin of someone you could give us the name of. Is one of the dead Sheriff Slone? I'm sure his next of kin can be found by his office. Why can't you verify his condition, is he dead or alive? Why are there Guilford County officers here, are they involved in this investigation or are they just guarding the sheriff of Guilford County. Have you been able to identify the body hanging outside the sheriff's condo? Did Sheriff Slone kill him, if not, who did? What happened to the Governor's security detail, were they killed? Were any civilians not associated with the Governor killed? When will you be able to provide us with the names of those killed and their relationship to the investigation?"

TJ smiled. Buck was being Buck. TJ and Buck Roberts were friends, had a mutual respect for each other, but Buck was going to do his job, Buck was doing his job. Dunham had a deer in a headlight look on his face. He was not used to answering questions off the cuff, he only answered questions that had been put before him in writing. He was not use to a live news conference. Dunham had working stiffs called public information officers who took these type questions, Dunham was a fish out of water.

Dunham replied, "Yes, we have identified the body outside the sheriff's condo, but we are not prepared to release the name at this time since it is part of our investigation. Nor are we prepared to answer your questions about any deaths attributed to this case."

Dunham was clearly shaken, a fact that did not escape Sheriff Pass. He stepped up and edged Dunham away from the mike.

"Mr. Roberts, maybe I would be better suited to answer your question. I asked the Guilford County Sheriff's Office to join us in this investigation. I think everyone would agree they have a vested interest. They also have resources which would be and already have been invaluable in helping us gather and decipher the evidence and information we have. They are working in conjunction with all our law enforcement partners under a mutual aid agreement. Their goal and ours is the same, justice, justice for all concerned."

TJ smiled, John had just saved Dunham's ass and Dunham was too dumb to know it. Every sheriff knew they were the true representatives of the people they were elected to serve. They did not have the cover an appointed bureaucrat like Dunham or even Director Sturgis had. They were elected by and served the people who were their fellow church members, fellow civic club members, neighbors for God's sake and folks they dealt with every day. Knowing they were who they answered to, and the sheriffs wouldn't have it any other way. Bureaucrats like Dunham looked at their job as a career. Sheriffs, the good ones anyway, looked at it as a calling. They were who their citizens wanted to hear from.

That's why the good ones never hid behind public information officers, they did the interviews.

The rest of the news conference was spent by reporters asking the same questions Roberts had asked, but in a different way and the answers being the same, the same but in different ways. The talking heads were already rehashing the same tired information, trying to put a spin on it that kept their viewers engaged. Dunham, Sturgis and Pass headed back to the house.

* * * * *

Corporal Howell knew one thing for sure, being on top of a water tower in Ocean Isle was no place to be in June. It was hot as hell. The rubber mat he sat on was the only thing saving him from being blistered by the metal of the water tower, and it was getting soft from the heat. The tent, because of the wind, was as much an aggravation as a help, but he wasn't about to take it down except to land the drone for a battery change, it was the only thing between he and Corporal Jackson and the blazing afternoon sun. They made the first battery change without a hitch, the second was coming up. The drone had been operating for about an hour and a half. He found that if he hovered at about 1200 feet, he could see all three of the properties owned by the realtor Swanson. He stationed the drone and watched the three canal homes from his hellish perch. He made a recon over each house before he took the stationary position. There were two houses on Concord Street and one on Monroe Street. During these recon missions, he ran a diagnostic infrared sweep on each house. Since it was so hot, and he was trying to get readings from a hot roof, the readings were light, nothing he wanted to make a judgement call on, but he did see something he felt the sheriff needed to know.

TJ answered the phone on the second ring, he recognized the number as being that of Corporal Howell. "Talk to me Corporal, are you hot up there?"

"Hot as hell, sir. I'll trade places if you would like?"

TJ laughed and replied, "Corporal, if I had your talent with those drones and you would take this headache I have, I would do it in a minute."

Howell laughed, he knew this sheriff and knew he wasn't kidding. Sheriff TJ Slone had been sheriff for a long time, but everyone who worked for him knew, when it came to work he was going to be right there with the best of them and if you were one of his people, if you were right, he was going to be standing with you no matter what, no matter who, he was going to protect and support you.

"Sheriff, of the three houses we are watching, I think we can take one off the list. One of the two houses on Concord has a bunch of children which have been keeping the doors on the house busy, going in and out. I've counted one older female and four kids ranging in age from eight to twelve years old. Looks like girls and a boy, with the boy being the youngest. It appears to be a family. Tax value information shows the house to be a three- bedroom, two bath home with about 1500 square feet of air- conditioned space. My infrared search shows what I believe to be six occupants, but because of the heat, I'm not prepared to stake my life or anyone else's life on that. My readings are coming from about 1200 feet to not alert anyone to the drone's presence. If the readings are correct, we have five of those six verified, which means the chances of this being where our victims are located is slim."

TJ heard the corporal and agreed. "How about the other two houses?" was the obvious question TJ asked.

"No movement Sheriff, not from either house on the outside since

I've been on station. The second house on Concord has five heat signatures as best as I can determine. The house on Monroe also has six, again as best as I can determine. I can give you a better read when the sun goes down and those roofs cool down. I can get lower. Sheriff, one of the houses on Concord has three fast movers."

"What the hell does that mean, fast movers?" asked TJ. "Sheriff, they may be dogs, big dogs or small children, the heat signatures move pretty quick. Because of the roof heat, I can't get a good picture of whether its human or not." Answered Howell.

TJ thanked the corporal and told him to concentrate on the two he felt may be contenders unless he called and told him different. TJ hung up the phone and reported Howell's findings to the others, they agreed, they were now down to two houses. Each had the sinking feeling in their gut. If they were wrong, they had nothing. There were no hits on the vehicle or boat they knew existed, although every cop within a thousand miles was looking for them. They couldn't approach the houses because these were some very dangerous people they were dealing with, and the lives of the officers, the neighbors and the hostages were at stake. It had been over twelve hours since the kidnapping, it seemed like twelve days.

TJ's phone rang again. He looked at the number displayed.

It was his daughter Monique. He let it ring, his heart sinking.

Brunswick County Chief Deputy Roy Ingram left his post in the hospital parking lot. Since identifying the woman, he felt the chances of anyone coming back was slim. He pulled his white Charger into the parking lot of the Marina located off of Thirteenth Street and Highway 17, the closest one to the condo. He was in South Carolina, approximately four miles out of North Carolina in Horry County. Brunswick County adjoined Horry County at the state line. Chief Ingram was playing a hunch. If he was wrong, it was a short ride back to his county, if he was right, it may give them the help they needed. He knew this was the largest public marina in the area. He also knew the owner, knew him to be a friend of law enforcement. Ingram parked his car and walked toward the marina office. Before he reached the office, he saw what he was looking for. A 16-foot Carolina Skiff was parked at the end of the dock with NC registration numbers. Numbers that belonged to Howard Wayne Swanson.

Ingram located the owner and asked about the boat. The dock it was tied to was for temporary use. It was used by boaters to tie up to when you picked up passengers, ice or bait, it was not meant for long term docking. The owner told Chief Deputy Ingram it had been there since before he had opened for today's business. They were not busy, so he let it slide. Ingram noticed security cameras around the marina and dock as well as around the parking lot. His request to see the security footage was met with no resistance. Chief Deputy Ingram laboriously searched the marina surveillance videos. He started at 2am and watched forward. There it was, the footage showed Azil Adula, pulling the boat up to the dock, tying it off and walking to a waiting Lexus.

This information only made the case against Azil and his team stronger. It also made the connection between Azil and Swanson airtight, which they would need to obtain a search warrant for Swanson's property. Ingram called Sheriff Pass.

John Pass answered the phone on the first ring and listened intently as his Chief Deputy explained what he had found.

"Thanks Roy, great job. Contact Horry County, get a search warrant and seize the boat. Ask if they will allow our people to handle the forensics, I suspect they will be happy to oblige. Take it to our compound for processing. Have our guys make up about fifty sets of photos of the two men and the woman, I want everybody looking for them and the Lexus. John, only law enforcement is to see the photos. Make sure you put it out to every agency in a hundred-mile radius, but stress law enforcement only."

John briefed the others on the latest developments. He kept the notice to a hundred-mile radius because he knew the more information out there, the less chance of keeping control of who got it. They had all they needed to tie Swanson and his property to the terrorists. Since they had his ring, he suspected Swanson was dead.

TJ listened to the latest development with both a sense of

excitement and dread. Excitement because there was movement, dread because they still did not know where the hostages were.

They did know the people who had them were very nasty people. Were they in one of the two houses owned by Swanson or were they somewhere else? TJ felt the houses were involved.

Swanson's ring in Santigo's pocket told him Swanson was dead. He was probably dead because they needed his house, hopefully one of the houses they were watching. Were the hostages still alive, that was the question. TJ felt they were. They were taken for a reason. His head ached, the Tylenol was helping, but not ending the pain, but the pain in his head was nothing compared to the pain in his heart. He silently said a little prayer, a prayer asking God to protect Tina, protect her until he could get to her and take over the job.

Corporal Howell had enough of Ocean Isle. The heat at 5 o'clock on top of a water tower was no way to enjoy a June day at the beach. It was hot, he and Jackson were not in uniform. They had both shed their shirt, pants and gun belts and sat on their rubber mats under a blue pop-up tent shielding them from the afternoon sun. They were in their underwear, shorts and T-shirts. Each time any bare body parts touched the metal platform not covered by the rubber mat they got a burning reminder of where they were. They discovered they needed to keep the batteries under shade so they would not overheat. They watched the screen of the laptop computer for any movement at the two target locations. The computer was literally sitting on a bag of ice wrapped in layers of plastic bags so it would not get too hot.

The only movement they had seen was at the Concord Street location. A male, approximately 6 ft tall, left the location walking a big dog, breed unknown. The dog had been walked about three times. The size of the dog could have easily been one of the fast movers he had spotted during his infrared search, but who were the other three he had not seen. At the Monroe Street location, he had seen no movement outside the house and the roof was still too hot to get a good reading on the number of people in the house and their position. Howell thought, Lord, let the sun go down.

Chapter Twenty

One woke *Four* up. *Three* had rummaged through the cabinets and put together a meal for the team, but before going to eat, *One* had a conversation with *Four*.

"*Four*, tonight we will be moving to a new location. The man I met with this morning has prepared a new location which is located about two hours from here. We will be moving the Sheriff's wife first. I will be leaving with her and *Three* about 9:30 pm, that should get me back here about 2 am. You and I will take the Governor and his wife to the new location. I need you to make sure everything is ready. I need you to protect the Governor and his wife with your life. He is the most important part of this operation. Can I trust you to be ready, to protect the Governor, to carry out your assignment? Can I trust you with this important assignment, can you do it?"

Four was both flattered and concerned at the same time. He knew he could do it, he just wondered why they did not all go together. He wondered so much that he did the unthinkable, he asked, "Boss, why are we not going at the same time, why are we spending so much time transporting these people?"

The last question was meant to have two questions in one.

The unspoken question, what was the point in all this? If they were going to kill them, it would have been done at the condo. Were they to be held for ransom, was that their purpose? *Four* did not like not knowing the plan.

One showed his displeasure at being questioned, *Four*, saw it in his face.

"We would be crowded if we tried to put six people in one car and we would draw attention. It is better to be cautious. Each prisoner must be in the floor of the vehicle when we transport them, out of sight. If you do not feel you can handle this assignment, say so. I will make other arrangements." *One* knew the last challenge would get the results he wanted.

"No boss, I can do it," said a contrite *Four*.

The meal prepared by *Three* was not bad, not great, but not bad. It was finished with little or no conversation. *Four* was pouting, but *One* was confident he would do as told. In about three hours they would begin the "supposed" trip to the next location. In actuality, *One* knew he and *Three* would be positioning themselves where they could see the area Samms was to pick them up. The seaplane was to land at the bridge area where locals launched their boats on the Intracoastal Waterway.

There was only a single roadway leading past a local restaurant, the liquor store and a bait shop. He and *Three* would not attract any attention because of the traffic on the street. The restaurant would close at 10 pm. *One* figured between the closing of the restaurant, the customers leaving, it being a Saturday night, the parking lot would have cars until 11:30 pm. He figured the restaurant crew would be the last to leave after cleaning up. Any cars coming in after their arrival at closing would be watched.

There would be no reason for new arrivals since the restaurant would be closing, unless they were picking up employees or they were cops. When the parking lot emptied, with just them and any cars associated with the people using the boat landing near the lot, it should be about the time Samms would arrive. He and *Three* would drive from the lot to the plane which would still be running. When Samms turned the plane, they would pull up to the plane. He and *Three* would load Tina Slone into the plane. Tina would be dead weight since she would be drugged just before they loaded her in the car at the canal house. *Three* would take the vehicle back to the parking lot and leave it. She would return to the plane by foot, load up and they would be gone.

The flight would be a short one. They were going 30 miles out to a pre-determined location, a location *One* would provide Samms once they were in flight. Twenty-four miles was twice what was needed to get out of the jurisdiction of American law enforcement, thirty would assure they were out.

At the pre-determined location, an Iranian freighter heading for Cuba would stop long enough to drop a lifeboat. The lifeboat would run parallel to the freighter until Samms landed. Samms would cut his engines and the lifeboat would pick up the passengers from the plane and again run a parallel course with the freighter.

Samms would take off $50,000 richer. After he took off the lifeboat and its cargo would be taken onboard the freighter. The entire switch should take less than five minutes. The flight from land to freighter would be just above the water to avoid radar.

Samms plane, a Grumman Mallard G73T, was actually built in 1950, before the pilot or any of the passengers were born. The plane had been upfitted with turbo engines instead of the radial piston engines it came with. There were only thirty-two in America and Samms had one. It had a top speed of 215 miles per hour and a range fully loaded of about 1100 nautical miles. That range and speed allowed him to pick up at sea and get to any landing area along the east coast. It had a payload of 5000 pounds of cargo or 17 people. Samms had used it many times to pick up either drugs or people. If it needed to be brought into the country, was illegal, and you could pay, Samms was your guy. The plane usually had a crew of two, but Samms decided in his line of work, just he would do.

Samms was experienced in this type of operation, he had done it before. He didn't make many trips, in fact he was lazy, he figured that was what kept him out of jail. He suspected the police had a suspicion about him, but he flew infrequently, choosing to go for the low risk, high reward jobs. The police didn't have the manpower and couldn't watch him do nothing, so lazy was good. This job would keep him foot loose and not working for a couple months. He wasn't greedy, but he was cautious and lazy. One had heard about him from a fellow terrorist who needed a way into America that was quick, efficient and discreet, all services Samms provided. One had used him before.

Whether it was people, guns, drugs or explosives he was your guy. He was high in price and low on morals. One did not like him, but he understood him. It was all about the money.

Samms always required twenty percent up front, non-refundable. If you missed your agreed time for pick-up, the deal was re- negotiated. If you had cargo, Samms was not going to help you load or unload. He was the best pilot *One* had ever seen. He would fly his seaplane so low that a jumping fish would crash into the undercarriage of the plane. The man was good and that was the only reason *One* used him. *One* wondered if he realized he was helping in the downfall of his country, he wondered if he cared.

One left the table and walked into the bedroom where the Governor and his wife lay on the queen size bed. He pulled a chair up close to the Governor. In a voice barely audible, *One* said, "Can you hear and understand me, if so, just nod yes." The Governor nodded.

One said "In a few hours I will be leaving with Mrs. Slone.

Her safety, her life is going to be dependent on you. I hope you remember all I have told you. I hope you comply. I think it would be very difficult for you to know the pieces of Mrs. Slone she will lose because you did not follow instructions will be your fault.

The deaths of your family members will be your fault. You let anyone know of our agreement, then it will be your shame and I will kill Mrs. Slone. If you do as we have discussed, you will be the next President. We will only ask you to recognize our rights as a part and place with the other nations of the world. We will be friends. We will be partners. Do you understand?"

Again, Governor Hart nodded. He understood. He understood he had no choice. He understood his life and that of his wife and Tina Slone's were in his hands. He understood he was forced into this position by a man who now said they would be friends, partners. He understood this man was crazy if he thought he would ever be friends with him, or anyone like him. He understood he was being asked to betray his country, Governor Matt Hart understood if he got out of this then he had some hard decisions to make.

One explained to the Governor again that he and Belle would be rescued within hours of his leaving with Tina. He explained Tina would be in a warm climate, comfortable and receiving medical attention within twenty-four hours. He admonished the Governor again to say nothing about his conversation but to tell his rescuers everything about what had happened, everything except about their deal. He explained how he needed to report he had not seen Tina Slone since the kidnapping, that he did not know what had happened to her. *One* explained he would be seen as a hero and everyone would rally around him. He was also told not to say anything to those he left to guard him.

One left the Governor. Matt Hart said a little prayer, a prayer asking God to protect Tina and to let this nightmare end with nobody else dying.

* * * * *

Tina woke from passing out to the feel of someone washing her face with a warm rag. She could smell the soap and the warm rag felt good on her bruised and battered face. Her finger was throbbing with every heartbeat reminding her of the horror she witnessed as the man cut her fingertip off using a garden shear, not once, but twice. Tina did not see who was washing her, but the touch, the gentleness, told her it was a woman. She could not see or speak because of the tape over her eyes and mouth. Her feelings proved to be correct about it being a woman when she heard *Three* speak.

"I am going to clean you up a little, I'm going to try and make you a little more comfortable. I will give you food and water, I'm going to do this until you do something, anything I don't approve of. Any attempt to escape or call out, I assure you, you will not like the pain associated with such a poor decision. Do you understand, if you do, nod."

Tina nodded. She thought herself a fool, for thinking this woman would have any sympathy or compassion for her. This woman was one of the people who kidnapped her and her friends. Part of the group that killed her husband. She was part of the group that cut her fingertip off. Tina Slone was heartbroken and in pain. Pain of the heart as well as her bruised and mangled body.

Stepping past her dead husband was something that caused her to hurt beyond words. The pain of watching her finger being cut off was shocking to the mind and her physical well-being.

Tina had been victimized, but she was pissed. She had been a fighter all her life. She had a history of not only fighting for herself, but those who could not fight for themselves. She did it as a nurse, as an elected official. She fought for her family, she fought for the people who elected her to public office. She was a fighter now taped to a chair, with tape around her eyes and mouth, dressed in her pajamas. She had a mangled hand and bruised face, but Tina was ready to fight. She was looking for the right time.

Ready to fight, but now was not the time, not the circumstances. Tina did not say a word as the woman took the tape from her mouth.

She accepted the bread and meat she thought was turkey pressed to her lips. The first bite taken in a dry mouth caused her to choke. The water given her out of the plastic bottle helped with the dry mouth and swallowing the sandwich. It was good to eat, but it caused her stomach to react with a low rumble. It had been hours since she had last eaten. It was as long since her last liquids. The stress to her body, both physically and emotionally were causing havoc with her system. Tina felt sure she had wet herself, yet her clothes were dry. She didn't know how long she had been passed out. She smelled. She could smell the dried blood and urine. She could smell the burnt flesh.

She would have never allowed herself to be in this shape under any circumstances. These were not normal circumstances. Tina did not know how long she had been a captive. She didn't know where she was or why. She had no ransom value; she was the wife of a sheriff. She was a small town elected official. Tina found herself feeling helpless but refused to feel sorry for herself. She knew if she got the chance, someone was going to pay for the death of her husband, for her pain. Tina was a fighter, she was just looking for the chance to even the score, hate was all she had left, she felt she had nothing to lose.

Three finished feeding Tina and cleaning her as best she could. She had no clothes to replace the pajamas soiled by blood and urine. *Three* felt sorry for her, sorry for her as any woman would for another. This woman had lost her husband, she was being used as leverage, for what, *One* had not shared with her. The torture and abuse Tina had endured was real, just as real as the blood she had washed from her face and body. The finger had been cut twice. It would be cut again to get rid of the burnt, dead meat from the heating iron and garden shears. Her training told her that, she would be lucky to survive without getting an infection. *Three* knew Tina Slone would endure more pain and suffering and there wasn't a thing she could do about it.

Chapter Twenty-One

Corporal Howell watched as the drone lifted from the platform on top of the water tower. It was programmed to return to the location it had been in all afternoon, silently watching the houses on Monroe and Concord Street. It was after 6 pm and the sun was beginning to sink in the sky, its lower position was causing the air to not be quite as stifling. It was still hot, just not as hot. Howell decided to run another diagnostic on each resident, to see if he could get a more positive reading on who was in the houses. He started with the Concord Street house. He saw immediately, though the sun was no longer straight overhead, the residual heat was still impacting his readings. The asphalt shingles were holding heat which meant his readings were faint at best. In the Concord residence, he saw what appeared to be at least five occupants. He knew from his surveillance a white male was one of the residents of the house and he knew they had a dog. He just didn't know for sure if the dog would be one of the other heat signatures. He was not willing to give an affirmative on anything unless he was sure, there was too much at stake to be guessing.

His check of the Monroe Street address showed similar results. He thought he could determine at least six heat signatures. Howell liked this residence as the location, but he was not confident enough to make that call to Sheriff Slone. He knew Slone had confidence his people would give him good information. Howell did not intend on letting him down.

They were a little late, a little longer than the three hours they had promised, but the media quickly forgot that fact when Deputy Director Dunham, Sheriff Pass and Director Sturgis stepped to the microphone.

Sheriff Pass started the news conference. "We have a little more information to share, if you are ready, we will begin."

The media were ready, they rushed the podium, placing tape recorders and microphones to the on position.

"We have identified the person many of you have shown on video or in photos. The person hanging outside Sheriff Slone's residence is Juan Santigo. He is here illegally, is a known mercenary who is suspected to have been involved in terrorist activity both here and abroad. He has no known religious or political beliefs that motivate him. It is felt he is a gun for hire and money is his motivation. Santigo is known to have been trained in the Special Forces of El Salvador and associated with the MS-13 gang culture. We're trying to gather information on any recent activity and recent associates. We have no further information at this time, but we will try to answer any questions you may have."

CNN reporter Kari Young started out. "This question is for Deputy Director Dunham." It seemed, the reporters had recognized Dunham was the weakest link, and like sharks smelling blood, they were going for him.

"If you were so familiar with this person, why had the FBI not picked him up before now? Did Sheriff Slone kill him? What about the other two? Who is the other dead person and who is the wounded person and what shape are they in?"

Dunham stepped to the microphone. He and the others had already discussed the questions they felt would be asked and had agreed on what the answers would be. He had been kicking himself since the first news conference, as he had not handled it well, he vowed to do better.

"You ask a legitimate question," Dunham started off saying. "We know of his activity because of intelligence gathered from informants and prior arrest. Finding him and stopping him is not as easy as knowing about him. As was stated, he was here illegally and I'm afraid our borders to the south are still very open to anyone who truly wants to come into our country. Your question about the other dead person's identity is not going to be released at this time, hopefully the reasoning behind this decision will become apparent in the near future. As to who killed suspect Santigo, probably Sheriff TJ Slone. We think ballistics will confirm that. Sheriffs Slone gun was found and had been fired. As to the health of the person in the hospital, the doctors have high confidence the person will survive."

"Andy Nance, ABC News, can you tell us if you have had any communications from the kidnappers, do you feel they are still in the area and why can you not be more specific about the names and identification of those killed or wounded, it has been over sixteen hours since this event started?"

Dunham looked frustrated as he answered.

"It has been sixteen hours, that fact does not escape any of us. The reason we have played the names close to the vest is the information and how we use it has impact on our investigation and information we might obtain. I understand you have a job to do, but so do we. There are lives at stake here as well as the privacy concerns of the families involved. You will get your information, but not before the needs of the families and the investigation are satisfied. And with that, we will have further information when it is available." Dunham walked away from the podium with Sheriff Pass and Director Sturgis following.

TJ Slone turned off the TV with just a touch more respect for Deputy Director Dunham. He had done a good job, he actually told it like it was, instead of trying to do the DC shuffle which they were so famous for in Washington. If Dunham kept that up, he may actually get to like him. TJ understood the air in Washington sometimes caused folks to forget their roots, to forget what was important. While he had many friends in high positions in both Raleigh and Washington, he always felt, they seemed to forget the world was not about them. Tip O'Neill, a former United States representative, wrote a book called "All Politics is Local". He was right, bureaucrats often forgot that. TJ never had.

A few miles away from TJ, *One* watched the live news conference. He watched and listened to the Deputy Director of the FBI update the news media. He was not impressed. They had said nothing, nothing except give the identity of *Five*. *Five's* identity was not going to cause any problems for his plan. His identity told them nothing. As the Deputy Director said, *Five* was a mercenary, a gun for hire, he could be working for anyone. The news conference had not answered the question he had. Who was alive, was it Slone, or was it his brother?

Sheriff Pass, Director Sturgis and Deputy Director Dunham returned to the Ocean Isle house with pizza and salad. Sheriff Pass also had news. It was not the news TJ wanted to hear. TJ's daughters were on the way. Monique had started out insisting on talking with Sheriff Pass. Pass told her he could not provide any information, using the FBI as the excuse, since they were involved in the investigation.

Monique was not one to take rejection well, especially when it concerned her father and stepmother. She was a fighter, sometimes when there didn't need to be a fight. She was head strong and on the way. TJ was sure the ride down would be with her sister in tow, though Monique was younger by a couple of years, she was more head strong, meaning hardheaded. Louise would be just as concerned but would be pragmatic and careful in picking her battles. TJ hated she and her sister were being put through this, but maybe this was for the best. He asked Sheriff Pass to bring them to the house when they arrived, without telling them anything. TJ did not want his daughters anywhere near the news media. He was afraid of how media would hound them for ratings points. He was afraid of what Monique would say or do. He could see how she could easily lose her cool, which would help nothing. TJ did not want her or her sister to have to go through any more unpleasantness.

Sheriff Pass could handle the request, he had just the deputy in mind to do it. He knew that once they got here, the first thing they would do was take their phones. TJ still thought the advantage of the bad guys not knowing he was alive could be a game changer. They would not be allowed to contact anyone else, not yet.

Monique and Louise were as different as night and day, Louise would be fine. She would want her mother back as much as TJ did and would do as she was asked. Monique was more emotional and more by the seat of her pants. TJ would have a tougher time dealing with her. Her heart was in the right place, he just needed her to use the brain he knew she had. It wasn't a job he was looking forward to.

Corporal Howell watched the screen which showed him what the drone was seeing. The sun was down, and while it was a warm June night, the heat of the sun was no longer putting a heat barrier on the roofs, stopping the heat reading sensors in the drone from picking out heat sources Howell would feel comfortable in identifying as actual people. As he looked at the Concord Street home, he verified five heat sources. He felt confident from the surveillance at least one was a male who he had seen walking a dog. In fact, he had seen him walking the same dog several times. It was a large dog of a breed he could not identify. It was large and short haired and obviously needed to be walked a lot. As he watched the screen, he felt confident of the male being in the house and as he watched he felt confident the dog was one of the signatures he was seeing. In fact, he felt there was probably only one other human in the house, the other three signatures seemed to be of the four-legged variety. He thought this because of the way they moved. Their movement was sporadic in speed. They went from slow to fast to slow. A child may move that way, but in his experience an adult seldom did. He felt sure the house only had two adults in it. He wasn't ready to make that call to Sheriff Slone yet. TJ liked valid information and now he was about 60/40 in his confidence level.

On the Monroe Street house, he was very confident there were six occupants in the house. He also noticed that only three of the occupants were moving. The other three had limited movement. Howell felt really confident in this but decided he would report both at the same time, in about an hour, when he ran another diagnostic test on the two houses.

TJ, Sheriff John Pass, Director Sturgis and Deputy Director Dunham finished the pizza and salad. TJ ate, not because he was hungry, not because it wasn't good, because it was, but because he felt he needed to. The pizza had come from PaPa's Pizza in Little River. It was a place just across the state line in South Carolina and was a favorite place for TJ and Tina. Tina loved the Baked Spaghetti. That thought alone would have taken his appetite away. Dunham, Sturgis and Pass had no way of knowing that. The restaurant was on the way back from the marina where they had gone to look at the boat being processed by the SBI and FBI. The guys decided to stop and pick up the pizzas on the way back, they would have no idea it was one of his and Tina's favorite spots. He suspected if they had known, to spare his feelings they would have gotten something else. It was getting darker outside, he didn't know why, but TJ had a feeling this was all going to be over soon, he just hoped it would end with Tina safe.

Chapter Twenty-Two

Monique hung up the phone. She was pissed. Nobody would give her any answers. She had heard the news reports about the kidnapping and death of some mercenary named Santigo. She had made additional calls to find out anything else and was told nothing. She didn't know if her father was still alive or dead. He couldn't be dead. He was her Superman. He had always been there for her. Even though he and her mother had separated and divorced when she was five, she always knew her parents were there for her, no matter what. She had the added benefit of having two moms. Tina, after becoming her stepmother, was also a rock for her. She wasn't blood, but she was definitely family. Now her father was either dead or hurt badly and her stepmother had been kidnapped. Her call to Chief Deputy Tom Powe got her nothing but a roadblock. She grew up knowing both he and his family, went to school with his son and he stonewalled her.

She knew bullshit when she heard it and what Tom Powe told her was unadorned bullshit. He said it was not their investigation, so he didn't know anything except what he had heard on the news. He said if he heard anything he would call. Bullshit. He knew something and there had to be a reason he was not telling her. Was he trying to spare her feelings, not wanting to tell her, her father was dead? Her stepsister Louise was willing to accept that, even though she knew Louise was worried to death about her mom and stepfather. Louise tried to get Monique to just wait, but she was having none of it, she was heading to Sunset Beach.

Her conversation with Sheriff Pass of Brunswick County had been just as futile. He also pushed it off on the FBI, saying they would have to contact her with any information and all their agents were busy on the case. Bullshit, bullshit, bullshit. Monique was livid, if she couldn't get the answers she wanted, she would make the three and a half-hour drive to Sunset Beach. Somebody was going to tell her something.

Louise was going with Monique to Sunset Beach. She knew her

stepsister was not going to take no for an answer. She also knew Monique was going to push everything to the limit until she found out what happened. Louise got that sick feeling in her stomach when she learned her mother was kidnapped but kidnapped meant she might still be alive. Monique did not know if her father and Louise's stepfather was alive or dead. Louise felt the same helpless feeling Monique felt, but in reality, what could they do? It was obvious to Louise the law enforcement agencies were doing everything they could, she felt the best thing they could do was stay out of the way and pray. It was out of their hands, but Monique wanted to be there and though she hated to admit it, in her heart, so did she. The media had a sound truck parked at the end of her driveway. Like vultures they were waiting for the opportunity to be the first to get an interview when her stepfather's fate was known. Louise understood they had a job to do, but their job meant pain for others. She had heard her father say about the news, if it bleeds, it leads. Only problem, this time it was her family doing the bleeding.

Captain Sonny Young and Chief Deputy Roy Ingram sat at the kitchen table both intent on the laptop computer screen in front of them. They were working on search warrants for the two houses on their suspect list. The information gathered definitely brought those houses into the sights as probable locations. One, if not both were involved, somehow. The boat and vehicle belonging to Howard Swanson, the fact he was not answering calls to his office or cellphone, had not opened his office or left signage on the door explaining why, was suspect in itself. Chances were good, he was involved or dead. Either of these facts, the boat, the car or the lack of communicating with any known associates were going to be good reason in legal terms to help establish probable cause.

They were hashing out the search warrants to have on hand when the time came. Things were a lot more complicated in legal terms then what it used to be. When they both started, a search warrant basically stated something along the lines of, they (who the search warrant was for) got it, we want it (whatever it was you were looking for), let's get it. Today the search warrant, especially one concerning terrorists, would have to stand the review of every court up to the Supreme Court, it had to be right. Captain Young knew, as did everyone else, the search warrant was the key to keeping them out of court, out of trouble. Key to winning or losing a case. With this bunch, no one was under the delusion they would go peacefully. Captain Young knew there would be gun play. Gun play, the captain scoffed to himself. There was no play involved, somebody would die, he just hoped it was not someone he knew.

Corporal Howell ran one more diagnostic before bringing the drone in for a battery change. The house on Concord Street showed lights and activity. Some of the blinds were open and you could see movement thru the blinds. It showed a presence of five life forms and he was confident that three of those life forms were not human. Monroe Street was all buttoned up. Lights could be seen, but they were not being overly used, like someone was trying to keep a low profile. In what Howell suspected was the living room, the light was constantly changing colors, the type light and color change a TV would make. There were still six life forms showing and three had been consistent, with little movement, the entire time the surveillance had been going on. Howell was ready to make a call and that call was to Sheriff TJ Slone.

TJ hung up the phone and faced the rest of the group. "Corporal Howell thinks he's narrowed the house down to one. He thinks the Concord residence is legit. He says he has lights, activity and believes they are just vacationers. He has five individual targets, three of which he says are fast movers, which usually means kids or animals. He said the Monroe Street house has six targets, three of which have stayed consistent the entire time he has been watching. Indicating they are either restrained or for some reason unable to move. He says the lights are at a minimum and the TV is on. He's calling Monroe Street as the greatest possibility of being the location of our suspects and victims."

Sheriff Pass said what was on everyone's mind. "We need to do a knock and talk on Concord." A knock and talk meant going to the location, knocking on the door and asking the questions that you needed answers to, either directly or indirectly. It was amazing how the simple act often got the information you needed. If the Concord house was not the right location, then simply asking a few questions could take them out of contention. If it was the suspect location, then there would be gun play and lives could be lost. That possibility did not escape anyone's thoughts. Howell's comment about the three fast movers gave everyone more confidence in his belief Concord was not the location.

TJ spoke, "John, if you feel confident, I think a knock and talk may be in order."

John felt confident. He knew getting this location out of the equation would cut their workload in half. It would allow them to concentrate everything on the target location. Honest citizens were always willing to cooperate with law enforcement, criminals were not. If the person was evasive or refused to answer the door or the questions, then law enforcement knew more investigation was needed. If they got the answers needed, then they knew they could take Concord off the list of possible locations. The officer sent to the door would be someone who was not intimidating in appearance or demeanor. Sheriff Pass had just the person. Officer Mona Sheppard was an experienced officer who had been a great asset for Brunswick Co. She was a good cop, a great mother, who mothered not only her own kid, but the young cops she helped train. Mona was dedicated and had the ability to access any situation quickly and make sound decisions. Sheriff Pass knew he could count on her to make a quick decision about which way to go after the door was opened.

Mona would knock on the door knowing she had two options immediately. If upon opening the door, she sensed danger or that this was in fact a possible target location, she would say she was looking for a person she knew was not there. After being told she was at the wrong house she would simply leave. The person in the house would hopefully be none the wiser. If she did not see anything that alarmed her, she would identify herself as law enforcement and ask if she could ask them a few questions. All this took place with a back-up officer in the car with her, ready to respond if needed, as well as a team in a vehicle close by. Mona would also have her cell phone on, in her pocket with the speaker on so the back-up could hear the conversation. It was a way for them to get the answers they needed without putting anyone in a lot of danger. It was risky, but it was a way to narrow the questionable locations and the odds were in their favor with the intelligence Corporal Howell had gathered.

The ride to the house with her partner was made just after a white van with the Brunswick County Special Weapons and Tactical unit parked in front of the house two down from the target house on Concord Street. The van was marked with a vinyl wrap proclaiming it to be a heating and air-conditioning work vehicle. It was anything but. Inside the van were six fully uniformed deputy sheriffs. Each wore tactical gear, including automatic weapons, flash grenades, bullet proof vest and night vision. The van held enough firepower to take care of a small skirmish, something everyone hoped and prayed would not occur.

Mona walked up on the front porch of the canal home located on Concord St. She adjusted the 9-millimeter Glock in the small of her back. She realized there was nothing wrong with the position of the gun, she wanted the reassurance of touching it, knowing it was there. Mona knew her partner in the car had eyes and ears on her, as did the SWAT team in the van. She also knew somewhere above her a Guilford County drone had eyes which were sending a live feed back to the water tower and the house where headquarters had been set up, just a couple miles away. She knew everyone was listening on the open cell phone set on a conference call in the cell phone holster on her belt. She knew all this, but she still wanted the comfort of touching what she knew was going to be her first line of defense.

As she approached the front door, she could hear Barry White singing in the gravelly voice she had heard so many times before. Her first husband had used Barry White to court her. His efforts at the time were appreciated and Barry's songs and music were definitely perfect for young and old lovers alike. She smiled to herself, thinking even the songs of Barry White could not save a marriage that had disintegrated into nothing but arguments and hard feelings. Her ex was jealous of her successes while he remained a street cop. Being married to a cop is not easy. When both are cops it's twice as hard.

Mona took a deep breath and knocked on the door. Her knock was greeted by a chorus of loud barks. There was obviously more than one dog behind the door she stood in front of. The barking dogs caused the dog's owner to shout out, "shut up, shut up now!" The dogs stopped barking, but Mona could hear them on the other side of the door and there was definitely more than one.

In a moment a white male, at least six-feet tall opened the door. He blocked it to keep the three Golden Retrievers who looked like they were clones of one another from rushing out the door.

"Yes, how can I help you?" The man said as he tried to keep the dogs back.

Mona looked beyond the man and could see a woman dressed in a robe. Her hair looked like it was tussled, not combed. Tussled like she had just gotten up, even though it was early evening. Mona could also see a hand drawn sign with ribbons hanging from the bottom, the sign read JUST MARRIED. Mona put the music, the sign and the dress, and what she counted as five occupants, just as Corporal Howell had reported, as no threat.

She made a tactical decision, not to alarm them by questioning them or identifying herself as a cop. "Is this the Craddock residence?" she asked, knowing it was not. She knew the house belonged to Howard Swanson, she also knew from the driver's license photo she saw, this was not Howard Swanson, she just hoped his name wasn't Craddock, the name she had just made up.

"No, you must have the wrong house," the man replied.

Mona replied, "I'm sorry for the intrusion." Mona pointed to the sign and said, "Did you just get married?"

The man smiled and replied. "Sure did, we're here on our

honeymoon. I took the sign off just as soon as we got away from the church. I was in a hurry to get down here and was afraid it would blow off the car as fast as I was going."

Mona followed up with "Beautiful dogs and they look like they're from the same litter."

"They are, they are our pride and joy. We couldn't leave them in a kennel, they're family, but as young as they are, as playful as they are, I have to walk them one at a time, and being cooped up inside they are pretty rambunctious." said the newlywed.

Mona thought of what Howell had described as fast movers, these dogs fit that bill.

"I'm sorry for disturbing you, please accept my apology along with my congratulations." Said Mona. She smiled and turned from the door. The newlywed responded with a smile and closed the door. Mona walked away confident that Concord Street was not their target location.

Mona got back into the car, her partner started it and backed from the driveway. They drove out past the mock air conditioning van with the SWAT team inside. They would stay on station until they were ordered to stand down. Mona took the open phone from her belt, speaking directly to Sheriff Pass.

"Sheriff, this is not our location. These folks are newlyweds. I verified five occupants in the house. Three of them are very large, very active Golden Retrievers. I saw the woman, and she looks like she has been in bed her entire visit, and she's not sick. I saw the Just Married sign and they're playing Barry White on the stereo."

Sheriff John Pass laughed. He had played a little Barry White and Lou Rawls himself when he was trying to impress his wife, then girlfriend. He didn't know if it worked, but it couldn't have hurt, he had been happily married for many years. He responded to his detective, "Thanks Mona, we heard, good job."

Sheriff Pass discussed Mona's findings with the rest of the group. They all agreed the full attention would be placed on the Monroe Street address. Chief Deputy Ingram and Captain Sonny Young deleted the search warrant for Concord Street and concentrated on Monroe St. The probable cause was strong. They felt that they could place the terrorist in the boat and vehicle belonging to Howard Swanson, plus the fact that they had checked every location owned by Howard Swanson except the Monroe Street location and had not been able to find or contact Swanson. They found his college class ring in the pocket of the terrorist killed by TJ Slone. The search warrant was going to be signed, but because it was a Saturday night, the chances of having it signed by a federal magistrate or Superior Court judge usually was slim. Federal magistrates and Superior Court judges didn't work on weekends. To have any case they made accepted in federal court, the search warrant had to be signed at least by a North Carolina Superior Court Judge. Their signature was required by the US Attorney. Both TJ and John Pass knew plenty of Superior Court judges, that would not be a problem.

Chapter Twenty-Three

Azil Adula knew better than to relax, even though he fully expected to be safely on an Iranian freighter heading to Cuba in a matter of hours. If he knew anything, he knew don't take these Americans for fools. They were like a commercial he had seen, with a ridiculous, pink rabbit advertising batteries. They just kept going and going and going. Even when they were beat, they kept coming back at you. He admired it but didn't understand it. Even in the face of death, they showed a certain arrogance that defied logic. He had killed many, by bullet, by knife, by explosions. He had even choked one young Marine to death, looking into his eyes. His hands and feet were tied so he could not resist. He saw a defiant young man looking back at him, even as his life slipped away. It took some of the joy out of killing a person when they showed no fear. These Americans were crazy. He did not take them for granted.

This was not over until he had turned Tina Slone over to his employers in Cuba. They would dock in Cuba 30 hours later or less. He would be met by his employer who would take delivery of Tina Slone and deliver enough money that he would never have to work again. He would be the telephone contact with Matt Hart as long and as often as they needed. Each contact would get him another half million on top of the five million he was being paid for the kidnapping. Five million plus expenses and his expenses were already over a million. He had padded the bill. He would not have to pay Number *Five* or his brother. *Five* was dead and his brother was either dead, captured, wounded, or in the hospital. He would not have to pay *Four* because he was either going to be killed or captured. As for *Three,* he had not made up his mind about her yet. After she helped him get Tina Slone on the plane, he could just as easily put a bullet in her head and leave her at the boat ramp. She was a nice piece of ass, but there would be plenty more just like her in Cuba. The expense money was all his along with the five million promised. He didn't need *Three,* after all, he was getting ready to be a very rich man. He even thought about killing that pig Samms, after he delivered them to the freighter, but thought better of it. He may need him in the future, it was worth more than the fifty thousand he demanded to keep that resource.

Thinking about it, he decided *Three* would at least make it to the boat. Killing her in front of Samms could make him hesitant about doing business in the future. *Three* would make it to the boat, whether she made it to Cuba was still up in the air.

Tina Slone felt the throbbing in her finger which had been mutilated by the gardening shears, twice. The pain from the cut as well as the cauterizing by the wood burning iron along with the smell of the burning flesh was imprinted forever in her mind. The only thing that gave her any sense of relief was the pure hatred she felt for the man who did this to her, to her family. She didn't know if TJ was alive or dead. She knew if he was alive, she would see him again. Nothing would keep him away from her. He wouldn't quit until he had her back. TJ's uncle had once described TJ as having no quit in him. It didn't matter what it was, a political race, a ball game, a card game, if TJ was in it, he was in it to win it. If TJ was alive, she felt sure he was working on getting her back. If he was dead, she was going to kill the son of a bitch who killed him and hurt her. The woman who cleaned her bloody, urine stained body, who gave her a drink of water and bite of food gained nothing by doing so. She was part of the people who did this, she would die if she got in Tina's way. Tina did not know how she was going to accomplish any of this, but the thought of it gave her purpose, it kept her going.

Three walked into the bedroom where *One* was lying on the bed. She shut the door as instructed by *One*. He motioned her to lie beside him. She thought more meaningless sex. She didn't want to have sex with him again, but she would. She was a slave to him and his whims. She hated the thought of it, but it was a path she had chosen, a path she could not get off of now. He was ruthless and though she liked to think she feared no man, she feared this one. They had lost two of their team and to him it was just business. It was like he didn't care. She shuttered as she thought he would have the same attitude if something happened to her. There was no love, no loyalty, nothing, it was business to him.

One pulled *Three* to him. He thought about having sex with her, maybe one last time, but there was no time. *One* whispered to her in a low voice, a voice *Four* could not hear, even if he were listening at the door.

"In about an hour, you and I will be leaving with Mrs.

Slone. Before we put her in the car you will give her a shot of the same sedative you have been giving the Governor's wife. I need her out and compliant for about three hours. We will be meeting a plane at a boat ramp on the Intracoastal waterway, less than a mile from here. We passed it this morning coming in. The plane is a seaplane that will take us to a boat offshore. We will arrive at the meeting point for the plane well before the meet. Mrs. Slone needs to be in the backseat and quiet until we get her on the plane and boat. Mrs. Slone will have no further harm to her, we need her alive. *Four* will stay here with the governor and his wife until he gets further instructions. Do not say anything about this to him, he does not need to know any of this. Do you understand?"

Three didn't understand. If they only wanted Slone, why did they take the other two. Something didn't add up. What possible use would a sheriff's wife be when you had a governor and from what little *Three* knew, the next possible Vice President of the United States. *Three* wondered what this was really all about. She wondered, but she knew better than to ask. She nodded she understood.

One sent her from the room, telling her to send *Four* in.

Four entered the bedroom as he was instructed to do. He saw *One* lying on the bed, beside him was a body indention he knew *Three* had just left. *Four* could smell the sweet essence he knew to be *Three*. He was both jealous and fearful of *One*. He also knew he didn't have a chance with *Three*, hell, he didn't even know her name. He did know she was good at what she did and would not hesitate to kill, she had already proven she was capable and would follow orders.

One motioned for *Four* to sit on the edge of the bed beside him as he swung his legs to the floor. As he sat down *One* started to speak.

"Brother, our journey is almost at its end. We will either be successful here on earth or we will be enjoying our rewards with Allah. In about an hour, *Three* and I will be leaving to transport the Slone bitch to our new location. You will be left to guard the Governor and his bitch wife. I trust this task to you. Are you the warrior I hope you are?"

Four nodded yes.

One continued. "Guard them with your life, they are the most important part of this plan. Do not allow anything to happen to them. We will check them together when I leave, I want them to be in the same condition when I return. I will return in about three hours. It is an hour and a half to our new location and an hour and a half back. When I return you and I will take them to the new location. Do you have any questions?"

Four once again shook his head, this time in the negative. "Allah Akbar!" Said *One*.

"Allah Akbar!" Responded *Four*.

Four had reservations about this whole thing. *One* said he was guarding the most important part of the operation, then why not move them first. It seemed to him you took care of the most important thing first. He felt uncertain, but he would say nothing, he would do as he was told.

One dismissed *Four* and busied himself gathering his weapons. In his waistband he carried a Glock Model 17. A 9mm which held almost a half box of ammunition with a magazine extender. He also had a smaller Kahr .380 in his pocket. This small caliber was meant only as a back-up and held seven rounds. After satisfying himself he was prepared weapon-wise, he turned his attention to the two money packages he needed. One package contained four stacks of hundred-dollar bills, each stack with 100 hundred-dollar bills. This made the remainder of the fifty thousand owed Samms for providing the plane and transportation to the freighter. The second stack contained five bundles, each bundle containing ten thousand dollars, totaling another fifty thousand dollars for the captain of the freighter. That made a cool one hundred thousand dollars for transportation alone. *One* thought it was easier to kill and take what he needed, except for the fact he could not fly a plane or captain a ship. Besides, it wasn't his money, expenses were part of the deal. *One* knew in a matter of hours he would be on a ship heading to Cuba with Tina Slone, a little damaged but still well enough to use as leverage to keep the next president of the United States in line.

The things required of Governor Hart, soon to be Vice-president Hart, would be simple and of little consequence in the beginning, but *One* was sure they would become more involved as they pulled Hart deeper and deeper into his involvement with their requests. His employers were paying the Cuban government well for their protection. He doubted the Cubans knew who his employers were holding in Tina Slone, and how they were using her to control Matt Hart. *One* smiled to himself. If the Cubans knew they held such a prize, a prize that could cause the third world war, he doubted they would be very happy.

Chapter Twenty-Four

Monique picked up her cell phone and dialed the number Sheriff Pass had provided earlier. She was leaving Whiteville heading for Sunset Beach. She was less than an hour away, less than an hour away from the answers she so desperately needed, answers she was going to have. Sheriff Pass answered the phone on the first ring, "Miss Slone, where are you?" Monique gave him her position.

"Come to Ocean Isle. Just before you get on the bridge there is a shop called "Rags Boutique and Beachwear". Pull into the lot, I will have someone meet you."

Monique wanted to ask why, but decided to pick her battles, a decision that was foreign to her. She wanted to get straight to it, but her father always cautioned her to pick her battles. Besides, she could make her point much better in person, she would wait.

"I'll be there in less than an hour." she responded.

Monique was divorced and had taken her maiden name back. The Slone name carried a lot of weight and respect. Her father always told her if you have an advantage use it. She didn't like to be dependent on anyone or anything. She had finally come to the realization she had spent too much of her life fighting against the tide. A fight which got her nothing. Now common sense was finally prevailing, if you have an advantage, contact, use it was good advice. She was finally using it.

Mona Sheppard pulled into the parking lot and waited. Her instructions were simple. Meet Sheriff Slone's daughters and take them back to the Cates home where the sheriffs were waiting as well as everyone else. She was to tell them to call their families and let them know they had gotten there safely, then she was to take their phones. Sheriff Slone told her his daughter Monique would be difficult about the phones, but to be firm and tell her nothing. Tell her it would all be explained to her when she got to the command location. Mona knew she could handle difficult people, she had before, but never someone who was trying to find out if their father was dead or alive. Never someone who had just driven 200 miles to get the answer, someone whose mother was a kidnap victim, maybe dead herself. Mona felt she could handle it, but she had to be careful how she did it. She tried to think how she would feel, but soon realized she couldn't imagine the fear, concern, sorrow these girls would be feeling. She had to handle this very carefully.

Mona watched as Monique and Louise pulled into the parking lot. Monique parked in a location where she could see everything, typical cop's kid, Mona was sure she picked the decision of where to park from watching her father. Typical cop move. Mona smiled. Her son watched her and copied everything she did. Monique probably didn't even know why she did the things she did, she just watched and copied what she saw her father do. Mona's kid was the same. Mona pulled next to Monique's car, driver's side to driver's side and rolled down her window.

Monique watched the car pull up to hers, driver side window to driver's side. The woman in the car rolled down her window, Monique did the same.

"Are you Monique and Louise?" Mona asked.

"Yes!" was Monique's short answer. The woman asking the question had a professional air about her. Her vehicle was a nondescript vehicle with no markings. Monique heard what she recognized to be a portable radio. The woman was probably a detective. She was attractive in her late forties or early fifties. Her eyes and demeanor said this was not new to her. Monique had met many like her who worked for her father. She always admired the sacrifice these women made in their own lives, with their own families to make it and to survive in what many considered a man's world.

Mona identified herself as detective Mona Sheppard. She asked if they had a nice trip and then regretted the question as soon as she asked it. Of course, they didn't have a nice ride, they were trying to find out if their parents were dead or alive. Monique's expression showed the absurdity of her question.

Mona decided to try again. "I'm sorry, that was a stupid question.

Let me start again. I'm sorry you ladies are going through this. I can't imagine what you are feeling. Hopefully you will have some answers in a few minutes. I hope you know we are doing everything we can to bring this to a happy resolution."

Monique didn't wait. "Are my father and mother alive?" Mona took a deep breath, direct, she liked that.

"Those answers will be provided by someone above my pay grade, but those answers are just a few minutes from here. I've been asked to have you call your families and tell them you got here safely and that you will call them later, that you will be meeting with the sheriff and Deputy Director of the FBI soon."

Monique quickly responded, "Why can't we call them when we know something? What's the point in calling with no news?"

Mona recognized Monique and her sister were the daughters of a cop. They were used to the blunt straight to the point kind of conversation. She decided she would use that tact.

"You need to call now because you are getting ready to go into a secure location. I will be taking your phones and securing them, you will not be allowed to make further calls until it is cleared by command. I'm sorry that is the way it is, or you go no further."

Mona hated to be so blunt, especially with the turmoil each of the girls must be in, but she counted on their genes kicking in and their cop DNA getting them to understand.

Monique looked at her sister Louise. These girls were as different as night in day. Though they were not blood kin, their lives as part of the Slone family, as stepsisters, made one thing for sure. They were united in the fact they wanted their parents back. Each in her own way was a force to be dealt with, but in this case they both realized if they were going to find out anything, they had to give in. Both girls started dialing their families.

After the calls, Mona collected the phones. She instructed Monique to follow her. Mona pulled out of the parking lot and turned left, not right toward Sunset Beach, but left to cross the bridge to Ocean Isle. Monique and Louise looked at each other. This was unexpected. Why were they going away from the condo where their parents and the Governor and his wife had been assaulted and kidnapped. This was getting strange. Mona then took a right at the end of the bridge road and headed to an area both girls were familiar with. The Cates, who were family friends lived at the end of the road they were now on. Both girls had happy memories of summer visits to the Cates home. In fact, it was those visits that convinced their mother and father to buy in the area. When Mona approached the security gate that blocked the road leading to the Cates home both girls looked at one another with a quizzical look, but, said nothing. Mona stopped at the gate, got out of the car and walked back to their car and said. "Use the code *7676. We'll be going to the house at the end."

Mona walked back to her car and entered the code.

Monique and Louise just looked at each other. They didn't need the code, they knew it, they had used it before. The house at the end, that was the Cates house, they had been there. Louise broke the silence, "What the hell?"

Monique thought the same thing her sister was thinking. Why were they going to the Cates' house? What did they have to do with this? Why did they have to call their families and give up their phones? Why was the command operation being ran from a house in a gated community and not from a Brunswick County Sheriff's Office or even a mobile crime command post on the scene? Who would come up with such a plan? As she asked herself this question Monique realized the answer was right there. Her father, he would do such a thing. He would choose a gated community to keep the media away. The Cates were family friends, they would do anything for her father. Her father would want to be out of sight, he would use his possible death or being wounded to his advantage, whatever advantage that might be. Her father had enough political clout to make the federal government and state law enforcement do it his way. Her father was alive.

Monique emotions were in a turmoil, as she thought, I'm going to kill him.

As they pulled in front of the Cates house and stopped, Monique turned to Louise and said, "Dad's alive. I'm going to kill him." Before Louise could respond, Captain Sonny Young stepped from the elevator which had been brought to ground level. Monique recognized him from the numerous awards presentations she had attended with her father. He was one of Guilford County's best, if he was here, so was her father. Monique was direct "Where is he?

Captain Young smiled, typical Monique, just like her father. "He's upstairs."

Monique ran up the stairs, not waiting to take the elevator, followed by her sister and Captain Young. After landing on first floor level, it was a few short steps to the door of the house. The door was full glass which gave a full open view of the Atlantic Ocean. It also gave her a full view of what was inside. She immediately spotted her father sitting at the same table they had enjoyed meals at in the past. His head was bandaged, and she could see the faint color of blood where the bullet had found it's mark just hours before. Her own feelings were mixed. She was glad to see he was alive, glad he was OK, but at the same time she was livid with him for putting her, her sister and families through the agony of thinking he was dead. Her father rose with a smile on his face as he saw her and Louise. That smile set her off, it was the same smile he had whenever he thought he had pulled something over on her. She was not in the mood.

TJ walked toward Monique with arms out-stretched to hug his youngest daughter, hers were out-stretched to push him away. "I'm pissed!" she said. "Why did you do this to us?"

"Mo, because I need the advantage of them thinking I'm dead and that maybe the person in the hospital is one of theirs. I need the advantage, so I can get your mother back."

Monique hated the nickname Mo, but secretly loved it when her father called her that. He was the only one she allowed to use it, she corrected everyone else. Hearing him and his explanation softened her demeanor, softened enough to accept the bear hug he was giving her. Louise joined in and they held a family group hug nobody wanted to let go. Each felt something was missing and each knew what it was.

Tina Slone heard the voices on the TV which had been on different news stations all day. The voices were muffled but when some of the reporters with deeper voices were talking, she was able to catch what had been the news of the day, the entire day and into the night. Though her eyes had duct tape around them as did her mouth she figured it was night. She could hear the activities early in the day and now, she heard nothing outside. The news she heard was about the kidnapping and deaths associated with the event hours earlier. She heard the reporter describe two dead bodies at the condo but was unclear about who had died. Was TJ dead? She felt sure the person hanging by the rope outside her condo was dead, she was not sure about the one on the balcony, but more importantly, she was not sure about TJ. The voices which she knew were her kidnappers were not as easy to hear, most of their conversations seemed to be whispered. She knew there were two men and a woman. She knew the man who cut her finger twice was in charge. She also knew if she had the chance, she would kill him. She didn't know how, but he needed to die.

When they did take the tape off her eyes to cut her finger, she found she was face to face with Matt Hart. She could see the pain in his eyes when they tortured her. She also knew it was nowhere near the pain she felt with the actual cuts. Seeing Matt in front of her established he was in the house somewhere as Belle probably was.

Only a couple miles away from Tina, unknown to her, at the Cates home where she had spent many wonderful days with family and friends, Monique, hurt, relieved and pissed, asked her father why her phone had been taken from her? Why it was so important the kidnappers think he was dead? Her father explained the kidnappers would be unsettled by the idea they may have a source for identifying the rest of the group.

TJ did not know Adula's crew did not know what the plan was or for that matter who each person in the crew was. TJ did know the person who they were pretending to be alive, was actually the brother of the mastermind of this kidnapping. TJ also knew that Azil Adula was a cold- blooded killer. He did not know Adula had lost his religion and though he would not have liked the comparison, he was no better than the dead Juan Santigo, the El Salvadoran mercenary. Azil Adula was in it for the money. Not the pocket change Santigo worked for, but serious money. The explanation about the phone was simple and Monique thought reasonable. She heard her father's explanation about the dead kidnappers, but she also thought of her family who were in the dark, just as she had been only minutes before.

Monique's offer to help was not well received, except by her father. The others in the room did not know her and probably looked at her as a nuisance rather than an asset. Monique looked at the Deputy Director of the FBI who had been introduced to her and her sister as was everyone else at the table. His look was one of aggravation, like he didn't like the fact she was here, much less the idea, she might be of help. Monique saw and recognized that look. Like her father she could read people and decided right away, she didn't like him. She had heard about him when her father ranted about those idiots in Washington. He was one of those idiots.

Monique figured he was a taker by what she had heard and what she saw in front of her. She figured him for the kind of guy that was quick to take credit for somebody else's work and would climb over your bones to get to the top.

The director of the State Bureau of Investigations she knew a little more about, he was familiar because he got the job her father had turned down. Her father liked him and that was good enough for her. Captain Young and Brunswick County Chief Deputy Ingram were known to her because she grew up with her father as sheriff, and being the Sheriff's daughter was sometimes a blessing, sometimes a curse. No matter what, she grew up knowing a lot of cops, and they knew her, her father made sure of that. She figured it was to make sure she knew she was being looked after or was it because her father wanted her to know she was going to be held to a higher standard because they knew whose daughter she was. Knowing her father, Monique figured it was both.

Captain Young had worked for her father for a long time and Chief Deputy Ingram worked for Sheriff John Pass who her father liked and respected. Monique knew that if he wasn't a good person, he would not be working as the sheriff's right hand, just as Tom Poe would not be working for her dad if he wasn't good at what he did.

Monique had a bone to pick with Chief Deputy Poe after this was over. She had grown up with him in her life, had gone to school with his kids and he kept information about her father secret, secret from her. Monique knew and understood why, but she still didn't like it.

TJ knew better then to tell Monique or her sister Louise that there was nothing for them to do. He also knew the mere suggestion they do something like cooking would be met with resistance, loud resistance. He was not going to suggest such a thing. He assigned Monique the task of watching the monitors which had been placed around the house. He asked Louise to change the stained dressing on his head. Louise took after Tina, she had the nurturing, caring quality about her. Raising her four kids, five counting her husband, a farm load of animals, Louise was a medical professional by job description and avocation. She quickly grabbed the first aid kit and started working on the bandage around her father's head. The bandage was stained from the blood from a wound she knew was not life threatening, but she knew probably caused him a lot of pain. It was still oozing blood, not a lot, but still enough to require another bandage. Louise made short work of applying the bandage while her father and the others continued a plan involving, from what she picked up, a location on Ocean Isle. That location really had their interest. Louise didn't ask any questions, that was not her style, but she intended on letting Monique know, she knew Monique would get the answers.

Chapter Twenty-Five

One looked at the clock on the TV cable box, it said 9:25 pm. In less than three hours he would be airborne, on the way to the Iranian freighter which would be the last part of the operation. What could possibly go wrong? If Samms showed, if they made the meet, got airborne and the freighter was where it was supposed to be, then a successful completed mission was in sight.

One walked from the bedroom, looked at *Four* and said, "It's time." *Three* went to her bag of tricks and removed the sedative and hypodermic she would use to knock Tina Slone out. *Four* followed *One* into the bedroom occupied by Governor Hart and his wife.

Three entered the room occupied by Tina Slone, Tina turned to face the sounds she heard as *Three* entered. Tina felt the small hands of *Three* as she took her arm, the same arm with the damaged hand. Tina wondered what fresh hell was coming and then she felt the needle as it pierced her skin. She felt the liquid as it entered her body. Panic as she thought, what are they doing to me. The needle did not hurt, just a little sting, the throbbing in her hand was still the dominant feeling. The soreness of the vicious slaps across the face took a distant second, so the needle stick was nothing. The fear about what the needle held and what fresh hell she was getting ready to endure, that weighed heavy on her mind.

$$* * * * *$$

The boat was not speeding through the water, but it was going at a steady moderate speed. It was heading south on the Intracoastal Waterway, heading past the canals which connected to it on Ocean Isle. It was dark, around 9:00 pm, but darkness had not completely taken over the night because it was early. There was the occasional boat, but boat traffic was very sparse. The boat was heading toward the canal that led behind the Monroe Street house. The captain of the small boat stated "I will give you a countdown from ten, when I get to one, go over the side. Don't hesitate, there are no street signs on these canals. You will be directly in front of the right canal. Your target will be the second house on the left, up the canal. Any questions?" The two divers clad in black rubber suits, with blackened faces, wearing black diving gloves and black swimming fins. both replied no. They did not wear air tanks or weight belts. They wouldn't need them. The only equipment they carried would be far more useful. Across the chest of each was a holster which contained a silenced model 17 Glock 9mm. It was a proven shooter no matter if underwater or out of the water. They also carried a waterproof flashlight which would probably not be used, but the old saying, better to have it and not need it, then need it and not have it. They had a waterproof radio which was connected to a wireless earphone under their rubber diving suit. They could hear it, nobody else could. The earphone also was used as a microphone when they pushed the transmit button on the radio, using the vibration from the bones in the face to help transmit the message they wanted to send. They also had a silenced assault sub-machine gun strapped across their back and divers knife strapped to their leg. In total they each had a hundred rounds of ammunition, communication devices and very simple instructions. If anyone tried to leave the Monroe Street location by boat, stop them, stop them by whatever means necessary.

"Ten, nine, eight, seven, six, five, four, three, two, one" shouted the captain over the steady roar of the outboard engine, never reducing speed. On one, Deputy Jackson of Guilford Co. and Deputy Jim Tillis jumped from the speeding boat into the dark waters of the Intracoastal Waterway for what would be a hundred- yard swim.

Deputy Jackson was not new to this type of water entry. During his time as a Navy Seal he had made hundreds of such entries, his fellow deputy, not so much. Deputy Tillis was civilian trained, he was used to easy fallbacks off a stationary boat in calm waters. Water marked by a diver's buoy and flag for safety.

Jackson wondered if Tillis's entry would unnerve him and if he would retain all his equipment. Tillis did as he was told. He dropped from the boat as if he were hooked to Jackson. They both hit the dark water making only one splash. The boat sped off into the darkness. Nobody knew they were in the water except themselves, the boat driver and whatever was in the water around them. Jackson was not afraid of sharks, even though he knew it was feeding time for these eating machines. He was concerned about speeding boats. They were in an open waterway, with black diving suits and darkened faces. Any speeding boater would never see them, they would be run over like bugs on the road and all the boater would hear is the thud of their head and body hitting the underside of the boat. Then you would need to worry about the sharks because there would be plenty of blood in the water.

"I know I don't have to say this, but I'm going to, just to put my own mind at rest. If a boat is heading our way, dive toward the bottom until it passes," said Jackson. Tillis just nodded in agreement. Jackson could see he was still on a rush from the entry. Jackson didn't mention his other concern. If that boat was dragging a net, shrimping, it could easily catch them and drag them along underwater and they would drown. Jackson knew it was a long shot, so why mention it, especially after seeing the look on his inexperienced young partner's face. They turned and looked toward the swim ahead of them and started off, two dark heads and bodies swimming through the just as dark waters toward the Monroe House canal.

* * * * *

Three left the room where Tina sat in her wooden chair, legs and arms taped to the legs and arms of the chair. Her eyes and mouth taped shut, her face bruised from the horrific beating, her hand and finger mangled by the two cuts made with the garden shears on her finger. Her clothes still smelled of urine and burnt flesh where they had cauterized each cut after making it. *Three* had tried to clean her up, but she could do little about the smell.

Tina Slone would have never allowed herself to be seen like this if she could help it. Tina couldn't help it, in fact Tina was trying to keep herself together, but felt she was slipping away. Her reasoning was getting blurred, it seemed as if she was drifting.

Tina's nurse training kicked in. They've drugged me, why, what was going to happen next? Tina tried to fight against the drug, but it was no use. In moments, Tina would be unconscious and dead to the world. She fought it, concentrating on the pain in her finger. She knew the adrenaline would help fight the drug.

One returned with *Four* from inspecting the Governor and his wife. They had checked to make sure each was secure. *One* knew they were, this was just window dressing for *Four*, a chance for *One* to stress the importance of what he was doing, when in fact it was not. *Four* was expendable, chances are he would be killed, killed and free to look for those 72 promised virgins. *One* thought to himself, good luck with that. *Four*'s death was of no concern to *One,* it would give him the cover he needed to make a clean getaway. The Governor and wife would be rescued, the Governor would be a hero. American's were suckers for someone who endured danger, they considered them heroes, they even had a special day for their veterans. What a soft bunch of idiots. *One* thought anyone who died for another was a fool, not a hero. He figured this was just some more of the religious garbage so many Americans believed in. *One* was through with religion, the only thing he worshipped was money and he was about to get a bunch of it.

Three reported Tina would be out in minutes and then she would be out for about three hours. Plenty of time to do what needed to be done.

Deputies Jackson and Tillis swam the last few yards to the dock at the back of the Monroe Street house. The swim had been uneventful, only one boat had passed, it was a pontoon of drunken college students. It passed safely behind them. Jackson keyed his radio three times to signal they were on site. They really didn't need to because Howell had been tracking them by drone. He had already reported their arrival to command, but it was protocol and needed to be done. Command keyed their radio twice, hesitated and twice again to acknowledge they received.

Deputies Jackson and Tillis, removed their fins, left them under the dock and climbed onto the shore, avoiding walking on the deck leaving any wet footprints for anyone to see. There was no boat at the dock, but if one arrived and they saw footprints leading from the water to the house, that could be a problem. They crawled under the deck where they would not be seen and placed their backs to the wall. Behind that wall was the enclosed bottom area of the house which housed the parking area. Their instructions were to contact command with any useful information, but now they busied themselves getting their guns prepared for anything that may come. Neither Jackson nor Tillis would speak, unless absolutely necessary. They used hand gestures or mouthed what they wanted to say if hand gestures would not work. Little had to be said. Each took a position at opposite ends of the deck. Still out of sight, but in better tactical positions if needed, they had the back and both sides covered. Jackson knew the front was being watched by a supposed air conditioning repair truck and a team of officers. Now they waited, waited for anything that needed to be reported. Any intel that may have a bearing on this case and the safety of the Governor, his wife and the wife of the Sheriff. Everyone now felt this was the location of the kidnappers and kidnapped. Jackson and Tillis waiting on a boat that may or may not come. Everyone waiting on a search warrant that had been prepared and was waiting for a local Superior Court judge to sign. In the van, the Sheriff's Emergency Response Team headed up by Captain Sonny Young included Guilford County and Brunswick County officers, all geared up and ready to go.

At the Monroe Street house *One* and *Three* readied the Lexus for their departure. Tina would be placed in the floor of the backseat, unconscious, hands, feet, eyes and mouth taped. *One* and *Three* would be in the front seat, pretending to be a couple on vacation in one of the prettiest places in North Carolina. The drive to the marina to meet Samms and his seaplane would be a short one. It would take less than five minutes to get there, but *One* intended on arriving early, so he could watch the area before Samms arrived. Once Samms arrived he and *Three* would be at the plane as soon as it stopped. They could be in the air before any police could arrive, he figured two to three minutes the plane would be on the water, at the boat landing, tops.

After take-off he would send Samms north, for about three minutes. Then and only then would he give him his true destination which would take them to the Iranian freighter which would be waiting in international waters. Three hours from now he would be safe, the only thing that could stop him was a hurricane or ship accident sinking the freighter. He had checked, the weather was fine.

Chapter Twenty-Six

TJ's phone rang, he picked it up on the second ring. He listened for a second and responded to what was obviously a question, but in a voice the others could not hear. He then said to the caller "the gate code is * 7676" and hung up. He went to Monique and whispered in her ear. Monique got up, walked out the front door and went downstairs in the front of the house.

Louise took Monique's seat in front of the monitors. All this had not escaped the attention of the rest of the room.

TJ informed the watcher on the outside of the house a friend would be coming down the road.

In a few short minutes, Louise stated "in-coming" pointing to the screen of the camera pointed at the only roadway entrance into the house. A red, late model F-150 slowly approached the house. One person could be seen inside. He appeared to be a white male, with a beard. You couldn't see it, but the hair was in a ponytail, a short one, but still a ponytail. The driver wore a John Deere ball hat that looked the worse for wear. You wouldn't look twice at him sitting, but when standing, you could see the professional bearing of a man who had military training. He looked like any redneck, All-American country boy. The only thing that looked out of place were the Oakley sunglasses. If you knew anything about sunglasses, you would know they were very expensive and they were actually a tool, a tool used by many tactical operators in the military. One of many expensive, tactical tools this man had.

TJ told Louise the stranger was alright, he's a friend. He radioed the same to the officers stationed around the house again to make sure nobody got jumpy. Monique met the stranger at the bottom of the stairs, shook his hand and told him to follow her. As they entered the front door, they immediately went up the stairs to the second floor and entered the bedroom on the left at the top of the stairs. TJ followed.

TJ thanked Monique and sent her from the room. When Monique got to the bottom of the stairs, every eye was on her. The looks on their faces said, what the hell's happening, who is this guy? Monique knew none of these answers, but she didn't let them know that. She loved he fact they thought she knew something they didn't. Her father had simply whispered, meet the guy in the red truck and bring him to the bedroom at the top of the stairs, he would take over from there. Monique especially liked the look on the Deputy Director of the FBI's face. He was pissed, but she expected he was in a constant state of being pissed and she didn't care. She thought it was funny.

TJ stuck out his hand, shook it and thanked the person for coming, like the man had a choice, he was a professional and did as he was told, having faith the ones doing the telling knew what they were doing and had his back. They didn't exchange names, there was no need. He knew he was to do as asked by the man in front of him. This man answered the phone he called and acknowledged the code word he was given. He was given the access code to the gate. He was greeted by a beautiful woman who took him to meet the man whose voice he recognized from the phone. He didn't need to know anything else except what he was expected to do.

Fifteen minutes later, TJ walked down the stairs followed by the mystery man, who immediately walked out the front door, down the steps into his vehicle, heading back out the only way from the house by land. He left with short concise instructions which nobody could confuse. Instructions nobody but him had heard. He left TJ a radio which was scrambled and could only be heard by the matching radio he had. It could not be traced and after activation it had a life span of 72 hours when it would then self-destruct, making itself useless and untraceable. Its parts were not traceable and was the best technology America had, but nobody would know it was American. Nothing was traceable.

TJ walked back to the table where Sheriff Pass. Director Sturgis and Deputy Director Dunham waited.

Dunham asked the question on everyone's mind. "Who the hell was that and what has he got to do with this?"

TJ said "Insurance, and that's all you need to know." That answer was not good for Dunham. He stood up, which caused others in the room to stand also, sensing things were about to get very ugly.

Dunham shouted the words in such anger that spittle came out with the words, "Bullshit, you don't tell me that's all I need to know, I'm a Deputy Director in the FBI. I'll tell you what you need to know, you don't tell me. You're just a county sheriff with a few connections which I don't give a shit about. You should have never been involved in this investigation and I'm getting ready to put a stop to it. You're through, it's over!"

TJ looked at Deputy Director Dunham and smiled. The kind of smile Monique, who watched with interest, had seen before. It was a smile that said, you're young, you're stupid and you're getting ready to be schooled. That was another smile Monique hated to see, but not this time, she couldn't wait.

TJ took out his phone, scrolled down a row of numbers and pushed a button. He handed the phone to Dunham and said, "you may want to go to a private area to talk with this person."

Dunham, took the phone, with a dazed look on his face, looked at the screen which caused his eyes to widen and walked away.

After Dunham walked away, TJ addressed the rest of the room.

"Folks there is a term called plausible deniability. That simply means what you don't know, you can't be held accountable for. I do not intend on putting any of you into a position that would compromise your ethics, violate anyone's rights or break any laws. This is still our investigation, the gentleman that just left is simply insurance in case something was to happen that would put lives or our country in jeopardy. Hopefully he will not have to do anything, but if our plans do not work, he is insurance.

Plausible deniability is for your protection. The person Dunham is talking to now will put his mind at ease. I don't really care if it is or not. I do care that you are protected, I hope you know that and trust me enough to take my word for it."

Nobody said a word, they didn't have to, they trusted TJ. TJ continued, this time directing his words to everyone, but looking straight at his daughters.

"Tina, I pray is alive. If she were here, she would tell you, we have discussed this among ourselves. We discussed different scenarios and discussed what we expected the other to do. We discussed kidnapping. You in the business know anything is possible, Tina knew it also. She also knows that I will be doing anything in my power to rescue her. Wherever she is, she is expecting me to come through the door at any time. I don't plan on disappointing her. If she is dead, then I will do everything in my power to bring her killer to justice. I don't have a death wish, neither does she, but neither of us can stomach the idea that evil wins, and we are willing to die to make sure it doesn't. She spent her life as a nurse fighting disease, raising our children to fight for right, peace and God's blessings. As a cop's wife she understood and accepted the pain and risk that goes with the job. She knew, as a cop, I had committed myself to doing whatever it took to make sure the bad guys lost, whatever the price. I plan on being with her again, in life or death, but I do not plan on dishonoring her by not carrying out her wishes. She's coming home, one way or another and those who did her harm are going to pay, one way or another."

No one doubted TJ, not any of his fellow cops or his daughters who listened with tears in their eyes. Momma was coming home, one way or the other.

Dunham came back into the room, head down and humbled. He handed TJ his phone.

"The Attorney General said I probably owe you an apology, please accept it." The words were there, but it was plain he didn't mean them. Dunham tried to hide his hate for TJ, but he couldn't. Even when he was outmatched his arrogance kept shining thru which TJ recognized as a true loser.

TJ felt Dunham was properly neutered, so he didn't press the issue. He didn't care about Dunham and his feelings, he had much more important concerns. He simply replied, "No problem, we have work to do."

Dunham did not know, nor did the others know, TJ was part of a secret group made up of the most influential members of the federal law enforcement community. The Attorney General was part of that group. Its purpose was to protect the United States of America, no matter what needed to be done. It operated within the powers of its members. It was made up of members who stayed out of sight, known only to the other members and those who worked for them, just like the man in the red pick-up. They had no official name, because they did not exist in any budget or any government department. The funding needed was drawn from the different departments involved. They were part of the legendary $350 hammers the government was accused of buying. A little here, a little there and they had the money needed to fund secret projects. They dubbed themselves the Garbage Detail and TJ reached out to them during a short phone call after reaching the Cates home.

The man in the red truck pulled into an ice cream shop at the end of the bridge road coming onto Ocean Isle. He walked into the shop and ordered a large cup of butter pecan, one of his favorites. He paid the high school age girl serving him. She waited on him, took his money, smiled and said thanks come again and never took the phone from her ear. The mindless chatter on the phone while serving him made the man in the red truck think, why in the world would her boss put up with that. He then just smiled to himself, thinking he was probably just as mindless at that age. It was the Marine Corps basic and Recon Sniper training that took that out of you. That and three tours in the middle east and the extensive work he had done for the NSA (National Security Agency), the type work few people knew about and even fewer spoke about. The agency was not just about gathering and distributing information, it had "Special" units who did special jobs. His unit was made up of just him. His assignments were just his responsibility. He suspected there were others like him, but he did not know. He was truly a lone wolf, a lone warrior. He knew it was his butt on the line and he knew he was the only one who would be protecting it. He had all the best equipment and any resources he requested. He didn't have reports to fill out, all his reports were oral, to the same person and he suspected was reported to others in the same way. He lived on cash advances and credit cards that he never got a bill for. He stayed in an apartment furnished and paid for by cash. His pay, while not much as a Gunny Sergeant, went straight into a bank account he set up in his real name. He was building his retirement one check at a time, one day at a time, but he had no interest in ever retiring. He had no family, no responsibilities. He worked when he was called, he trained on his own and answered to nobody other than the voice on the phone who gave him his instructions. The one steadfast requirement: Never be without your phone and always be ready to go. The things he was asked to do, usually involved something being shot or blown up. He seldom met anyone and any documentation about his assignment were destroyed after he verified and identified who or what they were.

He had received a phone call, hours earlier, instructing him to go to a particular location. The location was a coffee shop with computers folks could use to get into their sites. He was to use their internet connection to access a website which contained a photo of a terrorist by the name of Azil Adula. It had sketchy little information other than a photo. He was given a contact phone number and code word identifier and instruction to go to Ocean Isle quickly. He deleted the information he had accessed on the website after writing down the contact number.

Getting to Ocean Isle quickly was not a problem since he actually lived outside Camp Lejeune, the same place he was mustered out of the "official" corps. He was still a Marine, technically. He had the rank of Gunny Sergeant, had a military identification, could use any Marine facility, not that he didn't get some funny looks from the regular corps because of his appearance, but nobody questioned him. He was "special ops" they figured, and they figured right, but little did they know how special. He was similar to the Army's Delta force, except there was only one of him. On any operations he had fake identification which matched the fake registration on his truck.

He made the call to his contact number upon entering the island and ended up on Ocean Isle at a house located at the end of the island. The man who he met did not identify himself, nor did he expect him to. That was not the way things were done. It was obvious to him the man understood the program, he suspected he was a man with considerable experience and clout. He suspected this because his orders came from the highest levels and it would take someone with clout to reach his bosses. He also saw the vehicles and security around the house. The vehicles and demeanor of the people he saw screamed law enforcement. No matter how you tried to hide it, a black SUV with dark windows screamed cop or government. The people guarding the place screamed police, probably with military training. The only thing he couldn't figure were the two females. Who were they and why were they involved? He suspected this call had something to do with the murders and kidnapping in Sunset Beach all over the news. His suspicions were verified in the short conversation with the man he left the radio with. He activated the radios, giving him one, explaining they had a 72-hour life span. Explaining everything in the radio and its usefulness would end then. If he needed longer, he would have to go through his contacts, again.

He was assured by the man who gave him his instructions, the operation would be over well before the radio went out.

As the butter pecan melted, he heard the sound of what he thought was a whirring mechanical bug. He knew what he was hearing was the sound of a drone. He had heard it many times before. The uninitiated would not identify it as being anything but insect sounds. He looked into the night sky and saw a dark object without lights drop to the top of the water tower in front of the ice cream shop. He figured it had something to do with the man he just talked with. He wasn't the only one with a job to do.

The ice cream was great, the night was warm, the crowds were enjoying a nice beach day, but it was time for him to get busy. He pulled the truck into a corner of the public parking lot where hardly anyone was located. He backed into the parking space, exited the truck and casually walked to the back of the truck and dropped the tailgate. Inside was a gun box protected by numerous locks and alarm systems. He quickly opened the gun box. He knew what was in there and it was not time to get it out, yet. He just wanted to check once again to assure himself he had the equipment needed. He did. He closed the box after removing his sidearm and holster, which he hid in the small of his back. It was old school, but it worked for him. A Glock, model 21, Gen 4, 45 caliber was his weapon of choice. It fit comfortably in the small of his back. It was a big gun, but he was a big man. His second handheld firearm was a Glock model 43 9mm which he carried in a cross-draw holster on his left side, his weak side. While wearing it, he could draw and shoot from a moving vehicle, still driving, without losing any mobility.

In the locked and alarmed box was a MP 5, sub-machine gun, C-4 explosives and a LAWS rocket launcher. Again, old school, but highly effective and there were so many on the black market, tracing them would be very difficult, if not impossible. He also had a 50 caliber Barrett Sniper rifle. All his equipment was unregistered, which made attributing them to anyone doubtful at best. He was prepared to leave any of his equipment behind and just walk away, that was the nature of his job, his responsibility.

Nothing he had could be traced back to anyone, including his fingerprints. If someone ran them, they would come back not in file, but a message would be sent to his boss letting them know someone was checking. Even his DNA was not in file. It would show him to be a white male of Eastern Europe origin, which was not entirely the case. White male yes, European descent, partially, his ancestors were Saxon, but again, if someone checked, his boss would be notified. He didn't exist and in his line of work, that was a good thing.

He was known as the Garbage Man, nobody called him that, actually there were few who knew about him or what he was doing, it was a nickname he gave himself. He didn't mind it, in fact, the unknown group he worked for was nicknamed the Garbage Detail. So, being the Garbage Man made sense.

Unknown even to the Garbage Man, the Garbage Detail was made up of six people. The members were the President, Attorney General, CIA Director, Chief Supreme Court Justice, Sheriff TJ Slone and the Garbage man's contact person, the National Security Agency Director, the Garbage Mans real boss. This group was sworn to secrecy and took their responsibility very seriously. They seldom met, but the Garbage Man didn't know that, the only person he ever talked with over a secured phone was the Director of the NSA. His directions were simple. Meet the man he was directed to meet and follow his instructions to the letter. He didn't know the person he met, except to know that man had his instructions.

The Garbage Detail was seldom used. It was used only to protect the interests of the United States. The purpose of the six was to review and decide if those interests needed to be protected and time was a factor. The detail took care of situations that could lead to world war or conflict if they were not contained. It took the place of a using the military or small team operations such as a SEAL team or Ranger unit. It acted as a quick response unit. It gave the country and most of its leaders "plausible deniability".

The purpose was to take care of situations where lives and country were in danger. The operatives and there were several, were battle tested veterans who loved their country, could follow orders and worked alone. The only family they had, the folks they worked for or with. The President had the authority to take action, but sometimes action needed to be taken that was out of the public view and out of the bureaucracy that was Washington, DC.

The President wanted to make sure his actions did not usurp the Constitution but protected America. If he called a meeting, it was made in private over secured, scrambled telephones. The Chief Supreme Court Justice served as the legal authority as did the Attorney General. The directors of the CIA and NSA provided the necessary intelligence. Sheriff TJ Slone was the Washington outsider. He provided a perspective that was not DC influenced. He got the call to become part of the detail because President Turnage knew and appreciated TJ's common-sense approach. The President knew TJ to be ethical, adhered to the Constitution and could keep a secret.

Each member of the Garbage Detail, in the true spirit of the founding fathers, had pledged their loyalty, talent, fortunes and lives to America. Each decision had to be a six to zero vote, no dissention, which meant total commitment.

The President seldom called for the detail to activate. He called for the use of the Garbage Man in this instance because President Mark Elliot realized some outside group was trying to change the make-up and security of this country. The President also knew the country could not go through any more turmoil, especially after the recent assassination. The President himself had just learned of the group having been briefed after President Turnage was killed. He was briefed by the Chief Supreme Court Justice who had just sworn him in. As Vice President he had no idea the unit existed.

Sheriff Slone spoke with the Attorney General explaining his fears relating to the kidnapping. The Attorney General in turn spoke with the new President. TJ took himself out of the mix because he was the victim. The details vote was unanimous, all five agreed. The Garbage Man was told how to contact TJ. TJ was out of the vote because of his personal involvement, but TJ's commitment was far more than the others and they knew it.

TJ's conversation with the Garbage Man was short and direct. He gave him all the information they had. He told him about the Monroe Street canal home and the probable vehicle they would be driving. He told him what was expected. The instructions were simple. Protect anything that looked like a hostage, stop any suspects from getting into any form of transportation that would allow them to get out of range of his rifle or law enforcement. In short, stop whatever mode of transportation they were using. He was told help was going to be in the area. He knew law enforcement did not know about him.

He was given the radio frequencies for the operation so he could monitor what was going on. He was not to be seen, nor was his involvement going to be a part of any official record. Just a normal operation for the Garbage Man.

Chapter Twenty-Seven

One and *Four* took a drugged but compliant Tina Slone from the chair that had been her personal hell for the last eighteen hours plus. She smelled of urine and dried blood. Body odor, which would have never been an issue under normal circumstances, mixed with the other smells. Tina Slone was a proud, beautiful woman. An accomplished woman, now she was a drugged mess. She was practically carried down the stairs and placed in the floorboard of the Lexus parked in the basement garage. *Four* re-taped her feet together as he did her hands.

Because of the close quarters in back of the Lexus he taped her hands in front, it didn't matter, she was drugged, she could barely move. Tina was still taped across her mouth and eyes.

Tina knew she was being moved, she knew she was out of that damn chair, but she couldn't feel her legs except the sensation of her feet dragging across the floor. She also felt she was being carried by the two men she knew were her kidnappers. She couldn't see them, but the size of their hands as well as the breathing and voices told her who they were. She knew she was being carried downstairs because her feet would drag then drop.

She was definitely going downstairs, the same stairs she had been forced up hours earlier. At the bottom of the steps it was a short drag before she was thrown into the back of what she felt was a vehicle. She thought a vehicle because she bounced off the side of a seat and landed on what she knew was a floorboard wedged between the front and back seat. Even though she had been drugged and her thinking was muddled, she could sense some of what was happening around her. She could feel the hands and tape as one of her tormentors taped her hands and feet. She heard the car door close, she heard voices as they walked away. Tina fought against the drugs they had injected her with, was afraid it was a losing battle, but she struggled, fear and hate on her side.

Corporal Jackson, from his position under the deck of the Monroe

Street house, heard a noise through the wooden walls. It sounded like someone or something was being carried down the stairs in the basement. He could hear the opening of a vehicle door. He could hear voices but could not make out words. He heard the car door close and someone going back upstairs, this time not dragging anything. He had heard nothing but muffled conversation and what he suspected was someone or something being placed into a car. He felt confident he needed to report what little he had. He pushed the transmit button on his walkie, one push, wait, then two additional pushes in quick succession. He waited about ten seconds and then did it again. The purpose was to alert those listening that he was going to be making a report.

Protocol was they would not reply in words, only by keying their radio once to acknowledge they had heard. Words would be few on his part, over concern they would be heard since Jackson and his partner were there for recon and action only if needed.

At the top of the stairs *One* said to *Four,* "We will be leaving soon, my brother and I will be back in about three hours. Be prepared to take the Governor and his wife when I return.

Protect them with your life, they are our mission. Do not let anything happen to them. I'm counting on you."

Four did not know what to say, he understood none of this, it made no sense, but he nodded yes.

The squelch noise on the radio got everyone's attention at the command area, the room fell quite as they waited for the signal to be repeated. In a few seconds, the signal came again. Sheriff Pass picked up his pen, grabbed some paper and turned the radio up and a recorder on. Everyone else pulled a little closer. In a few seconds a muffled voice, known to those who knew him to be Cpl.

Jackson said, "Movement in basement. Car door opened and closed. Something loaded."

The transmission ended. It was muffled but understandable. It was not going to be repeated unless they keyed the microphone three short times. There was no need to, they heard the message. They could have used a cellphone and texted the information, but the chance of discovery was greater and took longer to transmit then the words. The words though few, said everything Cpl. Jackson knew. Now it was up to them.

One and *Three* picked up the guns they had brought with them. Both had side arms, but *Three* also carried a sawed-off pump Mossberg 500. It held a total of six rounds of double 00 buckshot. That equaled to twelve pellets in each shell the size of a small blueberry which left the barrel spreading out to make a very large kill pattern. It did not require a lot of aiming, it just needed pointing in the right direction. *Three* kept the shotgun close at hand, along with the Glock 9mm she carried and the S&W model 422 she had used to kill the highway patrolman earlier that morning. The 22 cal. was most effective at close range with a well-placed shot. With a silencer its shot sounded like the opening of a soda can as the air escaped. She could place the shot about where she wanted to. This same gun had ended the life of the couple at the canal home and the couple at the condo. This gun had taken the lives of five people in the last twenty-four hours and no one heard a thing. *Three* walked down the stairs to the waiting Tina Slone, lying in the back of the Lexus. As she looked in the back floorboard, she saw Tina was not moving, the drugs were working. Part of the gear she took with her was the knock-out drugs she had administered, but she doubted more would be needed. She gave her enough to get her on board the ship, she felt confident, she knew her job. *One* followed close behind, taking the driver's side seat, reaching up and pressing the button to raise the garage door.

Cpl. Jackson keyed the radio, one, wait, two more. One, wait, two more. Jackson spoke in a low voice.

"Vehicle leaving, vehicle leaving."

Cpl. Howell was also on the radio. His drone had seen the garage door go up and the back-up lights as the Lexus backed out of the garage. His voice was not muted, but loud and clear.

Sheriff Pass was on the radio telling his ground team of the movement.

At a bar at the end of Monroe Street, under the water tower, two Brunswick County deputies munched on nachos, casually looked toward the on-coming lights from the Lexus. They looked like beach tourists, except they both were drinking water and had been hogging the table for hours. They had endured the hard looks the waitress had given them. She had given up on the hope they were going to order anything that even looked like a large meal, which translated into a large bill which should have translated into a large tip. The waitress was pissed. These two were costing her money.

The Lexus pulled to the end of the road, stopped and turned onto the street heading toward the bridge road. The Brunswick County officers got up, placed a twenty-dollar bill on the table and began walking to their vehicle, a BMW confiscated from a local drug dealer. The twenty more than paid for the nachos and hopefully made up for hogging the table, but there was no time to wait for a bill or change. They got to their car just as the Lexus passed by the bar. Inside they saw a male and female, nothing else. They got into the car and pulled behind another vehicle, a red F-150 with a single occupant, which was between them and suspect vehicle. They reported what they saw. Sheriff Pass gave simple instructions, don't lose them, but don't get burned, help was on the way.

The drone had the Lexus locked in. It had the capability of locking onto a subject or vehicle and automatically following it.

Even if the Lexus had pulled into a convoy of white Lexus the drone would stay on the right vehicle, as long as it was in range of operator, and the range was not that great, so the BMW was important until additional help arrived.

The BMW stayed behind the red truck which was behind the Lexus. The Lexus turned on the bridge road heading toward the mainland. Both the BMW and the red truck turned and headed toward the bridge along with the Lexus. The red truck separated the Lexus and BMW. The deputy in the BMW wondered how long he could keep this position, it was perfect for a vehicle surveillance, the red truck was between them and the suspect vehicle. He knew help would be on the way, he had no idea help was already there. He did not know a drone was above following him and the Lexus. He did not know the red truck was on his side. Then it was over. The Lexus turned to the right, just before crossing the bridge. The Lexus turned without a signal, it was quick and deliberate. Had the officer followed it would have looked suspicious and out of place, he made the decision to cross the bridge, again following the red truck. The BMW crossed the bridge and immediately turned to cross back over, knowing the bridge was the only way off the island by car. The officer knew the only thing down that road was a bait store, liquor store, boat loading ramp and a couple of seafood restaurants. The bait store would be open, the restaurants would be closing in an hour or two and the liquor store was not open, but the boat landing was always open.

The red truck crossed the bridge and watched the BMW following him make a rapid turn heading back across the bridge. The Garbage Man figured it was a cop car. He didn't need to turn around. In the earpiece hooked to the radio on the seat beside him, his handler, the man he had met with, told him the Lexus had turned down the road and had pulled into the parking lot of one of the two restaurants on the dead-end road, the restaurant closest to the boat loading dock. He was told the Lexus parked but no one got out. The man in the red truck knew he needed to explore the area on this side of the intracoastal waterway. He was looking for a clear line of sight. It was almost ten o'clock.

One parked the Lexus in a secluded part of the restaurant.

He was not conspicuous, but there would be no prying eyes walking by the vehicle where he was parked. It was ten o'clock. Samms would be here in two hours, during that time, he would watch to see if anything in the lot was out of the ordinary.

One knew he was trapped, not the best tactical position to be in. There was only one way out of whether he was by car or foot, but he was leaving by neither. His thoughts were this would be unexpected. It was dangerous being trapped as he was, but it also gave him the element of surprise.

Samms was breaking every law and safety rule in existence. By landing and taking off from the intracoastal waterway at midnight, on a summer night when the waterway may have boaters and water traffic was not legal. *One* knew that, as did Samms, but Samms didn't care because he was being paid well.

One knew the risks were nothing compared to the surprise element. *One* also knew he had another hole card, to assure he was going to succeed in his mission.

The BMW took up a position just in sight of the road the Lexus had disappeared down. He was told to wait, not go down the road. He was told the vehicle was sitting in the parking lot of the last restaurant. He wondered how they knew that he was the only vehicle assigned to Monroe Street, so he thought. He had been on many surveillances and knew the only way they could know that is if someone in the car told them or they had eyes on. He figured eyes on. He looked out the car window for a plane or drone, he could see neither.

Cpl. Howell launched the second drone, the first being positioned over the Lexus. It was keyed in on the Lexus and would hover until the battery ran down and would have to be replaced. The second drone with a fresh battery would take the place of the drone over the Lexus. While bringing back the first drone Cpl. Howell ran it back over the Monroe Street address and ran another diagnostic test. He identified that instead of six occupants there were now three. The two in one of the bedrooms and a single moving person. Howell reported his findings, to include the fact that the Lexus held three occupants, two in the front, one in the back.

The Garbage Man found what he was looking for, just across the intracoastal waterway from the Ocean Isle boat landing, a mere quarter mile or so away. He backed the truck up into the high grass which ran to the edge of the water. The vehicle had switches that turned off the backup lights as well as the other lights while activating a night vision camera to drive by. The truck was in stealth mode. The Garbage Man pulled a black ski mask over his head and face. He exited the truck, no buzzers, no lights came on. He opened the rear of the truck and gun box taking out the 50 caliber rifle with military grade rifle scope on top. He laid on the ground and inched backwards under the truck. The grass covered the sides of the truck, the truck was over him. He could not be seen by anyone walking up on the truck. He figured people would figure him to be a fisherman, so the pick-up would not cause suspicion. The grass at the rear protected him from being seen from the water or the boat ramp which was little over a quarter mile away. He beat down the grass in front of him, giving him a clear view of the parking lot. He was set. The 50 cal. was his only choice. He was over twice the effective distance of the LAW's rocket. His instructions were clear, stop whatever means of transportation they were using. He knew the 50 cal. could do that. The MK211 Green tipped round was used against a hardened target. The Garbage Man knew it would wreck-havoc on any vehicle engine, stopping it in its tracks. That was his assignment, that would be what he would do. The Garbage Man also knew the Laws Rocket if used would cause too much collateral damage, possibly harming the hostage. He could not take that chance.

He looked down the scope, he could see the Lexus, he could see two people inside the Lexus, a man and a woman. He wondered what his target would be. The Lexus or another vehicle that would meet them. A boat coming in from the ocean or down the Intracoastal Waterway. Hell, they could even bring a seaplane in. It didn't matter, he could stop any of them and he would be packed up, on his way out of town before the smoke cleared and no one would know he was there.

Chapter Twenty-Eight

It was almost 10 pm, *One* was ready to play his hole card, what he felt would be a game changer. He pushed buttons on his phone.

"911, how can I help you" said the female voice who answered the call.

One went straight to the point. "I think someone is being killed on Monroe Street. I can hear furniture crashing and a woman screaming. I think someone needs to check on her."

"Sir, what is your name and what is the address on Monroe?"

"I'd rather not give my name." *One* said. Knowing the burner phone he was using would give no information except the number. He would destroy the phone after removing the battery so it could not be traced.

"I don't know the address, it's the second house from the water on the left-hand side of the street as you head for the intracoastal. It backs up to a canal. Please hurry, I think someone is killing her."

With that *One* hung up the phone. He stepped out of the car, removed the battery and stomped the phone. He threw the crushed phone into the canal behind the restaurant parking lot and got back into the car.

Three looked at him in disbelief.

"What are you doing, you just signed *Four's* death warrant. You know he will protect the Governor and his wife until they kill him. Just as you instructed him to do."

One looked at her with distain and started second guessing whether he would let her live or not. She questioned him, her life may well end between the pick-up point and Cuba.

"*Four* is an important part of the mission. His sacrifice will give us cover while we make our getaway. The recovery of the Governor is an important part of the plan. Why, should be of no concern to you," said a perturbed *One*, deciding she would not live, he would dispose of her at sea. His profit just got bigger.

Three was very unsettled by the brutality and lack of compassion shown by *One*. This wasn't a mission for *Four,* it was suicide. She realized *One* was hell bent on this mission and loss of life was of little consequence. He had no loyalty, he had no honor, no religion. He and she were the only ones to survive and she wondered if she would.

Sheriff Pass looked up as Chief Deputy Ingram ran toward him, radio in hand. "Ocean Isle PD just got a call to our target house. A domestic violence complaint, screaming woman, crashing noises from inside. The caller would not identify himself and hung up."

Sheriff Pass looked at the others at the table, TJ Slone was first to speak.

"Stop the Ocean Isle PD car. Just for a couple of minutes."

TJ picked up the radio and called Sonny Young who was sitting in the van just down the street, along with his team.

"Sonny, hit the house. Go as silently and as quickly as possible. You are going based on exigent circumstances, they just received a domestic violence call, screaming woman and crashing furniture. Silently, quick and silent, no flash grenade. You should have one, no more than two hostiles. You got about four minutes before the locals arrive sirens blasting." Young acknowledged he understood. TJ also told Young he would assign Jackson to secure the rear, he could put all his effort to securing the house.

Sheriff Pass got off the phone with the Ocean Isle PD. He had their assurance they would hold off the few minutes needed. They also noted it was his request, in case it was a legitimate call.

Sheriff Pass was pleased with what he had accomplished. He was not pleased with what he just heard from TJ.

"TJ, what are you doing?"

TJ held up one finger, signifying, hold on. He keyed the microphone on the walkie, calling Cpl. Jackson's call number. Under normal circumstances he would not have called, this was not normal.

In a hushed voice Jackson responded, "Go ahead."

TJ said in a short sentence "Have you heard anything from the house since the vehicle left?"

Jackson responded again in a hushed voice, "No".

TJ told Jackson Captain Young would be entering the front, he and Deputy Tillis would be responsible for the rear. Jackson understood and briefed his partner.

TJ turned back to Sheriff Pass and the rest of the table.

Monique and Louise were also paying attention, this was getting ready to be a game changer. TJ started out by reviewing the last couple of minutes.

"Ocean Isle PD received a domestic violence call to our target house. Cpl. Jackson said no unusual sounds from the house before or after the Lexus left, certainly no screaming woman. We have half the people in the house, half in the car, the drones have confirmed that. We're working on getting the search warrant, but now we have exigent circumstances, we don't need to wait. At worst we have two people in the house who are hostile at best one. I'm betting one. I believe the other two bad guys are in the Lexus, going to a meeting place, waiting for transportation. They are either splitting up the hostages or leaving with one. I think the call came from the two bad guys I believe are in the car. They have no need for the folks at the house, so they are being sacrificed so they can get away. The question is, which hostage do they have with them. I think they are providing us a distraction, something to keep us occupied while they disappear. I could be wrong and they may have decided they are in over their head and abandoned the hostages, but that's not likely since the drone has movement of one person at the house, if it was a hostage, why wouldn't they just come out?"

Nobody said a word. They all just looked at each other.

Finally, Deputy Director Dunham spoke. "You're putting an awful lot of faith in a lot of maybes. We could be making a mistake which could put our hostages at risk. I don't like it."

TJ looked at him with a look that easily showed the contempt he felt for the man. He made no attempt to hide it.

"I've got more to lose then any of you. I think it's the right call."

TJ looked at Monique and Louise, he could see they too thought it was the right call.

Sheriff John Pass dialed a number on his cellphone, the number of an Ocean Isle PD Sergeant.

"Sergeant, Sheriff Pass. In about two minutes you will be receiving multiple calls from the neighbors at the Monroe Street address.

The same address you got the domestic violence call to. When you get those calls, and you will, go in with lights and sirens.

Sergeant knows the call has already been handled. My guys are on the scene getting ready to take the door down. They may need your help. The call about a screaming woman is false. We think this house may be involved in the kidnappings and murders this morning. Sergeant, handle this like you would a domestic violence call. When you get there, find and report to a Captain Young on site. He will tell you what he needs. I will be there shortly."

The sergeant responded in the affirmative. Sheriff John Pass hung up the phone and prepared to leave the Cates home. Everyone around the table stood to go, including TJ Slone.

"Where do you think you're going?" Deputy Director Dunham said. TJ didn't have a chance to answer before SBI Director Sturgis jumped in.

"You know Dunham, you're starting to get on my main last nerve. I'm getting tired of your bureaucratic bullshit ways and I suspect everyone else is too. Where in the hell do you think he's going? In that house is probably either his wife or one of his best friends. He's going to find out which it is, just like any husband or friend in law enforcement would. Especially if that husband or friend is a real cop. You, you simple bastard, get your head out of your ass and shut the fuck up. This whole operation has been run without your help, everything we've gotten from you we've had to drag out of you. Ladies, (looking toward Monique and Louise), I apologize for the language, but I've about had it with this guy."

Louise smiled and Monique said, "I was about to tell him the same thing, don't worry about it."

Dunham looked like his sucker had been dropped in the dirt. As he looked around the room, he could see he had no supporters in the room. Once again, he had been burned.

Sonny Young took his team down the street at a double time pace. Lucky for them there was no traffic and nobody outside. His plan was to take the door down and swarm the living room area. Swarming, just as the word implied meant rushing into the room like a mass of angry hornets looking for a target, something to sting. Anything they found was going to get stung in the worst sense of the word. Cpl. Howell ran another pass and told them the two individuals were still in the same room they had been in all day, the front bedroom as identified by plans they had obtained from the records filed in the Register of Deeds and tax office. The other individual was in the front room or common room, just behind the front door Young and his team would enter. When the door came down, if he was a bad guy, he would go for any weapon he had. Young's biggest fear was the suspect may be wearing a bomb vest which could contain enough explosives to kill everyone in the house. If that vest contained ball bearing or any type loose metal object that could become a projectile, he could easily take out anyone close to him.

As they waited for the go signal, they had already discussed the options and possibilities. They had decided the only option was a head shot. They hoped it would not trigger a reflex reaction causing the vest bomb wearing suspect, if there was one, to push a detonator switch. All the other options left a higher percentage and possibility of something going wrong. Young knew this was a life or death situation for someone or everyone, every time his team entered into a building where a hostile subject was located. He knew that; his team knew that. They were all volunteers, they got nothing for the effort, no time off, no extra pay, nothing, nothing except the knowledge they made a difference. While they may have to take a life, today they had the chance to save lives.

Captain Young started using hand signals to communicate with the team. Because of the danger involved, the size of the door and the need for speed he had decided on a three-man entry team. One team member carried the battering ram. He would lead, knock the door down and fall out of the way. Young and the second officer armed with MP 5's with laser sights would enter, taking down any hostile they saw with an automatic three shot burst, hoping to immediately incapacitate the suspect if he was armed.

Cpl. Jackson heard the rustling noise at the front of the house. He hoped the suspect did not. Jackson was listening for it. Jackson motioned for Deputy Tillis to take his position. They moved from under the deck to a position closer to the water's edge where they had a clear view of the back of the house. They were also at each corner, so they could also see the sides. They waited. They didn't wait long.

Four watched the cable news. He had seen the same reporter reporting the same thing for hours now. They had nothing new. They had "supposed" law enforcement professionals who were giving their opinion and what if scenarios, but nothing new.

Four was getting bored. He looked at the clock on the wall, it was 10:15. *One* and *Three* had been gone about forty minutes.

The sound of the door being smashed brought *Four* to his feet. The gun he had been holding in his hand started to rise pointing at the two figures coming thru the door, it was a natural reflex. Each figure held what he recognized as scope mounted H&K MP 5's. He raised his gun just as the three-shot burst of 9mm rounds hit him square in the temple. He was graveyard dead and he didn't even know it.

One was too far away to hear the gunshots, but not too far to hear the sirens. They seemed to be coming from multiple directions. *One* smiled. They would be busy for hours. He would be long gone.

Sonny Young entered the room, sweeping from side to side with his MP5, looking for another target. The suspect lay on the floor with an increasing pool of blood flowing from what was left of the top of his head. The rest of the team entered the house and started clearing the rooms. Sonny entered the bedroom with the two subjects identified by the drone. On the bed Sonny recognized Matt Hart and his wife Belle. Both their hands, feet, eyes and mouth were duct taped. Governor Hart was awake, Sonny figured, because he was moving, but Belle Hart was comatose.

Captain Young jerked the tape from the governor's eyes, knowing going slow would have hurt worse. After the governor's eyes adjusted, the captain could see he recognized him. He cut the tape on the governor's hands and feet. The governor immediately turned to his wife and began taking the tape from her mouth and eyes. Young cut her feet and hands free. Belle Hart was still drugged and did not reply to the governor shaking her. The governor jerked the tape from his mouth, calling her name. She still did not reply.

Governor Hart turned to Young and begged, "Please, please help her."

"Governor, we have a team medic. He will look at her just as soon as we get you out of this house. We are still checking to make sure there are no booby trips, explosives or anything that would put you or anyone else in danger. We need you to come with us now," stated Captain Young as he took his arm and led him from the room and the house.

Belle Hart was lifted by another officer and taken to a position outside the house and placed on a waiting ambulance gurney. The outside of the house was full of cops, flashing blue lights and curious eyes from the adjoining houses.

One looked into the back seat on the floor of the Lexus.

Tina Slone lay quietly, her breathing shallow, but breathing. She was his cash cow. About now the governor should be rescued along with his wife. If not, the police had a hostage situation. *One* hoped Hart would remember their conversation, if not he would start taking pieces of Tina Slone, until she was dead, or he complied. *One* preferred the cash cow producing the money he could make acting as a contact person, a go between. He didn't care if Tina Slone lived or died. He did care about the money he could make keeping her alive. For a mere $25,000 a year, they had arranged for her to be housed and kept alive in a Cuban prison. It would be a difficult life for her, but she would be alive, the payments assured that. He had it all set up. He suspected she would be treated poorly, probably molested, after all she was an attractive woman, but she would be kept alive. *One* looked at *Three*. It was a shame she had to die, but die she would, but not before helping him get Tina Slone on that Iranian freighter just a couple of hours away.

One spoke to *Three*, not letting on that her hours were numbered.

"*Three*, what will you do when we get to Cuba, what are your plans?

Three thought about the answer, not because she did not know. She didn't know how to respond without upsetting *One*. She decided to tell an absolute lie.

"I will be at your service if you need me, if not I will return to the United States until my services are needed again to further our cause."

She had already decided she would never work with him again; this man was unstable and she doubted he was a true believer. It was plain he was out for himself, in her eyes, making him no better than the Americans she hated. No, she would take her money, take her fake passport and blend into a tourist group that now visited Cuba on a regular basis. She would book a flight into Mexico, take a bus north to the American border and cross using her fake identification, with the thousands of others that crossed each day. *Three* could not wait for this mission to be over.

Tina Slone heard the conversation between the man who had cut her finger, twice and the woman who had tried to clean her up, fed her and who had drugged her. Her thinking was foggy, but the adrenaline was helping her come around. She kept thinking about what these people had done to her friends, herself and her husband. She kept her mind focused on her pain, not because she enjoyed pain but because of her nurses training she knew adrenaline would get her out of this drug funk faster than anything. She thought about revenge. She thought about her husband in a pool of his own blood. She thought about life without him. She thought about her kidnapper's plan to take her to Cuba for God knows what. She thought about killing both of these people who were responsible for her being in a living hell. She thought about the fact she needed to be very still until the time was right, whenever that was. A body still racked with pain, but a groggy racing mind full of hate, hate for these people.

Chapter Twenty-Nine

The officer handling the phones walked up to Louise and handed her a cell phone. He said, "It's your father, he wants to talk to you."

All the blood seemed to rush from her body. She didn't want to talk with her father, afraid it was bad news. It had to be bad news, if it wasn't, he would have asked for Monique, she was his blood daughter, she was a stepdaughter. She loved him and knew he had been more of a father to her then her own, but she did not want to hear the news he may have. Louise sat down and took the phone. Monique stood beside her, holding on to her sister, she too had a sense of dread. Louise put the phone on speaker. Her voice broke as she said, "Yes, this is Louise."

"Louise, it's not your mom, she's not here. It's Governor Hart and Belle. They're safe, they have not been hurt. Louise that means your mom is in the vehicle, we know where the vehicle is, we have eyes on it, we'll get your mom back soon. Hang in there, honey, I'll get back with you soon. Louise, it's going to be alright." The phone went dead. Louise and Monique looked at each other and then hugged each other, each feeling like this hell would never end. They needed to hold onto one another for support.

TJ did not tell Louise everything. He picked his words very carefully. He didn't lie, and he was especially not going to lie to someone he loved, like his daughters, about something this important. He had already put them through hell by not letting them know he was alive, keeping them in the dark. He did not tell Louise they had found pieces of a human finger in the room her mother would have been in. He did not tell her there was the unmistakable smell of burnt human flesh and blood and a heating iron with burnt meat and blood in the same room. He may have to tell her these things, but not yet, not now. TJ had not seen those things. He had been told by the team in the house. He stayed in the car, sitting behind darkened windows, nobody knew he was alive, no one needed to know, yet.

Governor Matt Hart was checked out by the emergency personnel and given food and water. He was not asked about the kidnapping or his captors and he was wondering why. Belle had been taken to the hospital for observation. All her vital signs showed no problem, field blood test showed she had been drugged, the fear was she may have gotten too much of the sedative and could have problems from it. Governor Hart wanted to be at the hospital with her, he was tired. Much had happened in the last fifteen minutes, but he knew he would be questioned about what he knew, anything that might help. What would he say? He walked across the blood pool caused by one of his captors. The captor had a head wound that looked like someone had hit him three times with the sharp end of a pickaxe. He felt no sorrow, no pity, only rage. He thought of the pain Tina had suffered and he was forced to watch. He thought of what he had been asked to do and how they had told him she would suffer more as would his family if he did not do as told. He thought about TJ lying in a similar pool of blood, shot by which one he didn't know, maybe this guy. He knew Tina was gone. He knew she had not been part of the rescue. What he didn't know was what he was going to do. Sheriff Pass interrupted the Governors thoughts.

"Governor, we need to talk, can you come with me?" He led the Governor down a row of cars with flashing lights to a black SUV with tinted windows parked at the end of the line. The sheriff motioned him to the passenger side door as he opened the driver's side and got in. The Governor did the same on the passenger side. He closed the door and then got the shock of his life.

TJ said, "Matt, I'm glad you're safe and Belle as well, now who's got my wife and is she alive?"

Governor Matt Hart turned to see the person in the back, hidden by the shadows. He recognized the voice and was glad to see the face.

"I thought you were dead. I saw you in the floor, blood all around your head."

TJ smiled, "To quote Mark Twain, the news of my death is greatly exaggerated." He continued, "I was shot, and a head wound is a heavy bleeder, but it only knocked me out. When I came to, Sheriff Pass was talking to me and the ambulance driver was making entirely too big a fuss. You, Belle, and Tina were gone, and Mo was dead. By the way, Mo probably caused the death of the two I got. It was his alert that helped me surprise those two. Now Matt, we're going to need the whole story, but now I need to know about Tina. I need to know everything you know, and I mean everything no matter how small and trivial you think it might be."

Governor Matt Hart took a deep breath. He began the story when the kidnapping occurred. TJ stopped him.

"No Matt, Tina, when did you last see her, what kind of shape was she in? Do you know where they are taking her?"

Matt Hart grimaced. How much should he say? Did this change the dynamics of the deal he reluctantly made with the man he only knew as *One*. Could he lie to his friend? If it wasn't for him and his being offered the VP position, Tina Slone would be at home enjoying a glass of wine overlooking the intracoastal and Atlantic Ocean. Had this gone too far, what could TJ do, this whole thing was supposed to be over in about an hour, was there enough time?

TJ saw the hesitation, saw the change in attitude, felt there was some kind of internal battle going on in his friend's mind. TJ had seen the same reaction as an investigator hundreds of times before, with suspects who were trying to decide whether to lie or tell the truth. TJ did not like what he was seeing. Matt Hart, closed his eyes, took a deep breath and began.

"The last time I saw Tina, she was alive, a little worse for wear, but alive. I don't know where they are taking her, but I think she will be kept alive." He stopped there.

TJ felt like his heart would burst from his chest out of pure rage. He had never hit any suspect who he had been questioning, nor a complainant and certainly not a friend, but he wanted to pummel his friend. He wanted to knock his head right off his shoulders.

"A little worse for wear, Matt, we found parts of her body in the room she was kept in. We found a heating iron like you get with a wood burning kit with dried blood and human flesh. We found a chair with duct tape on the arms and legs which also contained blood and probably urine. A little bit worse for wear, Matt, I'm within a gnat's hair of knocking the hell out of you. You need to start giving me something or what you just went through will be child's play."

Matt Hart knew he was walking a fine line, he was torn. TJ couldn't stop this. It was too well-planned. Everything *One* told him had come to pass. He was rescued, it happened like he was told it would. He was safe, Belle was safe. They had kidnapped him with military-like precision, killing who knows how many in the process. He was told Tina would be safe as long as he complied. He was just trying to save Tina's life and protect his family. TJ was just emotional. He could fix this. When he became Vice President, he would put the entire weight of the government behind getting Tina back. He could make this work.

In a voice more like the voice of a politician, not a friend or husband, the governor spoke directly to TJ.

"You can't stop this TJ. These people are too well connected. When I become Vice President, I will use every resource at my disposal to get Tina back. She will be fine. TJ you just…"

TJ did not allow him to finish the sentence. It was automatic, he didn't think about it, he just let instinct and rage have its way. His left hand, his weak hand, darted forward. Around the head rest of the seat the Governor was sitting in, hitting him squarely between the nose and lip. Blood immediately spurted from the lip, busted by the fist belonging to his friend.

TJ only hit him once, the only regret, he didn't have a shot with the right, which would have done far more damage.

"Matt, we've been friend's a long time, I hope we will still be friends after this. That will be decided by what comes out of your mouth next, so choose your words carefully. I know where Tina is, she's only a couple miles from here at most. She's in the back of a Lexus, in what shape I don't know. She's obviously waiting with her captors for another form of transportation. It could be another car, a boat or a plane. I don't know which, but I do know it will not leave this area. It will not be taking my wife off this island and it will not be taking these assholes to freedom."

A bleeding Governor looked at the face of his friend, knowing what he said was true, TJ did not lie. TJ was not a man who liked the sound of his own words, in fact he used the John Wayne idea of speechmaking, speak slow, speak low and speak little. Matt Hart knew he was wrong, there was something TJ could do, and he was going to do it, it was he who could do nothing, nothing except tell his friend what he knew.

TJ listened to what the governor knew; it wasn't much. He explained what he was supposed to do to assure Tina's safety and that of his family. TJ could not believe how diabolical the plan was. After the original kidnapping, the continuance of the plan depended on the governor doing what was asked of him as Vice President and eventually President. If he did not, they would continue taking body parts to use as leverage against the Governor/Vice President/President until he complied, or Tina was dead. Then they said they would start on his family, maybe a second cousin first, a favorite aunt or uncle. The governor had no reason to think they could not or would not do what they threatened, after all they kidnapped him, and he had protection.

There was no way to protect all the people he loved.

TJ knew something the kidnappers did not take into account: Americans have a history of doing the impossible. Two hundred and forty some years ago many had signed a document proclaiming themselves and those they represented to be free. The men who signed the Declaration of Independence committed their fortune, their life and their honor to make sure their rights and those they represented were preserved. It was a commitment every true American upheld today. There would be no tribute paid, no extortion permitted, no living in fear. This was America and men such as himself were committed to make sure it would stay that way.

Matt Hart told TJ the leader told him that tomorrow Tina would be in a place where she could get medical help. Knowing who the leader was, TJ surmised there was only one place a radical Jihadist could get to in that short a time frame. A place where they could seek refuge, feel safe. Cuba. TJ also figured it had to be by boat or plane. Since it would be virtually impossible to get a flight into Cuba unless it was by seaplane, private seaplane, TJ was at a loss for which it would be. Boat, plane or both. While he didn't know how, he knew when. It would be soon. He also knew the chances of someone else dying was more than a possibility, it was a certainty.

Chapter Thirty

Mac Samms started flipping switches on the plane dashboard. He had already done the pre-fight check and knew everything was as it should be. He had taken one precaution, he had just enough fuel to get where he was going and get back with enough to spare for a trip to refuel. He didn't want to be able to go further in case his employer had plans he had not discussed.

Samms did not like surprises. Surprises like taking his plane or trying to force him to go somewhere he did not want to go. There is no honor among thieves and criminals, Samms did not trust his employer. Hell, he really didn't know who the guy was. He also did not trust the guy at the dock he used when refueling. He didn't know if he had a direct line to some cop who might be interested in his comings and goings. He did not need any extra attention tonight. A full gas tank could be the type thing that would cause suspicion, especially as expensive as aircraft fuel was.

The $10,000 he had already been paid was safely hidden at his house, hopefully to be joined by 40,000 friends later. Samms knew this trip was going to be quick and easy. The flight out with his cargo, the trip back, just he and his money. He would fly wave top high on the way out to avoid radar. The only way he would be found on radar was if there happened to be a Coast Guard Cutter or Navy ship in the area. Even if he was picked up on radar, the chances of anyone getting to him before he had unloaded his cargo and was airborne again were slim. It was a chance he had taken before and one he felt comfortable with. If they did pick him up, they would track him back to his docking area. If they searched the plane it would be empty. His answer to their questions, he was working on his plane and the fight was a shakedown flight. His excuse for the landing at the boat landing, fuel problems.

Emergency landings were permissible. They would be hard pressed to prove different. Samms pushed the start button, it was time.

Cpl. Jackson and Deputy Tillis sat on the dock putting their swim fins back on. They had a new assignment. It was about a half mile swim to the loading dock at the Ocean Isle bridge. Tillis knew where it was since he put his boat in the water there at least once a week. It was a longer swim then he was accustomed to. He never had a need to swim that far at one time. Their assignment, go to the loading dock, stay in the water to put whatever came to that dock in a crossfire. Whatever it was, was not to leave the loading ramp, whether boat or seaplane. If it was a car, the officers on the ground would take care of it. Jackson assumed the Sheriff and team would be the stopgap at the dock to the left of his position.

One checked his watch. The restaurant parking lot was clearing out, the only cars remaining were employees, cleaning and preparing for the next day. Nobody had paid attention to them as they left, why should they. A man and woman sitting in a dark parking lot. They probably thought it was someone too cheap to get a motel room. No matter what they thought, in a very short time they would find an empty car at the water's edge and they would be long gone.

TJ went to the back of his vehicle, the one that Captain Young had brought with him earlier this morning. He opened the gun vault and opened a gun case holding a Model 19, 4-inch barrel 357 magnum. It was old school, a revolver that had been used by many law enforcement agencies in the early 70's. In fact, this gun had been carried by TJ as a deputy sheriff. It had been modified with a target hammer and target trigger. The grips were rubber for a better grip and the trigger had been polished so fine that in single action you didn't pull the trigger, you just thought shoot. It was old school in an improved configuration. He checked the cylinder to make sure it was loaded with 357 Super Vel ammunition, 150 grain, a light bullet, jacketed hollow point which produced a devastating impact on whatever it hit. He knew it was loaded and ready. Checking again seemed to calm him. TJ slid the gun into the small of his back, along with a speed loader of six more rounds in his left front pocket.

TJ got into the driver's seat of his vehicle and followed Sheriff John Pass's SUV. They pulled out of Monroe Street heading for the street the boat loading ramp was on. Behind them a van containing Captain Young and his team followed. They pulled onto the boat ramp road stopping at the liquor store at the beginning of the road. A Brunswick County sheriff's car had pulled in and blocked the road. He would let cars out, but nobody was coming in. All the vehicles were out of sight of the loading dock and restaurant parking lot. The drone was still above and reported the suspect vehicle had not moved, Cpl. Jackson and Deputy Tillis had completed the swim in record time. Jackson was proud of Tillis as his sheriff John Pass should be. He accomplished the swim without a hitch. They floated just off the loading dock, just off to the right, out of boat traffic. If something came in from the water, like a boat, they were within sight and shot range of anything they needed to see or shoot. They were ready. It was low tide, Jackson and Tillis could stand with the water coming up to their waist, but instead they stayed low, just their head visible. Their faces were blackened, they could not be seen.

The Garbage Man using a pair of night vision binoculars watched the boat ramp. The suspect vehicle had not moved. The parking lot was almost empty. He spotted something else that caught his attention. There were two heads in the water off to his left, obviously sitting there watching. He watched them swim in, position themselves and then just squat and watch. He figured them to be cops, it they were not, they may become targets.

Samms was within minutes of the boat ramp, he decided to make a pass down the intracoastal toward the ocean before landing. He wanted to see what the landscape looked like. He needed to see where the boat traffic was. He started lining himself with the waterway and adjusted his altitude to get the best visibility where he could still see and determine what he was looking at. He began his run. There was very little boat traffic. It was just before midnight. The only boats on the water were the ones who were anchored or hard-core flounder fisherman under the bridge.

Samms approached the bridge, rose up to give the bridge ample space. When he landed, he would actually land below the bridge.

Another broken law unless it was an emergency. He looked to the right and spotted a sheriff's car blocking the road going down to the boat loading ramp. His heart stopped. He looked again and saw nothing but the sheriff's car and two vehicles sitting in the parking lot at the beginning of the ramp road.

Samms first thought was to break it off, call it quits, head back to the barn. Then he thought of his employer's words.

"You don't show up, I will hunt you down and make you regret it." He wrote it off as a bragging bad-ass wanna be. He also thought of the other possibility. He may be for real. He may really be a bad ass. If his guess was right, he was responsible for the death of two highway patrolman, a sheriff, and kidnapping three people. God only knew how many others. Besides maybe the cop car had stopped one of those other vehicles. He hoped that was the case. He hoped the officer would not come down to investigate a plane landing. He had masked the plane numbers, another violation, but he did not want bullet holes in his plane. If the cop came down the road, there was no doubt knowing the circumstances there would be bullets.

Samms was under a time crunch, he had to land, or he was going to be late and late was not an option. Samms prepared the plane for landing.

As the plane passed overhead *One* started the car. It was time. *Three* adjusted her seat looked back at Tina and thought to herself, this will soon be over.

TJ watched as the plane, a seaplane, passed overhead, flying low. He watched as it made a wide turning pass as if it was getting ready to land. So, it was going to be a seaplane. He was both surprised and worried. He knew unless the pilot was blind, he could see the road was blocked. There would be no element of surprise or so they would figure, but TJ had more than one surprise. TJ sent Sonny Young and his team on foot down toward the boat ramp, their instructions were simple. Do not let the people in the Lexus leave, but keep collateral damage to a minimum.

Sheriff Pass had geared up and went with Captain Young's team. TJ started his vehicle and waited until he heard Cpl. Jackson tell him the plane had touched down and the suspect vehicle was moving to meet it.

Samms dropped the plane to the water, something he had been doing most of his adult life. It was effortless, but anytime you were completing a controlled crash, which was what a landing was, there was risk. This time the real risk was a police car he had spotted on the ramp road as he prepared to land. He dropped the seaplane about a hundred yards from the ramp so he would coast under the bridge, up to the concrete boat ramp. He increased the power as he reached the shore, turning the tail rudder to swing the plane around. He ended up with the plane facing out toward the water. He idled the plane down and rushed to the rear door to open it. As he opened the door, he saw the Lexus moving toward the plane. He knew yelling would do no good, the engine noise would drown him out. Samms frantically started motioning for the Lexus to come on.

One was pleased, Samms was right on time, they would be airborne in minutes, the plan would be complete. He would have another successful mission under his belt. He watched as Samms motioned him to come on, he was ready for the mission to be completed also.

One pulled the car up to the plane and stopped. *Three* was already out of the car, opening the backdoor, reaching for Tina, to get her out of the car. *Three* had her up and was carrying her from the car to the plane. She was carrying in a fireman's carry, like a bag thrown over her shoulder. She reached the plane and Samms was screaming at her over the engine noise. *Three* dropped Tina at the plane door entrance, turned and started to motion for *One* to come on. Screaming something he could not hear. She had dropped Tina in the door of the plane and had drawn her gun, something was wrong.

The Garbage Man watched the seaplane land; was this the transporter for the hostage and their captor? His answer came as he saw the Lexus start to pull down to the plane.

He racked a shell into the 50 cal., he sighted and pulled the trigger. He made a small adjustment in barrel alignment and pulled the trigger again. Two shots, two seaplane engines out of operation.

The noise of the engines was cut in half after the first shot but nobody noticed except Samms. The bullet crashed into the plane engine tearing metal and stopping pistons as it passed through, tearing out bigger and bigger chunks as it went. Samms knew from the engine sound or lack of it, something was wrong. When the second round hit the second engine, doing just as much damage as the first, the engines stopping, Samms knew this was no accident. He knew it had something to do with the roadblock he had spotted. *Three* knew something was wrong because of the engine noise and the fact Samms had screamed to her he spotted a roadblock at the entrance to the boat ramp road. *Three* had a sense of doom, she could see this operation going down the crapper.

Cpl. Jackson watched as the female carried who he suspected was one of the kidnapped victims from the car to the plane. He heard the engine of the plane sputter and stop. Then he heard the second engine sputter and stop. He saw two muzzle flashes from across the waterway. He figured it was part of the team. He knew it caused some excitement at the plane. The female who carried Tina to the plane pulled a gun holstered at her side. Jackson took aim, he didn't know where Captain Young and his team were, but he knew a gun in the hands of a terrorist looking for a target was a problem. Jackson sighted in and pulled the trigger, twice. The distance was about 50 yards, an easy shot for a SEAL trained shooter. *Three,* Maria Garcia was no more. She dropped dead at the door of the plane right in front of Samms, two well placed shots took her breath away.

One turned to look as he ran for the plane, he saw nothing, nothing but a set of headlights driving toward the plane, very slow and deliberate. The lights of the black SUV were on high beam, it stopped about thirty yards from the plane, lights illuminating everything in front of it, washing out everything behind it.

The Garbage Man watched as the SUV stopped. He figured it to be law enforcement of one kind or another. He watched as one of the two heads in the water fired and killed the female who had carried what he figured was the hostage. He watched the person in the car run toward the plane. He watched but he did nothing. His job was over, he had stopped the mode of transportation, all except the car they arrived in. He racked another round into the chamber, aimed and pulled the trigger and the front grill, radiator and engine in the Lexus were turned into a metal hash when the bullet impacted each.

Everyone heard this shot. Those who were in law enforcement or the military, knew a 50 cal. had spoken. *One* knew the sound and suspected that was what had happened to the plane engines. He heard the round hit the car about the same time he heard the sound of the shot, that meant the shooter was close by.

He expected the shooter was military or military trained, which meant he could probably hit anything he wanted up to a mile away or more. This shooter was close. He looked around and figured the shooter was across the intracoastal waterway, it had the most unobstructed views. *One* ran to the plane and placed it between himself and the waterway. He looked down at *Three* as he jumped over her dead body. He didn't know where the shots that killed her came from. The plane should have blocked her from the shooter he thought to be across the Intracoastal. Samms stood in the doorway of the plane, the dead plane that was going nowhere unless it was towed. *One* thought Samms looked like he was in shock. He was of no use to *One,* he had no plane, he had no need for a pilot and this operation was looking more and more like a dead end. *One* shot Samms with a double tap to the head and chest. Now Samms was just something else he did not have to worry about.

Tina Slone was still groggy, but she could fathom what was happening around her. She felt pain as she was dropped into the plane, but she did not cry out, she was still pretending to be drugged. She heard what she guessed was the pilot as he was shot by the leader of the kidnappers. He fell from the plane in a heap on top of the woman who had carried her to the plane. Tina could not see that. She was still taped across her mouth and eyes as well as her hands and feet. She realized her hands were taped in front of her, she didn't know why. Little did she realize that *Four* had been too lazy to do the job right. For her it was a lucky break.

Tina moved her hands up to her mouth, hoping her movement would not be noticed. She pulled the tape from her mouth, placing her taped hands across her mouth, she pulled the tape up from her eyes, not removing the tape because that would be noticed. She made just enough space to see. She saw the leader who had cut her fingers standing outside the plane, gun in hand. She saw a car beyond her captor with its high beams on. She started tearing the duct taped hands with her teeth, all the while keeping her eye on her captor, the man with the gun.

One heard the door on the black SUV slam shut. He saw a huge man with a bandage around his head walk in front of the headlights. He could not make out the face of the man, but he suspected who it was. *One,* without looking away from the approaching man, pointed his gun at Tina Slone in the doorway of the plane.

The Garbage Man looked down the rifle barrel and the scope and watched who he recognized as the man who had given him his instructions. He was walking toward the plane and the kidnapper. He did not seem to be armed, but he knew that was not a given. He also knew he had no further targets unless the man from the car, now hidden by the plane, showed himself, so he waited.

"Sheriff Slone if I'm not mistaken," *One* said, the whole time looking at Slone, but his gun pointed at Tina.

"Yes Mr. Adula, one and the same," replied TJ. Tina's heart skipped a beat. TJ was alive.

One was not surprised Slone knew his name, he hated to admit it, but he had a lot of respect for local law enforcement, especially TJ Slone's sheriff's office. It had a reputation of being cutting edge and you were not sheriff as long as TJ Slone without doing something right. He knew when he planned this operation Slone would be a force to be reckoned with, that was why he had intended for him to be killed.

"I had high hopes you were dead. You should have been.

Since you are not, I take it my brother is."

TJ stopped walking about twenty yards from Azil Adula. It was a range he was comfortable with and it allowed him to see everything and gave him wiggle room. His hands were in plain view. The radio strapped to his waist was locked in the talk position, his team could hear everything.

TJ answered his question.

"Your brother is dead, as it appears is everyone else on your team. Everyone except for you."

Azil smiled. He caught the veiled threat in his statement and tone. This is a man who thought he held all the cards; he did not. Azil pointed with a motion of his gun. "I still have her. I still have options. I see you are not armed, or I hope you are not. Even if you were I can and will shoot her before I die."

"Not yet," TJ said, talking to Azil, but really talking to his team which he knew was listening to the open mike.

"Let's discuss your options," TJ said as he looked beyond Azil to his loving wife lying on the floor of the plane, a wife who he could see was moving slightly as she worked on the tape around her hands.

TJ continued. "You could give up. We could stop this before anyone else has to die. So many have already died and for what? Besides our prisons are a lot nicer than the ones in other countries."

Azil smiled at TJ's attempt at a joke.

"I don't think so. You could let me go and I will promise not to come back."

Both knew he was lying, and both knew TJ was not going to let him go.

Tina finished chewing thru the tape, tearing the last couple of inches, finally freeing hands that had not been free in almost twenty-two hours. Tina knew she had little she could do, her feet were still taped together, her eyes partly covered and a mad man had a gun pointing at her. What she did have going for her was an intense hate for the man who had kidnapped her, tortured her and ruined her home. What she did have going for her, she recognized the voice of the man standing in front of the blinding light. She knew TJ was alive, she knew he was going to do something. They had this conversation before, alone and with friends. TJ had always said he was not ever going to go along with a bad guy with a gun. He was going to wait for the chance, he was going to do something. TJ had told her and their friends this every time they traveled together. Tina didn't know if the friends believed him, but she did. Tina knew TJ would do something. It probably would not be pretty. She also knew she was going to provide him an edge if she could.

Azil Adula knew he was at a disadvantage, knew he was probably going to die, he just wanted to take one or both of the Slone's with him. He knew if he pointed the gun away from Tina Slone someone in the dark would drop him like a bad habit. He didn't know where it would come from. It might be the same shooter that took *Three* down, it could be someone else. He knew they were there. He knew they were good, after all they were Guilford County Sheriff's deputies or so he suspected. He really wanted to take TJ out. He should be dead anyway. They would probably have succeeded if he had died. He made a tactical mistake not pointing at him, but pointing at her, when TJ pulled his car down to the plane. A mistake he regretted. He had figured she was his leverage; he was wrong. TJ Slone appeared to be unarmed, but he wasn't taking that for granted. Somewhere in the dark were at least two shooters, one took out the plane, one took out *Three. One* would feel better if he had his gun pointing at TJ Slone, since his wife was drugged. He knew though if he took the gun off Tina Slone one of those two shooters would shoot him. *One* realized his options were few.

"Adula, your plan lacked the right team. You had a mercenary who had skills, but whose greed gave us all the information we needed to identify your little group. The kid you left at the house was no match for the entry team, he was out of the picture in less than a second. Your brother had skills, but he was foiled by a dog who heard him and Santigo on the roof. The little lady at your feet was probably the best you had, but her visit to the hospital gave her away. I suspect that was your idea, to see who was alive. To see if it was your brother. Connecting all the dots gave us you. I've heard a lot about you. Your reputation seems to be over blown. In my estimation this was pretty sloppy, as operations go."

TJ was trying to distract Adula. Trying to make him mad. Mad people made rash decisions. He knew he had shooters, but he did not know if they had a shot. He also knew Adula had a gun pointed at the woman he loved, someone he would do anything for, even die.

Adula listened to the words, words that made him angry, words that he knew were probably a fair representation of this whole operation. He knew also TJ Slone was trying to make him angry. It was not over yet.

"Sheriff, while I appreciate your thoughts, you forget I still have a gun on your wife. As you also know, she has experienced a little discomfort. Her death is up to me, I still have options and you still have a live wife. Now the question is, how are we going to get your wife back to you and me go on my way without having to deal with your silly justice system."

TJ knew everyone was listening on the active radio strapped to his belt. He had started this conversation so they would know what the situation was. It became painfully apparent to him, nobody had a shot, or they would have taken it.

Tina, with her hands free, looked for something she could throw. She had enough of this asshole. She heard him talking about options. She decided she was going to reduce his options if she had the chance. Tina held her hands together, so it appeared they were still taped.

She saw what she needed. It was nothing to throw, but something to shoot. Beside the door was a fire extinguisher. She hoped it was charged, she prayed it was charged. Tina, in a motion as fast as her drugged body allowed, reached up and grabbed the fire extinguisher, flipping the toggle switch on its top to the locked position activating the spray, pointing the hose at the back of Azil Adula. Out of the hose came a spray of white foamy mist, forming a cloud, which covered the entire door, spilling into the night. A cloud so thick you could not see through it. As soon as she fired the extinguisher she rolled to her right, hopefully out of the sight of the bullet she knew would follow.

TJ saw Tina jump toward the door, for what he did not know. Then the cloud of white foamy mist filled the door. Azil heard motion behind him, turned just in time to get a face full of powdery spray. He fired into the white powdery white mass of a cloud that was the door of the plane.

Little did Azil realize the spot he was shooting into, the spot Tina Slone occupied seconds before, was now empty. Tina was lying in the aisle to the right of the door. His bullets hit the empty plane floor.

TJ reached into the small of his back, pulled the S&W 357 from the holster and dropped to one knee. He wanted to fire upward knowing Tina was on the floor of the plane, thinking if he missed or in case the bullet was a pass thru, he did not want to hit her. Kneeling, his shot would be on an even trajectory. His position was on an incline and Azil was downhill. He fired twice, just as he had trained all his life. He watched the bullet impact the left temple tearing a golf ball size hole from Adula's head. The second bullet just barely crazed the back of his head as the impact of the first bullet caused his head to turn. TJ knew there was no need for a third shot. Azil Adula was dead. It was over.

TJ ran for the plane, calling Tina's name. He jumped on the plane and through the fire extinguisher fog saw his wife lying on the plane. He rolled her over, saw the blood-stained tape covering her mouth. He ripped the tape from her mouth causing her to cry out. TJ held her head to his chest, so glad she was alive. Tina looked up at him, tears in her eyes.

"Where have you been?"

The Garbage Man crawled from under the F 150, placed his rifle into the gun box in the back of the truck, locked the back of the truck and drove away into the night.

The next few minutes were like a fire sale with cars and deputy sheriffs swarming the area. The first on the scene were Captain Young and Sheriff Pass. With them was the team medic who immediately started looking at Tina's wounds. TJ immediately went to the body of Azil Adula. He wanted to make sure there was no sign of life, though he knew the 357 round was more than up to the job of ending his sorry existence. TJ then took out his phone and made the call he wanted to make. The deputy at the other end handed Louise the phone at TJ's request. TJ handed the phone to Tina. A mother spoke to her daughter. The horror was over.

A red F-150 was speeding down highway 17 toward Wilmington and the cell phone rang. The driver of the F-150 said hello. The voice at the other end said two words.

"Thank You" and the phone went dead. That was all that needed to be said. That was more than the Garbage Man usually got.

Chapter Thirty-One

One Week Later

TJ sat in the seat, the folding kind that because of his size he always felt nervous about. Those things were not made for men his size. He wore his black suit, not because he wanted to, but because the event called for it. It was not every day you attended the swearing in of a new Vice President of the United States.

There were two hundred people in attendance which was an intimate gathering by Washington standards. Assorted friends, family, and co-workers were in attendance, and of course the press which would share the experience with millions.

To his right sat his precious Tina. It had only been days since the kidnapping. Her face was still swollen and bruised.

Make-up took care of the bruising, but the swelling would take time. Her finger was bandaged with a flesh colored dressing, but you could still see it was a bandage. The cut could not be repaired, her finger would heal, but had to be cut again to repair the damage done by the gardening shears. It was the mental scars TJ worried about, and time would tell how they would heal.

The hours after rescue sparked a media frenzy as TJ knew it would. He took a back seat, letting Sheriff John Pass, Director Sturgis and Deputy Director Dunham take the lead as it should be. Deputy Director Dunham grabbed the microphone and held it like his life depended on it, making his involvement sound like he was an integral part of the operation. TJ made sure the Deputy Director's boss, his big boss, the United States Attorney General knew the truth. He was sure this did not make him any points with Dunham, not that he cared. His team, after the required de- briefing, quietly packed their gear and headed home. TJ, Tina, Louise and Monique followed them in a caravan of vehicles all Guilford County bound.

Tina insisted she wanted to be treated at home, in Guilford County.

Besides their home at Sunset was a crime scene and would be the focus of law enforcement and the media for days.

She was debriefed as they worked on her in the hospital, preparing her for the trip home. John Pass made every accommodation. The emergency room doctor, the same one who worked on TJ put up little resistance. If she was like her husband, what was the point?

No big deal was made about TJ's team and family being there, TJ wondered how the media let that slide. He figured there was so much other red meat with all the dead bodies this operation had produced they let it go. The Garbage Man silently disappeared back to where he came from, to wait for the next call. No one brought up or questioned who made the shots that took out the plane and car.

No one asked about who shot who or what. The information given the media was correct, just not complete.

The Chief Supreme Court Justice approached the podium set up on the White House lawn. He was joined by the President, First Lady and the Vice President to be and the new VP's family. The Justice began by saying repeat after me.

"I (state your name) do solemnly swear." The new Vice President to be repeated, "I, Nancy Carver, do solemnly swear."

TJ looked to the seat at his left, at the facial expression of his friend Governor Matt Hart, soon to be Secretary of Labor Matt Hart, split lip and all. He had turned down the job of VP.

"Any regrets?"

Matt Hart smiled, his wife Belle looked around him and said, "NO."

The reception at the White House that followed the swearing in had even more folks involved. Senators and congressman not invited to the swearing in, made a point of being at the reception. In Washington it was always about being seen at the right places, with the right people. The media had their favorites, the ones they could always go to for a sound bite. This was the very thing TJ hated about DC, the reason his two favorite things about Washington were the Smithsonian and seeing the place in his rearview mirror. He sat at his table surrounded by many folks in his estimation who were not real. With the exception of Tina, Matt and Belle, he thought the others at their table were no longer part of true America. and that was sad.

Tina on the other hand was glad to be there, so TJ was glad for her. At the table with them was Belle, Matt, two Senators and their wives from states that President Mark Elliot needed to carry. The purpose for them being at their table was to be swayed by Matt, the future Labor Secretary, to support some legislation President Elliot needed their vote on. It was DC, you didn't let a good reception go to waste when politics could be plied. No tragedy or opportunity missed. TJ was looking for the door, he was ready to go.

Attorney General Sam Poage approached the table. TJ saw him coming from across the room. He could tell by the look in his eyes, their table was his destination. His arrival was slowed down by all the folks at other tables who spoke to him as he walked by. He really didn't take long with any of those folks. He seemed to be a man on a mission.

"How's everybody doing this fine beautiful day?" a smiling AG Sam Poage said.

"Matt, Belle, Tina, TJ, I'm so glad you folks are safe. I know it was a horrid experience. This is a troubled world we live in. Nobody should be subjected to what you went through. I can only imagine what it has done to each of you personally. I wanted to give you my heartfelt condolences."

They each thanked him and the senators and their wives, added their well wishes, which was exactly what Poage wanted to happen. It opened up a dialog at the table about the event making it OK to talk about. It also brought Matt and the senators into a bonding moment. Again, let no tragedy go unexploited.

"Mrs. Slone, I wonder if I might borrow your husband for a little shop talk? I'll try not to keep him long." said the Attorney General. His question was more of a directive than a request.

"You keep him as long as you want. He hates these things anyway and will probably be glad to get away," Tina's replied.

TJ was glad to get away. He eagerly followed the Attorney General out of the ballroom.

TJ was no stranger to the White House. He had been there many times before in the short tenure of President John Turnage. It didn't take him long to realize they were going to the Oval

Office. The Secret Service agent at the door did not appear to have a sense of humor. TJ expected none of them did, especially now, since they had recently lost a president. He recognized the Attorney General, he looked long and hard at the large man with him. The large man with a raw looking scar on his left forehead.

TJ and the AG were led into the empty Oval Office. It truly was a remarkable place. The artwork, the keepsakes donated by other leaders, right down to the Resolute desk which was a gift from England in the 1880's. You could not help but be impressed by the history made in that room, both good and bad. TJ was not easily impressed, but this room, impressed him.

Chapter Thirty-Two

President Mark Elliot entered the Oval Office followed by Secret Service Agent David Epsom. His entry caused TJ and the Attorney General to scramble to their feet.

"Gentleman, please remain seated, we're all friends here," an amused president stated.

Handshakes were passed around. They truly were friends, had met and shared bread and drink often in the past. They were friends, but one of them was the most powerful man in the world and protocol required that be acknowledged.

"David, I need the room and I need ears only," President Elliot's words were directed at his Secret Service agent. The agent silently but quickly left the room, talking into the radio microphone attached to the cuff of his jacket. He could be heard to say, "Oval Office, should be ears only." What this meant was the rooms recorders were to be shut off. Normally everything in the room was recorded and documented. It was a system put in place after the Watergate Nixon debacle. It had been a security feature that was welcomed by most presidents, not so much by others who forgot during passionate moments.

President Elliot got straight to the point. "Gentleman, I have mixed emotions about our little club. I'm a little uncomfortable with the fact we are possibly violating the rights of individuals in the pursuit of expediency and security. TJ, the recent case involving you, your wife and Matt and Belle Hart is a prime example. Did we go too far? Could it have been handled differently?

TJ was trying hard not to lose his cool and demeanor. After all he was getting ready to address the president of the United States.

"Mr. President, I understand your concern. I'm also concerned that we don't violate anyone's rights, even the rights of someone as heinous as Azil Adula. I take my participation in this club as you refer to it, very seriously. In fact, before I consented to join, your friend and mine, President Turnage and I had some very serious conversations. I'm sure you are aware this club was his idea. His thoughts, which I concur with, were that its decisions are serious enough to require unanimous consent from members who are sworn to protect our Constitution. My role was to provide insight that may not have been tainted by what some refer to as the Washington flu. The Washington flu being tedious bureaucracy and political posturing. The decisions are made without the stench of partisan politics. The safety and welfare of our republic is the only consideration, not the emotional bonds of politics or family ties. That is why I removed myself from the last decision, because it involved my wife. I would like to think I would have made the right decision no matter who was involved. I know the decision made was the right one. Azil Adula is dead, that was his decision. He could have given up. Now, as to the club. It is a resource available to you. Just as you rely on your generals, your cabinet, your staff, you rely on six people to make a decision right for this country. It is a quick response team that avoids the quagmire that is the Washington swamp. It takes the politics out of it, the ability to respond with appropriate speed and efficiency is injected. It is always the least that can be done, using a sole operator, to derive the best possible results. It gives you and the country breathing room."

TJ took a breath. He did not know if he had said enough or too much. The look on the president's face did not tell him one way or another.

Seeing his demeanor, TJ continued.

"Just as you have the authority to send a missile halfway around the world without congressional approval, you have the right to take military type action if it impacts the welfare of our country. You have direct control over this action without having the bureaucracy. It is on a smaller scale and has a direct report result. You are not telling a general, who tells a colonel, who tells the major who orders the lieutenant who orders the sergeant who tells the private who pushes the button. It is much more efficient."

Attorney General Poage jumped in. "Mr. President, your concern may be the domestic aspect of dealing on American soil in this case.

We too have struggled with this. Our laws dictate that violations of local laws are handled by local authority. That is fine when you are dealing with local problems, like car thieves, burglary, drug dealers or worthless checks. In the case of an international terrorist, local law enforcement is quickly outmatched. The actions of our group gives a more level playing field and the ability to act as quickly as possible. In this case, every legal avenue was utilized. Every action taken was legal and above board, even the action taken by our operative. A police officer could have taken the same actions our guy did. The difference, he had the expertise and the equipment to do it. He did his job and disappeared. In effect, our folks are members of the Joint Terrorism Task Force, just like TJ and several of his personal. Our guy was an added resource. The only problem, he is paid by a military branch of service which some will argue makes this a violation of the *Posse Comitatus Act*. When this law came into effect in 1878, I doubt congress had any idea what we would be facing in today's world. We feel the *Insurrection Act* which gives you authority to deploy troops on American soil, gives you the right to deploy a single operative.

This could be cleaned up, but not without congress and the political machinations involved with congress coming into play."

President Elliot still looked as perplexed as he was at the beginning of the conversation.

"I hear what you are saying and agree with the need for expediency. My problem is accountability. Are we being true to our oaths, to our responsibility?"

"Nobody says making sausage is pretty, but most everyone likes the results. I don't have problems sleeping at night because of this. A lot of other things keep me up, but this is not one of them. I do realize, as I think President Turnage did, the people who make these decisions must be committed to this country and its ideals. Whether you feel comfortable with that is going to have to be your decision." And with that Attorney General Poage leaned back into the couch. The Oval Office was silent.

President Elliot broke the silence, standing up, since it appeared to meeting was over. "Gentleman, you've given me a lot to think about. I will be giving it the attention it deserves. Thank you for your service."

TJ kept his seat. He wasn't finished yet.

"Mr. President, you've got a big problem we need to discuss. You have a serious leak in your office or connected to your office."

President Mark Elliot looked at Sheriff TJ Slone with a look of dismay and a flash of indignation. Nobody liked to be told their operation had problems. The president was no different.

"What are you talking about Sheriff?" the president said, again taking his seat.

"Mr. President, who knew you had offered Matt Hart the job of Vice President? Who knew he was coming to Sunset Beach to decide? Who knew he would be staying with me? Now the answer to the last two, Sunset Beach and staying with me could have come from the Governor's office. The first, offering Matt the job, had to come from yours. This whole operation was too intricate and well planned to be spur of the moment. You have been considering this for weeks. You knew well before you asked Matt, who else knew? Matt called and asked to come down three days before he was kidnapped. He knew then, when did your office know for sure and ask him?"

President Elliot was a little taken aback. He was unsure of the tone TJ was using. Was he being accusatory, or was he being inquisitive?

"Sheriff, are you suggesting my office had something to do with this kidnapping? I can assure you it did not."

"No Mr. President, I'm saying the information had to come from here in Washington. Azil even explained to Governor Hart, now Secretary Hart, he had connections. Very good connections that would let him know if he was not living up to the arrangement, he was forcing Matt into," said an unapologetic TJ.

"Sheriff, don't you think that may have been the boasting of a terrorist meant to keep the Governor in line?" answered the president.

"No sir, that doesn't explain them knowing you had offered him the job or the fact he was coming to visit me. That was information that you and your office had. The two pieces of information alone had little value. The two pieces of information together had great value. Your office had the two pieces of information in time to allow appropriate plans to be made." TJ couldn't be any plainer.

An exasperated president replied, "I guess we will never know, you killed the person who could give us the answers."

"Not necessarily, there may be some links to his connection."

AG Poage spoke up. "The only thing we found on Azil was money, guns and forged identification. They will lead us nowhere. We found a phone, or parts of one, where he stomped it outside the Lexus."

TJ smiled, "No, Sam, there was another phone."

"There was no phone, I saw the evidence inventory list." "I took the phone. When I checked the body, to make sure he was dead," replied TJ.

"You took evidence, you know not to disturb evidence, you know there has to be a chain of command. TJ, have you lost your mind?" said a shocked Attorney General.

"No, Sam, what I knew was there was not going to be a trial for Azil Adula. He lay dead at my feet. His co-conspirators were all dead, along with a long list of innocent victims. What I knew was anything we took from them would be placed in evidence for a long time if not forever. I also knew there were persons that would breathe easy knowing they were dead, who could care less about the innocent victims. Person or persons who would continue betraying this country by trading information, costing lives for their own twisted perverted reasons. What I knew was the leak had to be coming out of this office or an office associated with this one. I knew I could not take a chance on the only piece of information we had at our disposal that would allow us to find this traitor to be compromised in any way. I also knew I was part of this case and I have treated it as evidence, marking it and cataloging it into my evidence locker, in my office where I know it is safe. The only thing I did not do was issue a seized inventory sheet. A problem a rookie lawyer could get around if they explain the concerns with doing it the normal protocol way.

What I do know is we have an opportunity to find the person just as much responsible for the deaths and misery associated with this case as Azil Adula. The best part, they don't know we're coming."

TJ finished his reply, knowing he had made his point. "I hope you want the traitor brought to justice as much as I do."

Attorney General Page and President Mark Elliot looked at each other, then at TJ. They did. They both realized a problem they thought was over, just got bigger.

Chapter Thirty-Three

"Ok TJ, where do we go from here. What is the next step, do we get my FBI involved? You seem to be driving this train" inquired the Attorney General, not in a happy way.

TJ knew the answer would not please the AG, but it needed to be said.

"No Sam, your folks draw too much attention. Your folks may be involved. When they enter a case, by being the FBI they come across as being heavy handed. Everything they do is a federal case, which it is, but they act like it's all that matters.

People resent that. People are intimidated. We need a softer touch, by folks who are used to dealing with regular folks on a daily basis. Sam, that's my folks. I would like a junior analyst/agent, one you can loan my office. One whose absence would not cause any raised eyebrows when they get a temporary assignment. An assistant that will be so new they have not been tainted by the FBI mentality and group think. I know if the bureau hired them, they will have the abilities needed. I also know in today's environment the bureau will have vetted their background. Young folks have shorter histories, thus shorter times to hide transgressions. It needs it to appear you are doing us a favor. In fact, you are. I don't need their supervisor knowing what they are working on. I need someone who can work with my folks. I'll give you back an employee better trained and hopefully with a success under their belt that will help their career. We've got a lot of work and a short time to do it."

Attorney General Poage did not like what TJ suggested.

He did not like it, but he knew TJ was right. The FBI did seem to take all the air out of the room when they entered a case. Their attitude seemed to be a holdover from the J. Edger Hoover days.

The FBI were some of the best in law enforcement, problem was they felt others were not as good. Local law enforcement often felt the bureau marginalized their efforts. TJ would get what he requested.

The ride home was uneventful. The reception ended and the

remainder of the day and evening was spent with Matt and Belle at their new townhouse. They did not leave until almost midnight. For TJ driving through the hills of Virginia in the early morning hours was a treat. He loved the quiet time. Those hills were what Tina described as Virginia dark, especially so at 2 am. The roads were winding and desolate. Tina slept softly, curled up in the front bucket seat of their SUV. It was a treat for TJ because the solitude of the ride gave him time to think. There was plenty to think about.

Tina stirred, opened her eyes, blinking them several times to adjust to the interior lights of the car. She looked at TJ and smiled. A smile TJ lived for. He loved her and together they had built a great life. When he looked back at her after checking the road, she had already closed her eyes and was once again drifting off. She was amazing, she seemed to be able to sleep anywhere. Just another thing he loved about her.

TJ's request for a young new assistant was purposeful. He knew a young, new person would be driven to do a good job. They had a reputation to build. He remembered being that way, he liked to think he still was. He also knew the FBI could and would hire only the best. He knew they would have checked their background all the way back to the birth canal. They would have checked not only references listed and unlisted but things like Facebook, Twitter and all the other electronic services young folks seemed to live by. He knew the chances of this person being the leak were zero. They would not have the access needed or the inclination to be a traitor. They were new clay to be molded and he knew just the potter to do it. TJ also felt the leaker was probably a career employee. A person driven by greed, love or the conviction they were not appreciated. They may have been passed over for a raise or a promotion. They may figure what difference did a little information make. In their mind they probably thought they were just spreading a little water cooler talk. What would it hurt? They probably thought they were a good American. They were wrong.

Debbie Lynch walked into the office carrying a cup of coffee that looked like a soft blonde hair color. The steam was rising, and the smell had a hint of vanilla. Just the way TJ liked it.

"What's this. You, bringing me coffee. You made it very clear when I hired you years ago, bringing coffee was not the job of an Administrative Assistant. Not that I'm complaining, but are you going soft on me or are you getting ready to set me up for something?"

"Get over yourself," Debbie replied. "It was the end of the pot and I wanted a fresh cup."

They both laughed. Their friendship was one that had built over the years. TJ had watched her grow as an employee and person. He watched as she grew from where she once described herself as JAS, just a secretary, to the person who was actually running the day to day operation of the Sheriff's office Admin.

Section. He watched her children grow up and have children. He watched a marriage fail and her remarry with a much better fit.

They were not just boss and employee, they were friends and family.

"Sheriff, I just got a call from Agent Sybil Ames of the FBI. She said she was assigned to you for as long as needed. What am I supposed to do with her? What is she going to be doing? Do I need to provide office space? What's up?"

"When is she arriving?" TJ quickly replied.

"Tomorrow morning, she will be here by 9 am," Debbie answered.

"No, we don't need office space. She will be sharing space with Chief Deputy Powe. She can use his conference table as a desk. She will need a secure phone and computer. The phone and computer are not to be part of the county network. They should be independent of it. Get our computer guys setting them up immediately. I want it ready before she gets here. Get her an entry fob and key to his office. Can you get all that done?"

Debbie smiled. "What is it you say, nothing is impossible, the impossible just takes a little longer. I can get it done. It will ruffle a few feathers, but it will be done. Now the question was, what is she going to be doing and does the Chief know yet?"

TJ knew he could count on Debbie. "She's doing the Lord's work and no, he doesn't know yet. Send him in when you leave."

Debbie got up to leave, knowing she was not getting a direct answer to her question. She was good with that. If she needed to know he would tell her, but their relationship required she make one more gig at him. "Oh, by the way, you're welcome. Don't get used to having coffee delivered."

Chief Deputy Powe walked into TJ's office carrying a pen and notepad. He was used to these meeting and knew that an assignment could be expected.

"Have a seat Tom, you will not need the notepad." Tom sat in the chair directly in front of TJ.

Tom Powe was TJ's second chief deputy. His first TJ had helped get an appointment to US Marshal. Tom had been with TJ since the beginning. They had worked together as deputies. They had worked together in Raleigh. When TJ was sworn in, Tom came along as head of his reserve unit. They were friends. Tom was one of the few people he would trust with this assignment.

"Tom, I need you to clear your calendar for the next week. I have a special assignment for you. I need you on it. I'm taking all other responsibilities from you. Can you make it happen?"

In the years they had worked together, Tom knew TJ had never given him an assignment he could not or would not do. He could do this, and TJ knew it. The difference, he had never given him an assignment to be worked, excluding his other duties. This interested him.

"I can," replied a confident Tom Powe.

TJ explained to his chief deputy that tomorrow, an FBI agent/analyst named Sybil Ames would be joining him on the assignment. They would be working together to break down and gather any information they could get from the phone TJ had taken from Azil's dead body. He explained they were looking for the source of information that had been the leak and cause of the kidnapping and death of so many. TJ explained the information they gathered should be compartmentalized, for their eyes only.

He, Tom and the analyst would decide who else would know about what they found. They would have the assistance of the US Attorney in the Middle District for any subpoenas for records needed. Any request for information needed from any federal agency or private company would come from the Middle District AG, to keep suspicion away from them as to who might be asking and why. The people getting the subpoenas would not question the Middle District Attorney General, they might a request from the sheriff's office if they tried to get the information from another source or Attorney General. Attorney General Poage would make sure they would get any assistance needed. TJ instructed they trace each number that called the phone or that received a call from the phone. They would identify the position of the phone from the time it was purchased to when TJ took possession of the phone.

The phone company could do that. They wouldn't want too, but they could trace the position of the phone within a range of 50 ft each time it was used.

Tom understood why he was being relieved of all other responsibilities. This was going to be a monumental task. He was afraid to hear the answer to the next question he asked.

"Sheriff, you said clear the next week. Do I take that to mean you want the answer by the week's end?"

TJ smiled. "Not necessarily Tom, if you can finish sooner, I'll take it."

Chief Deputy Powe also knew this investigation was going to require travel. He suspected one of those trips would be to Washington, DC. He also suspected the answers the Sheriff were looking for were going to make some folks very uncomfortable.

Chapter Thirty-Four

Sybil Ames arrived at the Sheriff's office at five minutes before nine. This was her first off site assignment. It was actually her first real assignment. She had been given what she felt was busy work in her short stint as an FBI agent. She didn't know why she was chosen. Her only instructions were to report to Sheriff TJ Sloane for her instructions. Sheriff Sloane would tell her what she needed to do. The Attorney General himself gave her instructions which was highly unusual. He told her to go home and pack, but he could not tell her for how long. She was given a bureau credit card and a bureau car. All things strange to her, new agents did not get these things. Not at first. Certainly not from the AG. Since this was her first field assignment, everything was a first. She was determined not to fail.

She took a deep breath and got out of the car. Though it was only about twenty yards from the parking lot to the door, it looked like a mile.

Sybil Ames was met and led into the sheriff's office by a woman who introduced herself as the sheriff's assistant. A nice woman with a professional air about her. She immediately put Sybil at ease. The sheriff's office was a large, paneled space with high ceilings and a fireplace. It was more like a formal living room with a desk. It had a couch, five chairs in front of the desk, facing the chair behind the desk. A conference table with six chairs was at one end of the room. The room was full of awards and plaques. There were photos of the sheriff and a lot of well- known people, both political and otherwise. In one of the chairs facing the desk, a man approximately 6 ft. tall with dark hair and a moustache, wearing civilian clothes. He was not wearing a jacket and a gun and holster could be seen on his belt. The belt also held a star on a badge holder. The man in front of the desk watched as she entered the room. Behind the desk was a larger man dressed in a red pullover golf type shirt. Embroidered on the shirt was a sheriff's star on the left chest. On the right chest it said, TJ Slone, Sheriff. As she walked in, both men rose from their chairs. She loved the South, the men here were gentleman.

TJ Slone, according to the shirt he wore, stuck out his hand to shake hers. He had a warm smile and a firm grip. He also had a scab across his forehead on the left side of his head. It appeared to be healing nicely. Sybil had done her research. She knew this scab was the result of being shot by the man who kidnapped the Governor of North Carolina, his wife, the sheriff's wife and killed several people, plus the governor's dog. Sybil suspected, though many thought the case was over, the case may be why she was here.

After the introduction to Chief Deputy Tom Powe and the Admin. Director Debbie leaving the room, the three sat down at the conference table.

Sheriff Slone was not much for small talk. He jumped straight into the case. It was just as she suspected, tied to the kidnapping and murder case. He laid out what he suspected was going to be found on the phone they were to dissect. He suspected it contained the identity of the leaker. He stressed the importance of keeping the information in their group. He stated the leaker could be anyone, so everyone was a suspect. The last revelation was a little unsettling to Sybil. She wondered if someone in her agency was involved. She wondered how she was going to handle that. She didn't know if Sheriff Slone was a mind reader or what? He answered the question she had but did not ask. After finishing the briefing, he entered a number in his cell phone. In short order it was answered.

"Sam, TJ, I'm going to put you on speaker phone. I have Agent Ames and Chief Deputy Powe in the room with me. Is there anything you would like to add? I just gave them a briefing."

The Attorney General spoke. Agent Sybil Ames knew it was the Attorney General because just a day before, he gave her instructions.

"No TJ, just as you know, finding this person is important to the country. Agent Ames, listen and learn from Sheriff Sloane and his team. You answer to him and only him during this assignment. If you get any grief from anyone in the bureau, let TJ know, he will handle it. Good luck guys." The AG hung up the phone.

TJ Sloane looked at the agent and asked, "Any questions?" Agent Ames had a million questions, she settled on one. "Yes, why me?"

TJ smiled, of all the questions she could have asked, had he been her, that would have been his first. He liked this girl.

"Agent Ames, you were picked because you are young, energetic, hungry to do a good job and most important you have no preconceived notions about your importance. You have no preconceived baggage as it relates to investigations. You were not in the bureau as a graduated agent, in the know, when this case started. Chances of you being complicit are zero, meaning you are not a suspect. I suspect you will work your ass off, and I expect nothing less. Since you graduated the academy, I suspect you are smart. I need that. If you stick with me, I'll make you famous.

Does that answer your question?

Agent Ames nodded yes. TJ answered that question and many more. TJ Sloane was connected. He and the AG were on a first name basis. She had an idea he knew others in DC. You just did not get an agent of the FBI assigned to you with orders to do what was asked without some real horsepower. He had been sheriff a long time. He obviously knew what he was doing. He said he would make her famous, she suspected that was not an idle boast. She wouldn't mind being famous. This may be a great career move for her.

Tom Powe and Agent Ames left the sheriff's office went into the Chief Deputy's office and closed the door. Chief Powe showed Agent Ames her new home for who knew how many days. The end of the conference table held an Apple Air computer and a Samsung 10 phone that Debbie had delivered. The table also had a door key, an access key fob and the codes for the building alarm.

She also had a small, printed card with the sheriff's phone numbers as well as those of the Chief Deputy and Debbie. There was a walkie talkie with a note designating her call sign as being 1202.

The sheriff's call number was 1200, the chief's call number was 1201. Debbie had forgotten nothing. In fact, unknown to Ames, as usual she had gone above and beyond the expected.

TJ was happy with his two-person team dedicated to finding out all they could about a single piece of evidence. He knew somewhere in the diodes and electrical connections in that phone was the identity of the person who gave secrets to what was the third most feared terrorist in the world. Secrets used to try to control one of the leaders in our country. They just needed to find that bit of information.

TJ had asked they begin looking at all calls, phone locations, text and caller identities from the week prior to the kidnapping. Agent Ames and Chief Deputy Powe were going to do that, but not first. First, they wanted to know the location of where the phone was bought, who bought it, and in whose name the service was purchased. This would give them the basis for all the other information they needed. They set up a computer program to form an information tree, the name of the phone's owner needed to be first.

It took less than an hour of searching the phones identification number to establish it was sold and activated at Tysons Corner, located in Mclean, Virginia, just outside Washington, DC. The store was contacted and as expected, the store was hesitant in giving out any information over the phone. Agent Ames asked the clerk to hold and placed the call on mute.

"Chief, we'll have to get a subpoena to get the information."

"What's the clerk's name" chief Powe asked.

"Toni, I think was her name." replied a confused agent. Chief Powe took the phone off mute.

"Toni, Chief Deputy Tom Powe here, how are you today? Toni responded, "Fine thank you."

"Toni, I understand your concern about giving out that information over the phone, you don't know if I'm really who I say I am. Toni, I respect and appreciate that, but Toni that information is really important and is of national security interest. Toni, if I sent a local uniformed Fairfax County deputy, and ask him to ask for you specifically, could you help us?" a friendly, father-like Chief Deputy asked.

Toni responded she could and actually sounded eager to help. Chief Powe said a deputy would be there within the hour and ask for her. He asked for security reasons she keep the call to herself. He then hung up the phone, picked up and looked through his phone, found what he wanted, immediately called the Fairfax Sheriff's office. He asked the person who answered their phone for the Chief Deputy. When the Fairfax County Chief got on the phone, they began with a little small talk. Chief Powe asked his counterpart to send a uniformed officer to visit Toni and get the information needed and to include any video, they may have on the transaction. He told the Fairfax Chief deputy he would be sending the request directly to his attention by NCIC (National Crime Information Center) which would be verification he was who he said he was, since it would come from one sheriff's office terminal to another. All this was accomplished in less than five minutes.

Agent Sybil Ames was amazed. This was not the way the Bureau would have handled it. They would have hung up the phone got a subpoena and marched in the store serving it and probably interrupting their day and business. She said as much to Chief Powe.

"Agent Ames, folks, good folks, naturally want to help. They don't like to be pushed and they certainly will not respond well to intimidation. If you give them a chance, they will do whatever it takes to do you a kindness. You push them they will only do what is required. They need to feel valued and not taken advantage of. That is how local law enforcement handles things. When you get a heavy-handed situation, you run into resentment and stonewalls" explained Chief Powe.

Agent Ames realized she had just had a demonstration about what good law enforcement was about. She was learning. She realized her academy training fell a little short.

The Fairfax County Chief Deputy called back with the information requested. His deputy had a lot of success. The phone was purchased by an Amir-Hossein Sief. He used an American Express card to make the purchase and prepaid for three months of unlimited talk, text and data. He purchased the phone eight days before the kidnapping, two days after President Mark Elliot announced he was preparing to make a Vice President pick. Mr. Sief wanted the phone number and phone listed to his daughter Savi. He told the clerk, who remembered the sale, the phone was a present for his daughter. The clerk remembered the sale because of the difficulty in spelling the names. The names were definitely not as common as Smith and Jones. The store had provided security film of the transaction, along with copy of receipts and the name of the clerk. All this was sent to the Guilford County. All this was accomplished by the respectful interaction with the store clerk. Lesson learned.

Chapter Thirty-Five

It was after lunch. The team had been behind closed doors for about four hours. Surely, they had something by now thought TJ. He opened the door to the office.

Tom Powe broke into laughter.

"I'm surprised it took you this long to check on us, it's been about four hours" he said.

TJ laughed. Agent Ames just looked a little perplexed.

She did not realize how hands-on TJ was.

"So, have you solved it yet?" An inquisitive TJ asked. "Not yet, but we are closer than we were" said Powe. "The phone was purchased in Tyson Corners, Va., just outside DC. It was purchased by a man who used an American Express credit card in the name of Amir-Hossein Sief. We have a subpoena for all information related to the card being hand delivered to American Express by an FBI agent. They will wait on the results, which he will transmit to us. A store video of the transaction identifies the gentleman to be none other than Azil Adula. We are waiting on the credit card information which should allow us to track location and timeline by its use. We have broken down the phone numbers called by this phone, as well as to the phone calls to the phone, during the days around President Elliot's announcement about a future Vice President. These numbers are being identified based on the most frequently called first. We are not seeing anything alarming yet, other than the fact several numbers got multiple calls."

The sheriff was impressed, but not surprised, his Chief Deputy loved a "hunt": the thrill of finding out something hidden from the normal person or missed by them. The idea of solving and exposing criminal activity was an adrenaline rush every real cop knew and worked for. This team was going to be great.

"Good job, guys. Hell, you'll have this thing solved by the end of the day," said the sheriff as he exited the room.

"He's kidding right?" Ames asked. A smile was the only answer she got.

The rest of the day was spent recovering and cataloging numbers into a computer program designed to put the numbers in date, time, and frequency, into an Excel type spreadsheet. The spread sheet produced would show the probable importance of each number. They also recovered and were cataloging the items deleted on the phone. This list of numbers would be entered into the FBI joint Terrorism Task Force computer to see if they were connected to any other phone or case. They would issue subpoenas for name information when the first part of breaking the numbers down was finished. They prioritized their request from most called to least called. To Agent Ames, this was tedious, but she realized it was necessary.

Chief Deputy Powe had his wife join them for dinner at Lucky 32, an upscale restaurant in Greensboro. The food was great, the conversation was not about the case, but it was talking law enforcement. She heard a lot of stories about the sheriff's office. She could tell from the stories, the folks in this office were family.

When Agent Ames returned to her room at the Sheraton Hotel, she could see the message light blinking. She called down to the desk to find she had a call from Deputy Director Steve Dunham who requested she return the call. Ames knew who Dunham was, but had never talked with him. She wondered what the call was about. The hot bath she had in mind would have to wait.

It was after 10pm. Had it not been a deputy director she would have waited until morning to return the call. The phone number provided rang only twice before a female voice picked up saying "hello".

"Deputy Director Dunham please," a surprised agent asked. "Agent Ames," the voice at the other end replied, "This is Katie Williams, the deputy director's assistant. He asked me to call you and get an update on the work you are doing and to report back to him."

Sybil Ames was silent and confused. Why was an FBI deputy director's assistant calling wanting to know about an investigation she was working? Was this some kind of test? How should she respond? Her response was guarded.

"I'm sorry Katie, but I'm not at liberty to discuss my case over a non-secure line. If the deputy director would like to call me tomorrow at the Guilford County Sheriff's Office, I would be happy to talk with him or he can call the Attorney General if he would like an update," was all Ames could think of to say.

The phone call quickly ended with Williams stating she would pass that along. Katie Williams hung up the phone thinking, Agent Ames is working with the Guilford County Sheriff's Office, both interesting and disturbing.

The next morning when Agent Ames arrived at the sheriff's office, she found a very excited Chief Deputy. The numbers were all entered for the time period they were reviewing. The computer had shown there were five numbers of interest. These five numbers when contacted were all in close proximity to the White House when they were called. They were within a quarter mile of the White House.

Ames was confused.

"Chief, so they are close to the White House. Why is that important?"

Chief Powe smiled. "Agent Ames, where are you from?" "Iowa" was her answer.

"Agent Ames, in Washington, the closer to the White House you are, the more powerful your agency is. The more access you have to the White House and its secrets. If I was a betting man, I would bet one of these five numbers is the leaker we are looking for," a gleeful Deputy Chief said.

Agent Ames looked at the numbers. One immediately jumped out at her. That number caused her much concern.

The telephone calls could be triangulated to give the location of the caller and the person being called, but first the owner of the numbers called needed to be identified, and subpoenas were issued to do just that. Again, the US Marshal serving the subpoenas would wait for the information.

Deputy Director Dunham was not happy. TJ Sloane. That man was a huge pain in his ass. Slone had not been very complimentary in his report to the AG after the Adula affair. TJ's friendship with the AG was not something Dunham anticipated when he took on the responsibility of the kidnapping investigation. Had he known he was so connected he would have played the whole thing differently. What should have been a boon to his career turned out to be just the opposite. Dunham was curious about why a new agent was pulled and sent on a special assignment. An agent practically just out of the academy. Finding out the agent was sent to Slone quickly turned this assignment into a huge pain in his ass. The agent indirectly worked for him. He was not given a reason or asked if she could be used. The order just came down from the Attorney General. He wanted to know why. He had asked his assistant to call the agent and ask for an update using his name. It would have been awkward for someone of his rank, not knowing what his agent was doing. It should have worked, but the agent was evasive. He had her called at her hotel because he did not want her around whoever she was working with when the call came in. What was she doing? How did it relate to Azil Adula, if it did? Why was he left out of the loop? Did the Attorney General not trust him?

The five numbers were identified. Agent Ames and the Chief Deputy sat in front of the Sheriff's desk as he looked at the numbers and names associated with them. They were all identified except for one. That one not identified looked familiar, but TJ couldn't remember from where.

"Why is this one number not identified? he asked.

Agent Ames and Chief Powe looked at each other. Powe nodded to Ames, indicating she was to answer.

"Sheriff, there are some numbers that no subpoena will get identified. Some numbers that are so secret that they only have an identifying number so some clerk can't inadvertently find who the number belongs to. These numbers belong to a select group, such as the President, the Vice President, the Cabinet Secretary's, Directors of the FBI, CIA, NSA and all the other alphabet agencies. These numbers and phones are assigned to the directors and senior staff. Numbers that should be confidential. Getting this number identified will take the Attorney General to give the clearance."

"Fine," TJ responded. "Let's get it done." Ames and Powe looked at each other again. Ames spoke, her voice shaking.

"Sheriff, it's his number, it's the AG's number. The same one you called yesterday. I watched you dial it!"

So that was why the number was so familiar. TJ looked at the agent knowing what a turmoil she was probably having within herself. A new agent on her first case and she was getting ready to expose her boss as a traitor.

"Agent Ames, that is not the AG's number. He asked me to call him on his assistant's phone. He gave me her number. He knew I was going to call and about when. He knew he was going to be in a meeting. He wanted her monitoring the phone and to hand it to him when I called in. That was why he had so little to say. He was in a meeting. The purpose of the call was to let you know you were supported by him and should listen and work for me. Not that your revelation is not earth shattering, it is, but thank God, not as much, not against the Attorney General.

"Sheriff that is good to hear. I was afraid it was the AG, it's a relief to know it was not him. We have another problem. When I returned to my room last night, I had a call from a Deputy Director at the bureau. Not really him, but his assistant who had been instructed to get an update on the case. I told the assistant nothing but to call here on a secure line or for the Deputy Director to call the AG." Ames reported.

"Let me guess. Deputy Director Dunham."

Ames looked surprised. How did he know? She didn't get a chance to ask. The sheriff's next response answered the question.

"Asshole."

Chapter Thirty-Six

Mary Beth Payne was a career employee. She had worked for the Attorney General's office for 18 years. She joined after graduating from William & Mary University. She was at the top of her class and graduating from such a prestigious school of higher learning made her application sail through the process. It was the highlight of her young life, the last real highlight. Mary Beth lived a lonely life, just her and her cats. Lonely until a tall dark Arab man named Amir-Hossien Sief came into it. They met at the local food market. They talked about hummus. Their conversation led to coffee and a whirlwind relationship. He made her head spin. In a few short days, they had gone from grocery store banter to her bedroom. In retrospect she realized how foolish that was, but she had never been happier. He was so very kind, so very self-assured, so very gentle. He was interested in everything she did, especially her work. The first date over coffee, the second over dinner the evening of the first date. The third, the next night, she cooked. That night was the first night they had sex. Mary Beth had never moved this fast before, but it just seemed right. He talked about how important her job was, and how important she was. He made her feel important. She could not wait for his calls, which he made several times daily. Her heart skipped a beat when she recognized the number when he called. She was thrilled and had never been happier.

Mary Beth had access to everything the AG had. After all it passed through her to get to him. She was in a state of shock when she saw the photo come across her desk for the Attorney General. The dead man in the photo was Amir-Hossien. The report stated he was a terrorist named Azil Adula. The report said he was the third most wanted terrorist in the world. Mary Beth was sick to her stomach. She didn't know what to do. The man who had swept her off her feet was a terrorist. He had been using her. She knew it was only a matter of time before they connected her with him. She didn't know what to do.

The ride from Greensboro to Washington, DC took about five and a half hours with pee stops. TJ, Chief Deputy Powe and Agent Ames barely spoke the whole trip. What was there to say?

Their meeting with the AG took an hour, explaining everything they had found and deciding on a course of action. The look on the Attorney General's face said it all. He was sad and shaken. It was someone in his office that had assisted the kidnappings and the deaths in this case. Someone he considered a friend, not just an employee. It was the saddest day of his career.

The Attorney General decided Agent Ames and TJ would handle the interview. Agent Ames objected saying she did not feel she was ready for the interview in a such an important case. The AG told her to let TJ take the lead.

The townhouse was located in Georgetown. It was neat enough in appearance and was just the type residence a career government employee would have. Located close enough to mass transportation to walk. There was no need for a car. The townhouse was close to shopping and restaurants. In the window sat a grey cat watching them as they walked up.

TJ rang the doorbell, Agent Ames stood by his side. "Can I help you?" the well-dressed middle-aged woman asked after opening the door.

"Ma'am, I'm FBI Agent Ames and this is Sheriff Slone, can we speak with you?" Both showed the woman credentials.

"Come in, I've been expecting you" said Mary Beth as she turned and walked away. The look on her face, her shoulder slump and the way she walked away spoke volumes.

Mary Beth did not wait to be questioned. She explained the whole sordid affair. Sordid now, but it had been a dream come true until she found she had been used. She told how Azil had courted her. She explained how she was a stupid woman, a lonely stupid woman. TJ believed she truly made a mistake. He felt other than giving state secrets, she was a good, hardworking government employee. TJ actually felt pity for her.

Agent Ames felt sorry for Mary Beth and hoped she was not looking at herself years down the road.

Mary Beth finished her statement and then presented agent Ames her resignation letter which she had already prepared. She really was waiting for their arrival.

"Can you give this to the Attorney General? Please tell him how very sorry I am. I love that man. He has been so very good to me. He did not deserve this. I'm so sorry." With that Mary Beth broke into tears for the first time.

The leak about Matt Hart came about during one of Azil's overnight stays. There had been three overnight stays before Azil left town. She wanted to impress him, so she told him she knew who the next Vice President was going to be.

He laughed and told her he didn't believe her. She told him because the press had already named all the contenders. He challenged her with a bet. If she was right, a weekend in the Hamptons for just them. She picks the weekend.

She knew who was going to be the Vice President because the AG and his FBI, under the office of the Department of Justice had the responsibility of vetting the candidates. Her boss Sam Poage was told the offer had been made and that Governor Hart was going to the sheriff's condo in Sunset Beach to decide. It was just that simple and just that complicated.

Mary Beth asked if she was going to jail tonight, and if so, could she call a friend to take care of her cats.

TJ saw no reason to take her to jail. She was not a flight risk. She had no place to run. She was definitely not going back to her office. TJ wanted to continue the interview, but not there.

The FBI headquarters was the place for further conversation, but not tonight.

Mary Beth had confessed earlier she thought about suicide, but her religion, her commitment to doing the right thing told her she needed to stand up to her responsibility. TJ believed her. He did not believe she would kill herself. She was in love, or thought she was. She was stupid, but she was no traitor. TJ could see in her eyes she would do anything possible to try and make this right. He believed her and he felt sorry for her.

"Mary Beth, did Azil ever mention a daughter?" asked TJ. "Yes, Savi, I met her. A beautiful young lady. We went to dinner together, the three of us. The night of the second date. In fact, she called me today and left a message. I didn't take the call or return it. I recognized the number. I didn't know what to say. I guess she's not real either, like her father. I did wonder why she was calling. She must know the man she called father was dead."

"Did you believe it was really his daughter, how did they act together, did they look like one another or say anything to make you feel they were father and daughter?" asked TJ.

"I would swear she was his daughter, but my track record is not the best on judging people. She called him daddy and they hugged as if they truly loved one another. I have her number and the name of the guy she works for in Mexico if you want it."

"Yes please." TJ answered, thinking to himself, why did she call.

Mary Beth opened a notebook and removed a small business card. On the card was the name Savi Sief and a cell phone number. The number was one of the five top called numbers, Mary Beth's being another. The number on the card, which Sevi claimed was hers, did not come back to a Sevi Sief. The name of the company on the card was Gran Jefe' International, a transportation, import and export business in Reynosa, Mexico.

TJ asked Mary Beth the name of the man Sevi worked for.

"Jorge Manuel."

TJ's heart skipped a beat. Jorge was number four on the most wanted terrorist list. He knew because he helped prepare the list. It was suspected Jorge was a narco-terrorist, involved in drugs, human trafficking, extortion, murder, and rape to name a few. Reynosa, on the border with Texas, was his home base. He was part of the Gulf Cartel, one of the most feared and ruthless narcotics groups in Mexico. He had the local police and army in his pocket. If you wanted it and could pay his price he could get it or make it happen. He was responsible for killing several police chiefs who had decided not to take his bribery money. He also killed those who took the money and did not protect him like he thought they should. He was very rich and very powerful. He ran the Northernmost provinces from the Atlantic Ocean to the Pacific Ocean in Mexico.

TJ had a sinking feeling they had not heard the last of the Adula family.

A concerned TJ looked at Mary Beth.

"Mary Beth, I may need you to return that call."

Continuing Saga…

Sunrise at Sunset is the first part of a trilogy. The second book of the three is **The Garbage Man,** the third and last will be **The Garbage Detail.** The trilogy continues exploring and exposing the inter-workings of terrorist activity and criminal operations happening daily in our world. It is fiction or is it; the names certainly are. Plausible deniability is a very real thing. Failure to take action compromises our safety and security. So, if it is done, out of sight and known only to a few who are sworn to secrecy, is it right or is it wrong? Read these books with the understanding these type things can and could be happening now.

About the Author

BJ Barnes is a career public servant. He began his service in high school, continued through college, joined the United States Marine Corps, became a deputy Sheriff, was a bank fraud investigator and a law enforcement college instructor. BJ served twenty-four years as the high sheriff of Guilford County overseeing 652 square miles of county, 500,000+ citizens, 650 employees and a 64 million dollar a year budget.

He brings years of service and experience to his latest venture writing fiction. Or is it? As sheriff, BJ was part of many investigations, both as an investigator and a department head. He was a member of the Federal Joint Terrorism Task Force dealing with worldwide terrorist activity.

He served on many boards and commissions dealing with everything from the homeless, drug and human trafficking, immigration issues, terrorism, and many of the issues our citizens do not want to think about. His position gave him the experience to know who the players are on the seedy side of our society. That includes how they act, what they will do, what they have done, who pays for it, who they have compromised.

Now with *Sunrise at Sunset*, BJ is giving you a peek into the type of activity happening around our world every day. This is the first book of a trilogy and an intro into the real world of terrorism. Buckle up, it can be a scary ride.

Made in the USA
Columbia, SC
14 January 2021